THE MENTAL MARVEL

BOOKS IN THE ARGOSY LIBRARY:

DR. SKULL
LEWIS CLAY

ABBEY OF THE DAMNED: THE COMPLETE CASES OF MIKE AND TRIXIE, VOLUME 3
T.T. FLYNN

THE DEATH MESSENGER: THE COMPLETE CASES OF JIGGER MASTERS, VOLUME 4
ANTHONY M. RUD

BOX 991: THE COMPLETE CABALISTIC CASES OF SEMI DUAL, VOLUME 5
J.U. GIESY & JUNIUS B. SMITH

BLIND TRAILS AT TONTO: THE COMPLETE TALES OF SHERIFF HENRY, VOLUME 8
W.C TUTTLE

IN THE MURDERER'S BRAIN: THE COMPLETE CASES OF THE SCIENTIFIC CLUB, VOLUME 3
RAY CUMMINGS

THE LEGION OF THE LIVING DEAD: THE COMPLETE CASES OF MR. STRANG, VOLUME 2
CARROLL JOHN DALY

THE MENTAL MARVEL
FRED MACISAAC

THE ADVENTURE OF THE VOODOO MOON: THE COMPLETE CASES OF THE LADY FROM HELL, VOLUME 2
EUGENE THOMAS

MURDER ON THE FILM: THE COMPLETE CASES OF CANDID JONES, VOLUME 1
RICHARD B. SALE

THE MENTAL MARVEL

FRED MacISAAC

ILLUSTRATED BY
ROGER B. MORRISON

COVER BY
PAUL STAHR

POPULAR PUBLICATIONS · 2025

PUBLISHING HISTORY

"The Mental Marvel" originally appeared in the August 31–October 5, 1929 issue of *Argosy Allstory Weekly* magazine (Vol. 206, No. 2– Vol. 207, No. 1). Copyright © 1929 by The Frank A. Munsey Company. Copyright renewed © 1956 and assigned to Steeger Properties, LLC. All rights reserved.

Visit ARGOSYMAGAZINE.COM for more books like this.

THE MENTAL MARVEL

*Roger Thule, the youthful genius, knew
everything that came in books—but he had
a few startling lessons coming from life*

1

ANCIENT AT TWENTY-ONE

DR. TOM MARVIN descended the staircase of the Thule residence on upper Madison Avenue with heavy step, and found Theobald Thule awaiting him in the hallway.

"This way, doctor, if you please," Mr. Thule said nervously, opening the library door.

The celebrated mind specialist looked curiously round as he entered; the library of a rich man's house was always of interest to him, and this one was the sanctuary of a student. It was a room fully thirty feet by twenty, and, save for the window space, its walls were jammed with books, while at the upper end there were half a dozen bookstands upon the floor, giving the effect of a stack room in a public library.

The volumes, he could see at a glance, were selected for contents, and not for bindings; but, then, this was the home of his patient, Roger Thule. Dr. Marvin had paid little attention to his patient's father when he entered the house, but now he studied him curiously as he dropped into an overstuffed chair with the sigh of a solidly built man when he acquires comfort. Theobald Thule stood before him, his hands thrust under his coattails.

"Your opinion, doctor, if you please?" he asked eagerly.

Dr. Marvin rested shrewd blue eyes upon the thin face and sharp features of his questioner. For years he had been hearing of this man and his son Roger, and always had had a poor opinion of the father. His answer was, apparently, far away from the point.

"For a clergyman, you've done pretty well for yourself," the doctor remarked with studied insolence.

Anger flashed in the large pop-eyes of gray.

"I retired from the ministry fifteen years ago, sir," he said with asperity.

"And you found the show business pretty good."

"Will you have the kindness to answer my question, sir? What is the matter with my boy?"

"There is nothing the matter with him," the doctor snapped back, "except old age."

"Old age! Roger is only twenty-one."

"Old and weary and ready to quit. Your golden goose won't lay eggs any more, Mr. Thule."

The ex-clergyman had stopped beside his center table, and now brought his hand down upon it with a resounding thwack.

"You are offensive, Dr. Marvin. Have you no respect for a father's anxiety? What is the matter with my son?"

"What I said," replied the physician. "The mentality of a man of seventy is too much for the body of a boy of twenty-one."

"What is your fee, doctor?" Mr. Thule asked coldly. "I see I must summon a responsible physician."

Dr. Marvin shrugged his big shoulders. "As you please. Too bad. I had hopes of curing him."

THULE'S ANGER EVAPORATED.

"That's what I want," he exclaimed.

She said under her breath, "How diabolically clever he is."

The doctor nodded. "Then you must permit me, in my own way, to diagnose the disease."

"By all means."

"And it is necessary to talk very plainly. You seem sensitive."

"Ignore my feelings."

"Very well, Mr. Thule. You were a poor clergyman with an unusual education and an experimental mind. You began to experiment with your boy when he was a baby. At the age of five he spoke several languages and was a mathematical marvel; at ten he was an intellectual prodigy; at fifteen he was a Doctor of Philosophy."

"Roger is the brightest boy who ever lived," said Mr. Thule proudly.

"Exactly. I have no doubt you were actuated by proper motives in the beginning, and you had no purpose save his intellectual development, but that disinterestedness did not last long. You found the ownership of a prodigy more profitable than preaching the Gospel. You exhibited him.

He was a lightning calculator in vaudeville at the age of six, and for three years you toured the country with him."

"I admit that."

"At ten you had him lecturing on philosophy, and at twelve he filled two hundred dates with his demonstration of psychology. At fourteen he was a world celebrity with his refutation of Einstein's Theory of Relativity. You cleaned up a million on that kid, I should imagine."

Mr. Thule had seated himself and had controlled his anger with difficulty. "Suppose this is all true—what of it? I was poor. Roger's future had to be provided for. It will be his some day."

"In all probability he won't have any use for it," said the doctor dryly.

The father winced. "I assure you, doctor, I did not develop his mind at the expense of his body. I believe in physical education. Although he could not indulge in competitive athletics in college because he was six or eight years younger than his fellow students, I hired physical trainers for him."

"More drudgery."

"He is a splendid boxer, a master of jujutsu, an oarsman and an excellent tennis player. He is a big, strong boy; you saw that."

"I saw that he had been." The physician lifted a plump forefinger and pointed it at the father. "You stole his childhood, his boyhood and his young manhood. Instead of supporting him, he supported you. You deprived him of the comradeship of his fellows. A Doctor of Philosophy at fifteen? Criminal!"

"I deny your charges, and I say it is splendid that he won his Ph.D. ten years before the average scholar!"

More mildly the doctor continued: "I don't believe that boy ever had any fun in his life. Having no interest but the pursuit of knowledge, he has continued that. He has learned all that most men learn by the time they are ready for the grave. His illusions—they went at ten years of age. He is stuffed with the pessimistic preaching of the sophisticated and cynical savants of all the ages. Women? He ought to be tingling at the sight of a pretty girl, but he thinks love is only exaggeration of the importance of one woman more than another; matrimony is a failure, fidelity a fallacy, and the female sex only an inferior division of humanity."

"I taught him to honor and respect woman."

"My poor man, he passed beyond your teaching about the time he was nine. He knows everything, that boy. Why, he's even a Doctor of Medicine! He knows more about medicine than I do!"

"I shouldn't be surprised," snapped Mr. Thule, with a glint in his eye.

"WELL, THAT'S THE whole story. He knows everything, and he thinks nothing is worth while. Life is a bore, and while it's possible there may be something interesting beyond the grave, he doubts that. Anyway, he has soured on you, he doesn't want to live, and he is starving himself to death, taking a very slight scientific interest in his symptoms. When did he refuse to see or talk with you?"

"A month ago," admitted Mr. Thule, whose hard face had softened and whose lips were working with emotion. "It's killing me, doctor."

"Serve you right," Tom Marvin replied heartlessly.

Thule began to pace the room, clasping and unclasping his hands while the doctor watched him, half pitying, half contemptuous.

Finally Theobald Thule stopped his walk and stood in front of the physician.

"My apology, doctor, for what I said in the beginning. I am afraid you are entirely right. This did not occur to me because I thought that the boy had heard something about me that was responsible for this situation. He had always seemed happy, to me. Our life together was more like that of two scientists than father and son, but I love him, and I supposed he loved me."

"He doesn't believe in love of parents any more than love of woman."

"If his mother lived, I suppose she would have prevented my mad experiments. Truly I saw no harm in benefiting by his amazing talents. I never dreamed it would come to this. He truly seemed happy. I have accumulated much money, doctor. I would give it all to restore him to a healthy point of view."

"Do you mean that?" demanded the physician.

"I certainly do, sir."

"I'd like to see what I can do with him. He needs drastic measures. I'll wager if he were marooned on a desert island he'd decide he wanted to live, and would use his talents to provide for himself. Or if I could get him interested in a woman. She would have to be remarkable, to interest that boy. I'd drop everything and travel round the world with him if necessary, but it would take a lot of money, many thousands. What is your limit?"

"My last cent," said Mr. Thule firmly.

The doctor rose and threw his arm over the father's shoulder. "I apologize to you," he said. "Now I'll go up and see him again."

HE CLIMBED TO the second floor and tapped on the door of a front room, got no response and pushed it open. Lying in a big chair by the window was the object of the conference, the boy who was dying of old age.

Roger Thule had been handsome, but he was emaciated. He had black eyes which burned, set in a long, thin, white face. His forehead was high and thatched by long uncombed black hair, his nose was straight, the nostrils thin, the mouth well-formed though the lips were almost blue, and the chin sharp-pointed with a cleft in it. He wore a dressing gown and his long legs were resting upon a second chair. Only his eyes moved as Dr. Marvin entered.

"I thought I was through with you," he said indifferently.

The doctor was a solid, paunchy man with a small blond Vandyke beard, blue eyes, and a rather winning smile.

"You're quite determined to die, aren't you?"

"I have told you so."

"But why a long, lingering death? You know all about poisons."

"I am curious to discover if a man can will his own death. There are apparently well-authenticated cases of South Sea Islanders accomplishing it, and there seems no reason why it should not be done by a civilized man."

"How long did you say it was since you had taken any nourishment?"

"Six days since I have taken anything except water."

"Well, you haven't died in six days, so it seems evident that willing won't do the job."

"I am beginning to think so, but I haven't given up hope."

"Your treatment of your father is pretty rotten."

"Not at all. For years he hasn't loved me. He has exploited me like the owner of a six-legged goat. If I bothered with emotions I would hate my father."

"He has just offered me every cent of his fortune to spend in bringing you to a proper frame of mind. I think he loves you, Roger."

"It doesn't interest me either way."

"It's too bad, if you must end your life, that you can't do it in a way that would be useful to science. What if I expose you to deadly germs of some sort? You could write down your sensations."

"I'm not interested in helping the abolition of diseases. Too many people in the world now."

"What's your opinion on the prospects of a man marooned on a desert island?"

"If it really is a desert island, he will die of starvation."

"There was Selkirk—Robinson Crusoe," the doctor objected.

"That was a deserted, not a desert island."

"Suppose a man of your attainments were cast away: could you make a go of it?"

"I wouldn't bother."

"I wonder how much practical knowledge you have?" mused the physician.

"More than you think. My education has been many-sided."

"Your father tells me you are a boxer. Do you suppose, now, you could become champion of the world?"

"It's possible, with training. I am not interested."

"Humph! I doubt it."

"I would be obliged to build myself up physically, devote a year or two to intensive boxing; and then my understanding of the mental processes of my opponent would do the trick. But I couldn't defeat a gorilla."

"Hum. Ever been in love?"

"There is no such thing as love. Several women have thought they loved me."

"You are a very bright young man," the doctor said slowly. "However, you are wrong when you say there is no such thing as love. You are wrong to wish to die before you have experienced that emotion."

"Love is unsatisfied desire, a physical impulse, developed until it becomes a mania by the unwillingness of the woman to yield. Satisfy it and it vanishes. Conventions and the lack of initiative of ordinary men hold them to women afterward. In my case the mania is impossible because of my understanding of female psychology. I know exactly how to attract and win a woman, I will charm her so that she will not resist and the insanity of unsatisfied desire is thus avoided."

"YOU ARE NOT as brilliant as I thought you were," challenged Dr. Marvin. "Shall I tell you something, Roger? You are not a great mentality, you are merely a compendium of human knowledge. You have read more than anybody living, you astonish the world by your display, but what have you done? A scholar, yes, but what have you invented, what have you added to human lore? Have you commanded armies like Napoleon, or made discoveries like Newton or Copernicus, illuminated the world like Edison, freed slaves like Lincoln, composed great music like Beethoven? You are an arrogant bookworm, that's all you are."

"I see through you," said Roger with a half smile. "You want to reanimate my ambition. I'm not interested in improving this rotten world or benefiting it. It makes me very tired and I want to be out of it."

"So you know how to captivate a woman. Why, you fool, you have never met a real woman. There are a score of chorus girls in New York who could wind you around their little fingers."

"This conversation is fatiguing me," said the prodigy. "Women are simple, not complex creatures. It's just a matter of pleasing them, and the method is not complicated. You'll find half a dozen Greek and Latin philosophers who have put it down in black and white. I have experimented with several women, and always successfully. An exact science, my dear friend. You could do it. Given a stalwart physique and an attractive face, no intelligent man can fail."

"My opinion of you continues to lower. I think you're a fool, Roger."

"Please leave this room," said the prodigy with some acerbity.

"Wait a minute. Is there any especial reason why you have to die this week or this month?"

"Just because it pleases me."

"You are the first person who ever seriously assured me he was irresistible with women. Purely in the interest of science, I should like a demonstration. I happen to know a beautiful young woman who possesses rare intelligence. I should like to warn her of your pretensions, introduce you, and see whether you are an empty boaster or not."

"Warn her? Well, that wouldn't help her much."

"There is a complication. This girl is somewhat interested in another man and he happens to be the champion heavyweight prize-fighter of the world."

"The Abysmal Brute?" Roger's eyes for the first time betrayed interest. "It is a fact that women are attracted by the animal in men; a relic of the youth of the human race. Intelligent women are affected even more than ignorant ones. Of course the word intelligence in reference to women is used relatively."

"And you'd have as much chance against Steve Haverty as I would have against you in an argument on the Theory of Relativity."

"Is that so?" asked the man who wished to die. "Listen, my friend. If I so desired, I could not only take this woman away from Steve Haverty, but would go into the ring and take away his championship."

"As slangy folks say, 'Yeaah?'"

Roger almost grinned. "Yeah!" He lifted a weak hand and pulled a bellrope beside his chair. Almost instantly a nurse entered.

"I have decided to eat," he said. "Bring me some clam broth first and some soda crackers. For dinner I'll have two lamb chops."

2

CHALLENGE

"WOULD YOU, FOR one hundred thousand dollars?" asked Dr. Marvin.

"A hundred thousand dollars would be a great help to any girl," said Eloise Lane frankly. "What an arrogant and presumptuous coxcomb Roger Thule must be! I've been hearing about him for years, as a sort of educational freak. So he thinks that making a woman fall in love with a man is an exact science! Didn't he ever hear of the theory of mutual attraction or repulsion?"

Dr. Marvin chuckled. "He has heard of that, but he is certain it can be overcome. You must understand that he has heard of everything. His idea is that a man can move upon a woman as a skillful player moves his pieces upon a chessboard. Knowing the moves, he cannot lose."

"I get a hundred thousand dollars if I don't fall in love with him. It's not necessary for me to make him fall in love with me."

"Knowing what pitiful things women are, he couldn't fall in love," smiled the doctor. "All you have to do is to resist him, Eloise."

"It's really like finding the money," the girl reflected.

Dr. Marvin gave her a whimsical glance. "I'm not so

sure. He is a darn good looking cub. You're twenty and he's twenty-one. You can never tell."

"I'd much sooner take Steve Haverty. He's a man. Of course he is very ignorant, but he's young enough to learn and he is likable. He's really almost helpless."

"And you are actually saving a life. This challenge of mine prevented Thule from starving himself to death."

"Would he really have done that?"

The doctor nodded. "I'm sure of it. He is a strange youth."

"Well," she laughed, "bring on the prodigy."

Dr. Marvin had made the acquaintance of Eloise Lane a year ago when she was brought to him for consultation by her regular physician who was becoming alarmed at her mental condition. He saw a vividly beautiful girl of nineteen with corn-colored hair and great limpid sea-blue eyes, an adorable little nose, a determined, finely chiseled chin, an exquisite mouth, very sensitive, whose tenseness betrayed mental anguish; and a form that was lithesome and of surpassing grace.

He knew her by reputation, a dancer who had ravished New York. She had come out of nowhere, scintillated for a few months, and slipped into oblivion. In the second act of a blaring, blatant, musical hodge-podge sponsored by the most famous of musical comedy producers, the scene shifted to a sylvan glade in which appeared a shy, shrinking, half nude nymph who proceeded to dance to Stravinsky music in a manner to startle cynical New York. Overnight she became famous and for six months the big town was at her feet. And one night when the curtain descended she did not arise for her ovation from the heap in which she had crumpled. She had to be picked up and carried to her dressing room. Her heart had been overstrained and she could never dance again.

Several years of intense study and of painful experiences in cheap vaudeville in remote places, a struggle against poverty and inappreciation; then sudden success; but hardly had she tasted of the cup when it was snatched from her lips. She had to find a new means of livelihood, to begin all over again. But it was not this which was driving her mad, it was the urge to dance and the knowledge her heart would not sustain her. Her melancholia frightened her physician, and she had yielded finally to his plea that she go with him to consult the mind expert.

HER APPEARANCE CHARMED the kindly Dr. Marvin, and her melancholia distressed him. Having put her at her ease in his inimitable manner he asked her many questions which she answered artlessly, and from these answers he made his diagnosis.

Eloise was young, eager and ardent. Her love of dancing was great, but no greater than her love of lights, audiences and adulation; half her chagrin was because never again would she experience the wild ovations of a delighted crowd. Craftily he began the work of restoration.

"After all," he said, "you are very beautiful, very young, and you have a rich and lovely voice, as beautiful a voice as I have ever heard. I think you have a good memory, I know you are intelligent—there is no reason why you should retire from the stage."

"But I can't dance any more," she wailed.

"No, but you can act. You may become as great an actress as you were a dancer, yes, greater, and your career will be much longer. What is the greatest female name connected with the theater? Bernhardt; and was she a dancer or an actress?"

The sad eyes brightened; he saw a spark in them. "I don't know anything about acting," she said hesitatingly.

"Study it. You can learn. You have poise, grace, stage presence, fifty per cent of the qualifications of a great actress already. Think, Miss Lane, what an achievement, if, having made a reputation as a celebrated dancer, you should return and triumph as a legitimate actress."

"I am afraid that's not possible," she murmured, but her melancholy was dissipating.

"Anything is possible to beauty, intelligence and youth. You are brokenhearted because you can't come back," he continued. "But you can come back. Many dancers have become great actresses. Enter a dramatic school, study the lives of people of the profession. In a year I'll be sitting in a theater watching you make audiences laugh and cry and feel happy."

"I'm going to try," declared Eloise. "Doctor, I'm a different girl since I came into this office. Do you—may I come and see you some time?"

"Come any time and don't worry about my fee. I'll go to dinner with you now and then; it will pay me just to look at you."

So Eloise Lane became an actress and Eloise and Dr. Marvin became stanch friends. That was why he thought of her in the business of Roger Thule and why he set the reward for her services at such a high price. Roger's father deserved to pay for his folly, in his opinion, and Eloise needed money.

Great psychologist as Dr. Marvin was, he was not familiar with the mental processes and solid prejudices of theatrical producers. They knew Eloise Lane as a dancer and, therefore, she could not be an actress. The girl had studied hard and found it harder to get employment than to learn to read lines and act them. She had secured a small part now and then which she performed beautifully, but producers were blind and she was having a hard time keeping body and soul together. Then Steve Haverty had appeared on the scene.

Haverty was a powerful, decent, clean-minded and wholesome savage. He was handsome as a caveman might have been, and he was rich and famous and very much in love with Eloise Lane. In the ring he was terrible, a killer. Out of it, he was simple, kindly and likable. He had gone through grammar and high school without learning anything; he had been a truck driver, a stevedore, a soldier and now he was champion heavyweight pugilist. Even to an intelligent girl like Eloise he had a certain appeal.

Eloise had set her little jaw and determined to make good as an actress, and Steve wanted to take some of his money and star her. She was strongly tempted. Dr. Marvin was afraid she would marry Haverty, and that was another reason he wanted to use her in the case of Roger Thule.

A FAT, KINDLY, unscrupulous old schemer was Dr. Tom Marvin, who loved to pull strings and make his marionettes dance to his measure. He was flattered that his craft was superior to that of the mighty scholar, Roger Thule, Ph.D. All Roger needed was a demonstration that he didn't yet know it all, and Eloise would attend to that. And if Roger's arrogance led him into the prize ring against Steve

Haverty, the Abysmal Brute would teach him another much-needed lesson.

Meantime Roger had abandoned his strange determination to pass out of the world at the age of twenty-one. He was eating heartily and attending a gymnasium. Father Thule had made no objection to placing a hundred thousand dollars in escrow, Eloise would not have to marry Steve to become a star of the theater as well as to eat regularly, and the doctor was the center of a most enthralling experiment.

One month from the day that Roger boasted he would win the love of any woman living and would also take away Steve Haverty's championship belt, he called upon Dr. Marvin at his residence on Madison Avenue to meet Eloise Lane.

Eloise, whose contempt for the savant was almost equal to her curiosity as to what he looked like, saw no reason why she should not impress him with her own personality. Her long golden hair was braided and wrapped tightly around her beautiful little head. She wore a simple robe of white silk, very decolette, with a narrow gold belt around her waist, and to complete the Grecian effect she had on no stockings and incased her pretty little feet in golden sandals.

When she threw off her opera cloak in the presence of Dr. Marvin, the heart of that sophisticated old villain missed a beat.

"It's unfair," he said with a gnomish grin. "You don't have to bowl over this infant to win the money. All you have to do is to resist him."

"The conceited thing!" smiled Eloise. "It would serve

him right if he became mad about me, and I certainly don't intend to conceal any of my poor attractions. Who is going to be here?"

"Just you and I and Roger. And I'm going to have a call which will take me out of the house for a couple of hours. You'll dine *tête-à-tête*."

"Mr. Roger Thule," announced the servant. Eloise dropped into a chair, instinctively assuming a graceful attitude. Dr. Marvin leaned his elbow upon the mantelpiece. There was a fire in the grate below, for it was mid-November and the lights of the library in which the meeting was to take place were subdued. To the physician, gazing at Eloise, she looked as Helen of Troy must have looked to Paris upon their first meeting in the palace of Menelaus.

Roger Thule was ushered into the room, and it was the turn of Eloise to be impressed.

She had formed a mental picture of the intellectual prodigy which no description of Dr. Marvin could alter. She expected a head much too big for his body, thick-lensed spectacles, a cadaverous face, and a man small and spare of frame.

She saw instead a young man who was at least six feet tall, broad-shouldered, powerful, lean, long-legged and active. His glossy black hair was very thick, and it curled over his high forehead. The eyes were large, black and penetrating, and the face positively handsome, so regular were his features.

SHE SAW A flame in the black eyes when they rested upon her, a flame which vanished immediately. His smile, which revealed even, very white teeth, was very attractive. This was a fine big handsome boy; that he was the greatest scholar in the world was absolutely incredible. Was Dr. Marvin up to tricks? She shot him an inquiring glance.

Not having seen Roger for a fortnight, the doctor was surprised at the change in his appearance; the fellow was glowing with health and interest in life.

"This is Roger Thule," he said after shaking hands with the visitor. "Roger, meet Miss Eloise Lane."

Roger crossed the room and extended his hand to the girl who lifted a bare arm with an exquisite gesture and touch his big palm.

"I was led to believe that you were very beautiful," said Roger in a voice which was deep and caressing. "But you so far exceed my expectations, Miss Lane, that I am at a loss to express myself."

"Move one on the chessboard," said Eloise to herself. "Don't try," she replied insolently. "From what I have heard of you I doubt very much if you have met many beautiful women."

"Certainly none like you," he answered. The servants came in with cocktails, one of which Eloise accepted, but Roger refused his. "I am in training," he said gravely.

"Really? Do you have to train to study?"

He nodded. "I am studying pugilism, just now. It is my intention to meet and defeat the heavyweight champion, Steve Haverty."

Eloise choked on her cocktail and threw an amused glance at Dr. Marvin. "Holding out on me," she reproached. "Really, Mr. Thule, haven't you taken a lot on yourself?"

"No, I scarcely think so," he replied blandly. Eloise laughed out loud.

The servant entered. "Dinner is served, doctor," he said,

"but Mrs. Jackson has telephoned asking if you can drop in on her immediately for a little while."

"One of my neurasthenic patients. It makes her insane to deny her anything," Marvin explained. "You young things will have to dine together and I'll be back for the coffee. *Au revoir.*"

The servant threw open the door leading to the dining room. Eloise rose, took Roger's arm and permitted him to lead her into the other room where a small table was set for two.

"A conspiracy," she declared. "Were you a party to it, Mr. Thule?"

"No, indeed, but I am happy to be the beneficiary of it."

He seated her, sat down opposite, and inspected her with interest.

"What amazing hair you have," he declared. "You are a very astonishing young person, Miss Lane. A month ago I was so disgusted with life that I was contemplating getting rid of it. I realize now that I didn't really know life since I had not yet met you."

"Move two," thought Eloise, then aloud: "Cards on the table, Mr. Thule! Dr. Marvin has warned me of your intentions. I win a hundred thousand dollars if you don't succeed. What chance have you?"

HE SMILED. "NONE whatever. I was an egotistical ass to be badgered into this proposition. I never before encountered a girl of your type and all my theories fall to the ground before your hair and lips and eyes. Yet I am glad because I have had the privilege of meeting you."

She veiled her eyes with her long golden lashes because his gaze was so ardent. "Clever, how diabolically clever he is," she said under her breath. Aloud, "You will, of course, appreciate that I don't believe you."

"That is my misfortune. As far as I am concerned the game is over before it has begun. Try to find an excuse for me, Miss Lane. I am only twenty-one and all my life I have been a thinking machine, exploited by my father, cheated of my childhood and my boyhood. I have come into contact with few real people; my life has been spent among pedants and cynics like myself. You are like the breath of spring to a man who has known only Arctic winters."

"You poor kid," she thought with ready sympathy, then meeting the keen black eyes she stiffened. "That is known as the appeal for sympathy," she sneered. "Women, poor souls, respond instantly to it. Would you like me to be a mother to you?"

"I never knew my mother," he said sadly. "She died when I was a year old. If she had lived I should probably have been a normal person, not a freak."

Despite her armor, this penetrated to the warm little heart of Eloise. "You did get a terrible deal, didn't you?" she said less acidly. "Eat your soup. It's getting cold." Presently she inquired, "Why on earth are you going in for pugilism? Surely you don't think your education equips you to meet the brutes who work in prize rings."

"I am very strong," he answered. "My parent did not forget my physical training. I am very quick, I have boxed a lot in an amateur way, and in fact it has been my only recreation. Given equal strength, speed and stamina, intelligence will beat stupidity."

"A man may be very stupid in everything except his

profession. These prize fighters are specialists in their line even if they are ignorant as regards differential calculus."

"Granted. I should not make use of differential calculus in the ring, but of boxing science. And I do not expect to defeat Mr. Haverty immediately. I shall put in six months of intensive study of prize fighting before I challenge him."

"I wonder if you dream how conceited you are," she said, exasperated.

He smiled at her. "Doubtless I seem so to you. It is, however, nothing but well-founded confidence."

"I know Mr. Haverty. He is rather nice. I am considering marrying him." She flung this at him like a bombshell.

"I am sure you will reconsider," he said calmly. She boiled, then calmed herself.

"But why are you doing this? Why do you want to be the champion fighter of the world? Don't you think it a disgraceful profession?"

"Dr. Marvin told me he knew a woman who wouldn't fall in love with me, and mentioned that you were much interested in the heavyweight champion. It occurred to me then that it would be amusing to turn your affections to me and incidentally topple the champion off his throne. I was in a strange mood—denying myself food with the intention of dying. Crafty old Marvin was dangling all sorts of bait before me to make me want to live and, curiously, I snapped at this."

"BUT YOU SAID you had given up the idea of making me fall in love with you. Why not give up beating Steve Haverty?"

He laid down knife and fork, leaned on the table and

gazed into her eyes. "Because I must cling to one of my motives or I may slip back into my former mood."

"Why have you given up the first motive?" she dared to ask.

"Because, having seen you, realizing how sweet and lovely you are, I feared hurting you."

"But if I loved you and you loved me, it could not hurt me."

"It's because I could not fall in love. My child, I have the mind of an old man. With my knowledge of human nature it would be impossible for me to fall in love with any woman. That's why I cheerfully abandon this disgusting experiment."

Eloise pushed back her chair, rose and glowered at him. "You—you are just a poor fish," she exclaimed. "You couldn't fall in love? Why, a clever girl could make you eat out of her hand. You are afraid of hurting me! Alongside of you I am an old woman. Go on with your experiment, do you hear? Make me love you! You have as much chance as a man has of melting an iceberg with a cigarette lighter. And I hope you get into the ring with Steve Haverty and he knocks your conceited head off your shoulders!"

"My, my, my," exclaimed a new voice. "Quarrelling already? You're not married yet, children. Sit down, Eloise, and finish your dinner. Jones, lay a plate for me."

Dr. Marvin pushed Eloise back into her chair and pulled up one to the table for himself.

Eloise turned on him. "As for you, you old Mephistopheles, this deal is off. I hate the sight of that human encyclopedia over there. I'm going to marry Steve Haverty, do you hear?"

"All right, all right, just as you say," placated the doctor.

"Miss Lane, I issue a challenge," stated Roger Thule. "You have just made some assertions about me. I dare you to continue to see me and give me an opportunity to make you love me; and I dare you to defer your marriage with Steve Haverty until he has conquered me in the ring."

"That means forever," she replied. "You couldn't get a match with Steve. Nobody would pay to see him pulverize you."

"Then set a time limit of a year," he pleaded.

"That's only fair," Doctor Marvin declared. "Come, Eloise, be a sport."

"Very well, doctor," she said.

3

"PROFESSOR" WHIZ

THE PHYSICAL CULTURE Institute of "Professor" Whiz
Malone was located on Third Avenue in the East Forties.
Once it had been a sweat-shop where emaciated aliens
drove sewing machines ten hours a day for a pittance, and
it was still a sweat-shop, but now Professor Whiz drove
human machines who paid him for it.

The professor was a small man with unusually wide
shoulders and a face which had probably been homely
before it was battered in the prize ring. Whiz got his nick-
name because he was just that, a whiz in the ring, the speed-
iest, hardest hitting, headiest and snappiest welterweight of
the period, except that "he couldn't take it." Whiz was very
hard to hit, but when he was hit hard he lost his enthusiasm rapidly and was apt to lie right down on the floor of
the ring and let the referee count fifty if he wanted to. So
he passed into ring history.

Four years before, he had been an instructor in boxing
at Harvard and had lasted a year in that capacity, but
his inability to appreciate the importance of a faculty
member's refraining from bootleg whisky caused him to
he dismissed from the university with regrets. When Roger
Thule was taking one of his several post-graduate courses

in Cambridge he had studied boxing with Professor Whiz, learning a lot from him and earning the admiration of the old pugilist.

So, when he determined to take up prize-fighting seriously, he had thought of Whiz and enrolled in his gymnasium. There was a small, disorderly office inside the main entrance to the gymnasium, in which the professor made out his monthly bills, the rest of the establishment was open space and had a fully equipped twenty-four foot ring in its center.

There was a small running track, thirty laps to the mile; chestweights, rowing machines, and punching bag frames in the place—and some hard looking characters.

In the ring, Roger Thule was working out with one Dick Grogan, the thief assistant of Whiz. The professor sat in a wooden chair, in gym costume, arms folded, jaws thrust out, eyes gleaming. At the end of three rounds he ordered the contest stopped. Roger, perspiring freely, eyes bright, but breathing heavily, followed him into his office.

"What do you think, Whiz?"

"You're not bad, doc." He had called the sixteen-year-old Doctor of Philosophy "doc" in their college gymnasium days. "You're quick and your footwork is fair, but you ain't nearly as strong as you ought to be and they's a heck of a lot you don't know about the game."

"I am aware of that. It's why I'm here."

"Well, we can build you up, but it will take time, and we can show you a lot o' tricks and probably make a pretty flashy boxer out of you, but there's one thing I can't teach you and you probably won't never learn."

"What's that, Whiz?"

"How to take a beating and like it."

"I don't think it's necessary to like it. I think I can stand some hard punches."

"That ain't it, doc. No man ever became a champ that wasn't able to stand up to a batterin' and sort of get inspired by it—like it, that's what I mean. I never liked it myself and that's why I'm runnin' a gym. The real champion loves a fight; next to sockin' the other fellow on the button he likes to get hit—it makes him go in harder."

"Very well," he said calmly, "I'll teach myself to like it."

"THAT AIN'T ALL. A great fighter has to stay in there while he's getting slugged until he's knocked unconscious. Most of these bums don't know enough to quit and that's what makes them win. Now you take a highly eddicated guy like yourself, doc. You'd take just so many and your intelligence would say, 'Why put up with this when all I got to do is lay down and play dead for ten seconds,'—and that's how you'd lose."

Roger laughed. "I should think the idea would be not to be slugged."

"Yeah? Don't you kid yourself. Put two good men in a twenty-four foot ring and they're both going to get it plenty.

"Look at Tunney. Most as cultured as you are—anyway the papers cracked him up that way. He was the smoothest boxer ever won the championship since Jim Corbett, and Dempsey was just a slow-witted killer with a wallop like a pile driver. Tunney kept away from Dempsey for seven rounds, being so clever, and then Dempsey hit him seven times on the jaw with everything he had. I'm telling you they all get slugged. Tunney was a real fighter. He had a right to be knocked out, and he had plenty of jack already; he could of retired then, but up he gets, after the count, keeps away from Dempsey till his head cleared up, and then wore him down and won the fight."

"Well," said Roger Thule. "I want to be built up, as you say, and to be taught the game; and then we'll see what will happen."

"Your money is good. I like you even if you are a doctor of what-you-may-call-it, but you got more hard work in front of you than I'd want to tackle."

Roger Thule laughed cheerfully.

"Bring it on."

"Well, go out and jog around the track about fifty times and then call it a day."

When Thule had gone Whiz went into the gym and called Grogan.

"How's the amachure?" he asked.

Grogan grinned toothily. "Not so bad. He's quick and at times pretty good."

"You didn't lay a glove on him while I was watchin' you."

"Ah, I told you he was quick. And I didn't want to hurt a new guy. It discourages 'em."

"I seen him whip over that right of his, half a dozen times."

"Ain't I said he's quick?" protested Grogan. "But I bet he's got a glass jaw."

"Well, try to bust it next time you spar with him. *I* bet he ain't."

Grogan's eyes gleamed. "Want me to hit him hard?"

"Sure, if you can."

"You watch me," advised the assistant.

Thule weighed himself and tipped the beam at 179 1-2.

"Still suffering from that suicide spasm of mine," Roger muttered. "I can easily put on ten pounds in a few months. This is going to be rather amusing."

Dressed and glowing from a hard rub, Roger Thule went to the telephone and called the apartment of Miss Eloise Lane.

"May I call for you about six o'clock and take you to dinner?"

"I am giving somebody tea, but we'll be through by then. Come over," she said cordially.

"And how about a theater?"

"I would like to see 'Merrymen.'"

"That's easily arranged. Look for me at six."

"*Au revoir*, then, irresistible," she laughed as she rang off.

He hung up smiling at the telephone receiver. "If she hadn't been warned," he said to himself, "it would be much more simple."

4

THE ABYSMAL BRUTE

ELOISE LANE PAID a hundred dollars a month for two rooms, kitchenette and bath on the top floor of an old brownstone house in the east Fifties, and Roger tapped on her door after climbing five flights of stairs, to have it opened by the lady in person.

"Come in, Mr. Thule," she invited. "And there is a gentleman here whom I would like to have you meet. This is Mr. Roger Thule, Steve. Mr. Thule, meet Mr. Stephen Haverty, heavyweight champion of the world."

For the first time Roger looked upon the countenance of the man he intended to dethrone.

Steve Haverty had been sitting in an overstuffed armchair with his legs crossed, holding in his right hand a teacup not much bigger than his thumb. He was a huge young man with enormous shoulders and a suggestion of great bulk which belied him for, though he stood six feet two inches, he weighed only 196 pounds stripped.

His feet were very large and were made more conspicuous by gray spats over his narrow patent leather shoes. He had risen, a friendly smile upon his face, and, laying down the cup upon a tea table, he took several steps toward the visitor with outstretched hand.

"I heard about you, Mr. Thule. I seen you once when I was about twelve years old and you was a shaver. My old man took me to the theater when you was the Lightnin' Calculator."

Roger winced. He hated his showman days.

"You sure got a wunnerful brain, Mister," went on the heavyweight champion.

"Thanks," said Roger curtly, accepting the big hand which closed around his with a grip which made him wince. Roger's hand was not small, but a crushing grip was part of Steve's stock in trade.

"Take your corners, boys," mocked Eloise. The young men sat down.

Steve's hair sprouted like pigs' bristles, very thick and dark brown. He had a broad, low forehead, bushy eyebrows and a pair of small but pleasant brown eyes. His nose had been broken years ago and it had not occurred to the champion to patronize a facial surgeon, so the broken nose continued to make a good-natured face appear sinister. The cheekbones were high, the mouth large, and several of the big white teeth probably false. The chin was very heavy and he had what is known as a bull neck, which means that the neck helped protect the jawbone. It was his habit in the ring to sink his chin into his neck. Roger had seen pictures of his fighting face.

He wore a black cutaway coat and striped trousers, such a formal calling costume that almost nobody but Englishmen and prize-fighters wear them in New York. His vest had a white hem sewed on it and his necktie was plaid and contained a diamond stickpin. An ignorant man with money, all dressed up, thought the genius.

"Eloise told me that you were taking her out to dinner and the theater," continued the amiable champion. "It's all right with me."

His voice was heavy but not disagreeable and he evidently wore his company manners.

"I'm very glad of that," Roger remarked with a trace of irony. **"I'M STUCK ON** Eloise and I don't care who knows it," continued Steve, "but I ain't got any mortgage on her— yet." There was a suggestion of threat in the adverb.

"And you wouldn't have then, young man," said Eloise. "What do you think of him, Mr. Thule?"

"I find Mr. Haverty very interesting," Roger replied politely.

"What do you think of Mr. Thule, Steve?"

"Hey? Quit trying to ride us, Eloise," pleaded the embarrassed giant.

"What do you think of him?" she insisted.

Steve looked despairingly at Roger. "You can't do nothin' with 'em," he declared. "I think he's a nice guy."

"Take a good look at him. He intends to go after your championship."

Steve roared and slapped his hands upon his thighs. "Great stuff," he exclaimed. "I'll get even with him by goin' in for Deep Stuff like he does. How's that, Mr. Thule?"

"You are quite welcome," Roger said gravely.

"Same here. I have to take on anybody that the boxing commission approves of and my manager thinks can draw a big gate."

"She isn't joking," said Roger with perfect seriousness. "I am going in for pugilism and I may be good enough to challenge you yet."

Steve stopped laughing and appraised him. "You look big and strong, but I'm bigger and stronger. It's O.K. with me, Mr. Thule. Only what's the matter with the lightnin' calculatin' business? Getting too big for it?"

"I tired of it," said Roger with a smile. "I think there is more profit for less work in your business."

"I guess you're right at that," stated Steve. "Well, I got to go or I'll get put out. Don't keep Mr. Thule out too late, Eloise. When a man's in trainin' he's got to keep early hours."

Laughing heartily at this witticism, he shook hands and departed.

"Isn't he a dear?" asked Eloise.

"Rather a decent sort of brute," admitted Roger.

"He's not a brute, or a fool either," she retorted indignantly. "Your arrogance is really intolerable, and the more ridiculous because you are only a boy who has done nothing but swallow a few college libraries. Steve was miserably poor, had no education, and has made a million dollars by his courage and his skill with his fists. In a few years more he'll be a gentleman. You'll never be anything but a snob."

"Come now," he smiled. "You are rather hard on me. Just the same I can't understand how you can tolerate the society of a man who earns his living by beating human beings into unconsciousness. And those clothes of his, and his manners—he's uncouth."

"THERE IS SOME excuse for his being in the prize ring, but none for your going into it. It's just another form of your insolence. How you will be punished! Steve would have as much chance as a lightning calculator."

"No, I don't think so. Shall we go to dinner?"

"It's in the bond," she said still angry. "Otherwise I would select other company."

"Then I'm glad of the agreement. I find myself getting a lot of pleasure out of your company, even when you are furious with me."

"Look out or you'll fall in love with me."

He sighed. "I wish it were possible."

"Solomon was wiser than you, but in the end he had a thousand wives."

Roger laughed at her. "Solomon's wisdom has been exaggerated and so has the number of his wives."

They dined at the St. Regis, where he talked delightfully on many subjects. In the end she brought him back to Steve Haverty.

"I am very curious to know how you expect to beat him."

"I am afraid you would carry the information to the enemy's camp, my dear. I'll keep my plan to myself."

"Well," she said maliciously, "before the fight I'll tell him that I'll marry him if he defeats you. With that motive—"

"That would be a mistake. I know one always fights harder to win a great reward, but usually with less intelligence. However, tell him if you wish."

She turned her eyes on Roger Thule and they were hard. "I would hate you except for fear it might be part of your method. You think hatred is akin to love."

"On the contrary. Hatred is an emotion which is positive. Love is a figment of the imagination. Don't be afraid to hate me, Eloise."

"You bet I won't," she snapped. "Every time I see you I like Steve better."

5

"HIT ME!"

FOR A MONTH Roger worked with a physical instructor at home and for a couple of hours in the afternoon with the boxing instructors in the gymnasium. Shrewdly, Roger had confided his ambition to no one except Eloise, and her betrayal to Steve Haverty had no consequences because the champion thought no more about it. Steve was training now for a fight with a western aspirant which would take place shortly and he saw Eloise very seldom. She herself got a small part in a farce on Broadway and had little time for Roger, although she dined with him twice a week and sparred with him as usual.

To herself she admitted that she liked Roger; she liked him because he was such a boy despite his attainments, and because she didn't think he had a sense of humor. She liked him, but, as for loving him even if she had not been warned of his intentions, she could not have loved him. He was too austere, too formal, too vain.

The comments of his assistant and the boxers who had sparred with Roger in friendly fashion finally persuaded Whiz to put the gloves on with him. Whiz was not yet forty, a little slower than of yore but immensely clever, and he could probably have gone into the ring and kept out of the reach of the knock-out punch of the great Haverty for three rounds.

He took on Roger and fully a score of fighters and fighting men watched the three round bout. It was a good little man and a good big man. Roger's reach was more than three inches longer than that of the professor and all the craft of Whiz could not aid him to land a punch except when the big fellow was going away from it, while Roger reached his jaw and his ribs a dozen times.

At the end of the three rounds Whiz was puffing, and his opponent was breathing easily.

"Come on in the office," he commanded. When they were seated wrapped in their bathrobes he opened up.

"What's yer game, doc? What do you want?"

"I told you. I want to box well enough to take on professionals."

"But why? What's it goin' to get yer? You don't need the money. You don't want a broken nose or a cauliflower ear."

"Certainly not. I don't intend to get them."

"Well, you could go in the ring now and knock out plenty of second-raters, but a good big man would murder you."

"You didn't. You started some terrific ones at me just now."

"I'm not a big man and I'm a has-been. Lissen, doc. You can box. You're like a flash. I don't know how you do it, but you seem to know where a punch is goin' before it starts. Just the same, you couldn't stand up and swap wallops with a good two-hundred-pounder."

"That remains to be demonstrated."

"You make me tired. Now suppose you were up against Lefty Murphy or Phil Crowe or—or—"

"Steve Haverty," said the grave young man.

"Oh, Lord, not him. I'm talkin' common sense. Admit you could plant ten blows to their one; they would keep comin' in, and unless you knocked them out, no matter how smart you was in getting away, finally they would crack you on the jaw; then, curtains."

"But why should *I* fall, if *they* didn't when I cracked them on the jaw?"

"Because they can take it. Them fellows are hard as nails. They been scrappin' all their lives. A truck could run over them and not hurt them, see, and you was raised gentle. A knockout punch would knock you out."

"Yes? Whiz, you are supposed to have had a terrific wallop."

"I still got it. Don't you think I haven't."

ROGER THREW OFF his robe and stood up. He lowered his chin and faced the professor.

"Now land one of your haymakers on my jaw. Just as hard as you can."

"And lose my best paying pupil? Nix."

"I'm telling you do it."

"I'd break yer jaw, kid."

"Try it. You won't."

Whiz could not resist such an invitation. He threw off his bathrobe, measured his distance, set himself and swung his bare fist with every pound he had behind it. *Crack!* It sounded like a rifle shot.

Roger did not totter or fall. He lifted his chin and smiled at the astounded Whiz.

"I said put all you have in it," he said mockingly.

"Holy gee, I did! It's a wonder I didn't break my hand."

"Well, try a solar plexus now."

Whiz opened and shut his right hand gingerly. "I will not. Say, doc, you ain't human. That punch would have knocked over an ox. It would ha' felled Haverty. How do you do it?"

"I have complete mental control of every muscle of my body, Whiz. You wouldn't understand a scientific explanation. But have you ever seen a hypnotist stick needles in his subjects who didn't even bleed?"

"Yah, I seen that. Some kind of a fake."

"Not at all."

"Well, I didn't hit a muscle; I hit a bone."

"The jawbone was perfectly protected, that's all."

Whiz considered. "You had time to fix it," he declared. "You don't see the punch comin' in a fight until it lands."

"I can see it coming and I shall be ready for it."

"Well," said Whiz, "I believe this because I seen it. Say, doc, if you can do that you can be champion of the world."

Roger put on his bathrobe and sat down again. "That's my game. Whiz. Science is the worst-paid profession of all. My father made a lot of money out of me when I was a child because I was a freak, but I couldn't sell my services as a scientific man for five thousand a year to-day. Haverty will get half a million for his share of his next fight. It's about time science applied its principles to win the big monetary rewards."

"Yeah?"

"Do you think I could beat Haverty?"

"I don't know. Haverty is a bull in the ring. He comes like a locomotive and he hits like a steam hammer. Nobody ever hurt him yet, though everybody he ever fought has plastered him with punches. He's always wide open. Do you honestly think you can fix your muscles and bones for Haverty?"

"I think so."

"Then you could win on points, because you sure are fast enough to land on him. But you can't hit hard enough to hurt him."

"I know that. It's up to you to show me how. How would you like to be my manager?"

"You couldn't get a match with him without knocking out a dozen tough birds, and that trance act of yours mightn't work always."

"Besides that, I think I know how to avoid taking many blows."

"Well, you're green on ring tricks. I could wise you on those."

"Want to manage me?"

"Sure! You got to start to make a rep at once. I'll pick a palooka for you and get you on in some out-of-town club in a couple of weeks."

"And the demonstration I have just given you is between ourselves."

Whiz grinned. "You bet. My hand aches still."

"And because my father is sensitive I shall fight under an assumed name."

"That's all right. Only there's good publicity in a big scientific man making his debut in the ring."

"We'll save that to help the gate for the Haverty fight."

"Say, imagine me manager of a comin' champion! Take a shower now, kid. You don' wanter take cold."

ELOISE HAD CALLED Roger a snob, but she would have had

to admit that he behaved very considerately to the cauliflower gentry with whom he associated in the gymnasium, and he was perfect in his manner toward the rag-tag and bobtail he met at the Gaeger Club in East Brooklyn where he fought a preliminary bout under the name of Tom Moore with one Dinny Moriaty, a dock champion of the district.

It was a long, low, unsanitary structure, filled with the odor of bad tobacco smoke and fogged with clouds of it. Roger was down for a four-round go, and he found Dinny scowling in his corner when he entered the ring. The dock-walloper was a red-headed, long-armed and very hairy individual who hadn't shaved for a week and who looked as Attila's Huns must have.

The crowd knew Dinny and was with him and cheered him when he tore across the ring at the bell. Roger met him with a left jab which closed one eye, and then evaded with ease the shower of swings which followed. He boxed with the man for a couple of minutes, landing frequently enough and taking the swings on his forearms in a manner that hurt the swinger more than himself. However, the crowd wanted gore and smacking, and began to boo him immediately while it particularly objected to his footwork. When the bell rang the fans insulted him outrageously and demanded that he go in and fight.

The second round was a repetition of the first with Moriaty lunging and swinging and Roger pecking at him effectively but unostentatiously. He was wearing the man out, but the audience gave him no credit for that.

Toward the end of the round, Moriaty shouted, "Damn yez, stand up and fight," and then Roger did an astonishing thing.

"You can't hit," he said loudly. "Let's see you hit me."

He spread out his arms and stood unguarded. The savage opposite him was suspicious, but decided to take a chance and he started one from his shins which landed with a plop against Roger's stomach.

"Wow!" screamed the crowd.

Nothing happened. Moriaty looked dumfounded; the referee, who had rushed forward to count, drew back with the expression of one who has seen a ghost—and then Roger was all over the disheartened champion of the docks. *Wham! wham! wham!* to the jaw and the heart, only mechanically guarded, and Moriaty fell heavily to the floor and did not get up.

"If you do that again," threatened Whiz afterward, "I'll throw up this job. How did you know he couldn't hurt you?"

"I knew," said Roger. "Now find me a better man."

"Just a cheap kid trick. Showin' off, that's what you were," persisted the manager.

"I never show off," replied the fighter. "I've just demonstrated to a lot of people that it's impossible to knock me out. It will send my opponents into the ring half beaten before the bell rings."

"Well, there's something in that," admitted the manager. "Could you show me the trick?"

"Not unless you can read Hindustanee," smiled Roger.

"Huh. Well, see if it can tell you how to hit. You ought to ha' dropped Moriaty with one punch while he was surprised, and you had to use ten."

"You've got to improve my slugging," declared Roger. "That's what you are for."

6

A "COMING" FIGHTER

BOTH WISDOM AND prosperity are the proper rewards of maturity and experience, and cannot be supported without self-consciousness by the very young. Roger Thule would have been considered a charming young man if he had known no more than the average boy of twenty-one, but his extreme sophistication and the cynicism which it bred exasperated all with whom he came into contact.

Middle-aged men were annoyed to have what they considered a babe in arms contradict them and then demonstrate conclusively that they were wrong. Women saw the Ancient One in his black eyes, and avoided him, while men of his own age disliked him because of his air of patronage, and he in turn found them utterly uninteresting.

As for his father, long ago he thought he had discovered the mercenary spirit beneath the smug paternal manner, and the late repentance of the Reverend Thule, while it surprised him, had not restored the father to a proper place in his affections. Roger was an isolated being, without a friend or a confidant until he met Dr. Tom Marvin; but between him and the physician a curious comradeship had sprung up.

Until a few months before, the boy's zeal for knowledge

had been continually at fever heat; when all at once he lost interest in it, he had wanted to die.

Now he found himself amused and attracted by what he termed his two ridiculous enterprises.

"How many languages do you know?" asked Dr. Marvin one evening when Roger had dropped in unannounced, as he had formed the habit of doing.

"I speak seven or eight modern tongues rather fluently, but I am able to read some twenty-five or thirty, including all the dead languages."

"Amazing! I can jabber a little French and of course I read Latin and Greek, but that lets me out."

"It's no task for me to learn a language. I can memorize five or six hundred words of any tongue in a few days, and, being aware of the roots and methods of conjugation and declension of the basic tongues, familiarization with their developments and variants is no trouble at all."

"Do you understand Egyptian and Chaldean?" asked the doctor satirically.

"Oh, yes," said the boy simply, "and a dozen variants of the Chinese and East Indian. Persian and Arabic, as a matter of course."

"You're not a student; you are a siphon of knowledge."

"Not a bad simile," smiled Roger. "I learn with incredible rapidity. In the course of my studies of literature and languages I have picked up lore unknown to the modern world as not one per cent of the writings in any except half a dozen tongues have ever been translated. For example, magic, hypnotism, fakirism, occultism—"

"But that's all twaddle."

"Most of it; but there are glimmerings of light in the mass of misinformation."

"Look here, Roger," said the doctor sternly. "None of that stuff must be used in your affair with Eloise, I love that girl. I won't have it."

"You may be sure I won't hypnotize her nor magnetize her nor steal her soul. But I feel justified in making use of my understanding of the emotions and mental processes of the sex."

With a booming laugh the doctor tapped the student upon the shoulder.

"Pshaw! I'll bet my money on the guile of one small girl against all your alleged understanding of her sex. Woman is Enigma."

"An enigma is only a riddle, and there are few riddles which cannot be solved."

"Eloise tells me that you are a small boy with an overstuffed mind, and that so far you do nothing but bore her."

Roger smiled unconcernedly.

"Eloise is not telling you the truth," he retorted.

TWO WEEKS AFTER his victory over Moriaty, Roger stepped into the ring of a club in Yonkers, matched for a six-round go with one Bill Heffernan in the semifinals. The fee for his services upon this occasion would be fifty dollars, which was twenty-five more than he got for flattening Moriaty in Brooklyn. Upon this occasion Dr. Marvin occupied a ringside seat. So far, Rev. Thule was unaware that his son was participating in disgraceful pugilistic encounters.

Roger's physical development when he stripped in the ring caused the physician to open wide his eyes. There were no great bulging muscles beneath his satin skin, but the experienced glance of the physician recognized exceptional strength and power in legs, arms and torso.

Heffernan was another Moriaty, a little faster and less stupid. He tore into Roger, who retreated before him, content to block his blows. Roger's only offense appeared to be gentle taps upon the man's arms. The round ended without the scientist's attempting to reach the face or body of his opponent and without Heffernan's having laid a glove on him.

The second round was a repetition of the first, except that Heffernan was much slower, and Roger stuck his left in the man's face half a dozen times. Most of Roger's blows were without steam and landed on biceps and the forearms of the fighter.

The fight was very unsatisfactory to the public, who jeered and booed and wanted those "bums" thrown out of the ring. They commanded Roger to fight and ordered Heffernan to kill the four-flusher.

All through the third round this vehement criticism of the battlers continued as Heffernan grew more and more sluggish and Roger still unenterprising. Dr. Marvin's eyes were gleaming, for he thought he understood the scholar's plan of battle.

Heffernan came up for the fourth, a look of desperation in his eyes, and seemed to throw himself into a position of defense with difficulty. Again the pecking at his arms, and the doctor saw him wince at every tap of the gloved hands of his enemy.

The audience roared with laughter as Heffernan made a feeble effort to drive in his right and the unfortunate man's hands fell to his sides. A merciful crash of the right fist to the jaw and Heffernan dropped to the canvas, lay there conscious, but made no effort to rise. The referee, after the count, lifted the right glove of Roger Thule as evidence that he had won. The crowd could not object to the decision, but jeered and howled ferociously at victor as well as vanquished as they left the ring.

"I see your knowledge of anatomy came into practical use in that fight," observed the doctor when he sat in a restaurant with the pugilist and his manager half an hour later.

"I thought the guy was crazy," declared Whiz. "I told him to go in and box Heffernan for a few rounds, but that don't mean hittin' a man on the arms. You can't hurt a fighter that way."

"Oh, yes, you can," replied the doctor. "A drop of water landing on top of a man's head every few seconds would kill him or drive him crazy in a few hours. Heffernan's arms were paralyzed by the fourth round."

The savant smiled. "I was just testing a theory. Finding that Heffernan was too slow to hit me, I adopted one of the principles of jujutsu to boxing. If I had not knocked him out he would have been unable to come up for the fifth round, and they would have accused him of cowardice."

"Yeah? One wild swing might have busted yer little experiment, doc," declared Whiz. "I doubt if I can get you another match. The crowds don't like you."

"If they dislike me enough—it will make me a drawing card. They will throng to see me knocked out," replied Roger calmly.

"He's right," Dr. Marvin asserted. "For years Dempsey

was hated, and his first big gates were made by those who wanted to see him killed."

THERE WAS NO publicity as yet regarding the young man whom Whiz was managing; the fights were too unimportant. But upon the strength of the destruction of Heffernan, Whiz landed another semifinal in Jersey City with a wild bull named Jeff Maloney. The match occurred two weeks after the affair in Yonkers, and again Dr. Marvin was at the ringside.

"Tom Moore" was outweighed ten pounds by the slashing Maloney, and the fellow's reach was at least an inch longer. This time Roger decided to carry the fight to his opponent. He met him in the center of the ring in his rush, stepped upon Maloney's outstretched right foot, stumbled as it was yanked away, and was felled immediately by a right swing to the left side of the head.

He lay inert on the canvas, to the stupefaction of Whiz and the dismay of Dr. Marvin. At the count of nine he staggered to his feet and stood defenseless while the wild bull rained blow upon blow at head and body.

"Keep away! Box him! Bicycle!" shouted Whiz pleadingly, but Roger was out on his feet. He made feeble gestures with his arms which were impotent against the rain of blows, and then he began to crumple and lay prone. Again the count of the referee, the roar of the delighted crowd. Six. Roger stirred. Seven. He rose precariously to one knee. Eight. Dr. Marvin caught his eye and saw the light of intelligence returning. Nine! and he was up and in a position of defense.

Again came the slashing attack of big Jeff Maloney, but Roger was blocking now with some success, and when the blows did land he no longer quivered. Just as the bell rang he planted a hard left in the right eye of the Irishman; but it was Jeff's round by a mile.

While Whiz and his other seconds worked over him he lay inert for a few seconds against the ropes in his corner, and then began to listen to the hysterical chatter of Whiz.

"Keep away from him or he'll finish you in this round. Box him, you fool! Keep out of clinches, fight, and don't try any funny business."

"He won't hit me again," said Roger Thule slowly, and then the bell rang.

Maloney rushed, swinging with both hands. Roger evaded both swings and planted a stiff right to the stomach, caught an uppercut on the jaw which did not seem to faze him, then stepped back and scientifically closed the other eye of the Wild Bull.

Half blinded, Maloney tore in, and now the scholar evaded him easily. Straight rights and lefts went to Maloney's eyes and the big man staggered about no longer able to distinguish his opponent clearly. Maloney was comparatively fresh, eager to plant the knockout, unhurt except that he couldn't see. Roger was a blur, and Roger was never where his blows were driven. *Crash!* A heavy right crushed in Maloney's nose. *Thud!* He took one in the pit of the stomach. And more knife thrusts at the poor eyes. Now he was a blinded Samson, but the bell rang in time to save him.

"Great work," declared Whiz. "If you only could hit, now, you could finish him in the next. His seconds won't help those eyes much."

"It's brutal," gasped Roger, "but I had to do it. He was too strong for me."

"Did he hurt you?"

"He hurt me all right."

"Well, kid, you can take it."

MALONEY WAS A pitiful sight when he staggered forward for the third round. He was temporarily blinded, Roger was a black shadow, the bright lights pained him and he had no defense against the shower of thrusts and jabs save furious and abortive swings.

Half a dozen times Roger set himself and let go rights and lefts in hope of ending it, but the physique of his foe was superb; he kept his feet. However, the thing was such a massacre that even the gore-loving crowd wanted it stopped, and the referee finally pushed Maloney to his corner where he dropped into his chair and blubbered. The referee pointed to Roger, who thus won his third fight.

"What happened in the first round?" asked Roger of his two friends after the fight.

"You got a terrible lacing, kid," declared Whiz. "Say, I took no stock in you till I saw you knocked down twice and get up. You're no boxer. You're a fighter you are."

"*Twice?* I remember being knocked down. I stepped on his foot and got thrown off balance, but I only went down once, didn't I?"

"You got up again," said Dr. Marvin, "got hit with everything including the kitchen stove, and went down for the count of nine."

"Funny," mused Roger. "I remember going down and getting up. I was fully conscious then and I called upon a certain knowledge I have of muscular resistance. His blows did not hurt me after that."

"You mean you did not feel them?" asked the doctor incredulously. "How is that possible?"

"It's a sort of withdrawal of consciousness from a part of the body where a blow is expected. You know how you can make a section of the human body immune to pain by a local anaesthetic. Mine is a mental anaesthetic, doctor."

"Too bad you didn't use it the first time. It's the bunk if you ask me," commented Whiz.

"I was off guard," admitted Roger. "My mind was concentrated on recovering my balance and the blow caught me without armor. It won't happen again."

"This guy is a mystery to me," declared Whiz with a shake of the head. "Just the same, doc, you can't hit hard enough to bust a pane of glass. To-morrow we go in for that."

"I don't have to be a bone crusher if I can land on the right spot," Roger defended.

"However, I do need more instruction in hitting. I hope poor Maloney's eyes aren't permanently affected."

"So long as you don't kill them, you should worry," said the practical if brutal Whiz.

"See here, Roger," declared Dr. Marvin. "You have demonstrated to me that you are capable of becoming a brilliantly successful pugilist. It's even possible you may succeed in beating Haverty, but what of it? To-night you were within an ace of being knocked out. That blow on the side of the head might have killed you. You cannot always guard against accidents, and each opponent you meet will be more dangerous. Haverty is a master of his craft. Drop it."

"I'm going to beat Haverty," said Roger.

"But why?"

Roger scratched his head and grinned wryly. "I'm hanged if I can understand my own mental reactions on that subject. All I know is that I have got to do it."

"I can understand them," said Dr. Marvin. "You, my boy, are in love with Eloise, and you have yielded to the most ordinary and most primitive of motives. You want to show off to a woman."

"That's nonsense, of course," he protested. "Eloise is an agreeable girl—but, in love with her? Pshaw!"

"If you are in love with her and she fails to reciprocate, it serves you right for your arrogance."

"There are times, Dr. Marvin," Roger Thule said, with a return of his old offensive manner, "when I wonder if you are not an unusually stupid man."

"All right. Explain your fool motives in a better way."

THE NEWSPAPERS, AT last, took notice of "Tom Moore," and agreed that he was a comer. His two easy victories had attracted no attention but the fight with Maloney had been very dramatic. Maloney had floored "Moore" twice in the first round and hit him with everything he had at least ten times, and then the young fellow had come back and so cut up his opponent that the fight had to be stopped in the third round.

"Moore" was a comer and the Jersey papers commented kindly upon him. Even the New York papers found space for a paragraph or two. No matter how great a boxer he might be, no man in the ring wins respect until he proves he can take it. Gene Tunney was a fake champion until Dempsey hit him seven times and almost knocked him out in Chicago. Because the mighty boxer could take a beating and come back, he leaped into popularity.

Two days later Whiz signed Roger up for a main bout in Long Island City with Peaches Rosenbaum, a really good heavyweight, for three hundred dollars, win or lose.

Roger bore the marks of his conflict with Maloney. His face was badly bruised, his stomach turned blue and black, and he was sore for three or four days. He was vain enough to remain away from Eloise for a week until the scars of battle healed. He worked daily with Whiz, punching the bag, practicing blows, and building muscle until his preceptor was afraid he would go stale and ordered him to lay off for a few days.

"Those first two fights were just sparring matches, but this one took something out of you," declared Whiz. "You got to win on points against Rosenbaum and you need all your pep. You can't knock that guy out."

"Do you want to lay a wager on that?"

"Nix. And I forbid you to try, see? If you don't do what I tell you, you can get another manager."

"All right. But why?"

"In the first place I don't think you are strong enough yet, but there's another reason. There ain't so many good men in the heavyweight division and I don't want to get them scared of you. Beat Rosenbaum and I pick up another good match right away; knock him out and they shy away. There's more to this game than getting into the ring."

"I see your point. I must be good but not too good."

"Sure. Look at Harry Wills. He never could get a match

with Dempsey. They said it was because he was a black man; but if he wasn't such a good black man, he'd ha' got a chance quick enough. Look at Sharkey: he got a draw with Heeney, but he was a good boxer and he came near licking Dempsey. Heeney was slow as a coach so they picked him for Gene Tunney's last fight. Not that Tunney mightn't have battened Sharkey, too, but why take a chance?"

"I realize that I don't know as much as I should about the business," said Roger. "I must devote some attention to it."

"You devote attention to learning how to hit, and I'll tend to the business," declared Whiz. "Keep on doin' what I say and I'll have you in the ring with Steve Haverty in a year. And then God help you."

"Or him," smiled the exasperating Roger Thule.

Whiz scowled at him. "Danged if I know why I like you, doc," he declared. "You sure can get my goat."

7

TRAGEDY STRIKES

ROGER WAS LYING in his bed thinking, but not about the mighty philosophical problems of the universe which once had engrossed all his waking moments. He was wondering why he should be glad that Whiz and Dr. Marvin liked him, and how long it would be before Eloise liked him also.

He was aware that he was generally disliked for his superiority and his knowledge of it, and until recently he had been rather proud of it and accepted it as a tribute. It certainly had not bothered him. He had no fondness for anybody; he really knew nobody well enough to be fond of him except his father, and he considered that he had no reason to love him; for Theobald Thule had made Roger what he was for his own profit and glory, and his inordinate pride in his son was not paternal love. Even his recent concern and his willingness to spend part of his fortune to restore his boy to health struck Roger more as a grand gesture than honest repentance for turning a healthy commonplace boy into a thinking machine.

Roger usually breakfasted with Mr. Thule and occasionally dined with him. He was pleasantly respectful to his parent, but secretly was amused at the old gentleman's efforts to restore relations which had not existed since

Roger had turned wise eyes upon him at the age of twelve, to see through him as though he were made of glass.

He found himself feeling sorry for his father, now; and his new-found ability to experience emotions such as excitement, sorrow, and friendliness surprised him. He admitted that he got a distinct thrill in the ring, experiencing what must be the joy of battle. He found pleasure in the company of the beautiful Eloise Lane; he enjoyed his evenings with Dr. Tom Marvin.

He was softening and humanizing. He had built himself an imaginary pedestal, climbed on it and struck an attitude. He had supposed himself high above the interests and affairs of ordinary folks, and now he found himself pleased because he was winning an esteem not based upon his erudition but existing in spite of it.

"The next thing I know," he said to himself, just before he fell asleep, "I'll be fool enough to fall in love."

He had an appointment at ten at the gymnasium and had left word to be called at nine, but at half-past seven, Mrs. Jardine, the housekeeper, pounded with both fists on his door.

"Mr. Thule, Mr. Thule, get up!" she was screaming. "Your father!"

Roger always awoke with all senses alert.

"What's that? What about my father?"

"He's dead. He's been killed."

"I'll be right down," he said calmly, but he was shaking as he drew on a dressing gown, thrust his feet into his slippers, unlocked his door—he had formed the habit of locking it on the road in his theater days—and ran down to the lower floor.

He dreaded to touch the still form

Death was of no consequence in his philosophy, and grief a puerile emotion, but his eyes had filled and he was more bewildered and shocked than he had ever been in his life.

"Where is he?" he demanded of the hysterical woman who stood at the foot of the stairs.

She pointed to the closed library door. "In there."

Roger opened the door. His father sat in a chair before his table, his arms by his side, his head bent forward so that his forehead touched the table top.

THE YOUNG MAN stared, hesitated and then walked resolutely to his father's side. In the operating room of the medical school, for he had acquired a diploma as a physician and surgeon in a year of intense study, he had handled and even dissected the dead. This, however, was different; he dreaded to touch his father. It had to be done, though, and he lifted the head and pushed back the body with difficulty.

There was a bullet hole in Theobald Thule's coat on

the left side, over the heart. The coat was stiff with dried blood, there had been blood dripping upon the Chinese rug beneath as a small reddish blotch upon the deep blue of the rug gave mute witness, and there was a condition of rigor mortis.

Roger's lips were dry, his eyes were burning, and his tongue seemed paralyzed when he tried to speak to the woman who hovered at the door.

"Get the police," he said finally in a voice which was strange to him. "Father was murdered and he has been dead for many hours, seven hours anyway. Don't touch anything in this room."

"How will I get them?" asked the woman.

"On the phone!"

"It's in there. I don't want to go in."

"I'll get them."

He called police headquarters from the table phone and as he waited he saw that a sheet of paper had rested beneath his father's head and on it was written:

MY SON

At his feet on the floor Roger spied a fountain pen; then he had the desk man at headquarters.

"This is Roger Thule of—Madison Avenue speaking," he said firmly. "I have just discovered the murdered body of my father—" Despite himself his voice broke. "He was shot through the heart while working in his library. Rigor mortis has set in and the crime must have been committed around midnight. Thank you."

" 'My son.' "

His father had been beginning a note to him when the bullet struck him. He usually addressed him as "My son," and the pride in his voice had made the old Roger sneer.

He looked on the set face, grim in death, and again involuntary tears started to his eyes. Of course his father had loved him. His pride was really love. He had patiently taken the blank page of the baby, Roger, and had begun to write on it when most babies were prattling their first indistinguishable words. He wanted to make his child the most intelligent in the world; surely he could only be commended for that; and when the boy developed so amazingly and offers came to turn that precocity into gold, who could blame the half-starved clergyman for accepting?

True, he had liked luxury and had acquired a lust for money, but the money would eventually go to the son who earned it. To Theobald Thule there was nothing so sublime as knowledge, and the astonishing attainments of Roger, his scholastic victories, had seemed to the father the most worthwhile things in the world.

No doubt he had grieved deeply when the arrogant youth turned against him; probably he had even been bewildered, for he supposed himself a greater benefactor than any father ever had been, since he would leave his son not only wealth but culture beyond that of any young man living. The mental illness of his son had distressed him beyond measure; even Dr. Marvin declared that Roger's father meant it when he offered his last dollar for a cure. Of course he had loved his son.

Now, although Roger believed that what was before him was only a clod of earth and the spirit which had animated it was not immortal, he found himself on his knees beside the body saying over and over:

"Father, forgive me, dear father, forgive my pride and arrogance."

And when he rose there was a gleam in his eye. Roger Thule had added another to his new purposes in life: to find and punish the murderer.

IN TEN MINUTES the ringing of the front doorbell announced the coming of the police; two hard faced men in civilian clothes, an inspector and a detective sergeant.

"I am Inspector Horton," said the first, "and this is Detective Sergeant Jones. You are Mr. Thule, Jr.? You phoned us a few minutes ago."

"I am Roger Thule."

"Yes. Pretty sad business, Mr. Thule. Mind stepping out of the room for a few minutes?"

"Not at all. I'll go up to my own room and dress."

"Very good, sir."

When Roger came downstairs in ten minutes the officers were waiting for him in the hall.

"We've made our inspection," said Horton. "It's murder. Died by a bullet which entered the body above the heart, a thirty-eight caliber bullet. No gun, Mr. Thule?"

"I saw none."

"Well, we want a talk with you."

"Suppose we take seats in the drawing room," Roger said calmly.

The two officers settled themselves and crossed their legs. Horton was a squat, heavy-jawed man of fifty with sharp blue eyes, a stub nose and a heavy grayish-brown mustache. Jones was bald, round-faced, florid and pig-eyed.

"You are the son of the murdered man," began Horton.

"Yes, sir."

"You on good terms with your father?"

"Certainly."

"I heard of you. You're the 'Boy with the Mighty Brain.'"

"Ten years ago, when I was a child lecturer, they called me that," Roger said, annoyed to realizing that his cheeks were red.

"Didn't have any trouble with your father, lately?"

"Certainly not."

"What time did you come in last night?"

"About ten o'clock."

"See your father?"

"I saw a light in the library. I assumed he was there."

"But you didn't go in and speak to him. You weren't on such good terms."

"My dear man," said Roger with acerbity, "my father and I were scientists; we took our relations for granted, and we did not kiss and hug when we met. I usually breakfasted with father and dined with him if we both happened to be at home. I assumed he was reading or working and did not dream of disturbing him."

"And you didn't hear a shot?"

"No."

"Look here," broke in Sergeant Jones. "I seen you somewhere and your name wasn't Thule either. I seen you. Say, I know who you are—Tom Moore, the prize-fighter, that's who you are. This feller's a pug, inspector. I saw him fight Maloney over in Jersey."

Horton's hard eyes grew harder. "That right, Mr. Thule?"

"Quite," said Roger blandly. "I am a boxer and I fought Maloney."

"Cut him to ribbons, he did," declared Jones excitedly.

"I don't get this," the inspector declared. "How can you be Roger Thule, the scientific sharp, and Tom Moore, the scrapper?"

ROGER SMILED PATIENTLY. "It's very simple. I fight under the name of Tom Moore."

"What for? You're rich, ain't you?"

"It happens to amuse me to be both a scholar and a pugilist."

"And you used a fake name so your father wouldn't get on."

"Something like that."

"But he found out, there was hell to pay, you had a fight, he was going to disinherit you and you shot him!" rattled off the inspector.

Roger laughed outright. "Quite a theory. Only it happens that he did not find out, so far as I know, and we did not quarrel. If he had found out he would have done nothing about it save protest mildly. And I did not shoot him."

"You shot him," repeated the inspector. "And, before he died, he tried to write, 'My son shot me,' but only got as far as 'My son.'"

"Quite ingenious," said Roger. "I saw the sheet of paper on the table as I was phoning the department. I think he died instantly, but he had begun to write me a note just before he was shot."

"That's a likely story. You live in the same house with him and he writes you a note instead of telling you what he wanted."

"Father often wrote me notes which always began 'My son,' and had them sent to my chamber by one of the servants. It was a habit of his. I often wrote him notes. We were not ordinary father and son, Mr. Inspector. I take it, instead of looking for the murderer, you have decided that I must be guilty and intend to make no further search."

"I don't say you're guilty. I'm trying to get the facts," said Horton doggedly. "It's kind of queer, don't you think so yourself?"

"I'm sorry to say I don't."

"You got any money of your own?" demanded Jones.

"I receive two or three thousand a year royalty for scientific works I have written. I recently received fifty dollars for winning a prize fight, but my manager got half of that."

"Then you were dependent on your father," stated the inspector.

"In a sense. You must realize, however, that his fortune was made by capitalizing my talents as a child, and was held by him in trust for me."

"It was his money, just the same. How much is he worth?"

"About a million, I imagine."

"Which you inherit?"

"I assume so."

Horton looked at Jones. "Best motive in the world," said Jones.

"You said it," replied Horton.

"Meanwhile somebody killed my father and nothing is being done about it!"

"I wouldn't say that," grinned Inspector Horton.

"Know anybody who had it in for your father?" asked Jones.

"No. I know nothing about father's affairs. For years we have been strangers although we lived together. Of what he did with his spare time I have no knowledge whatever, any more than he knew what I was doing with mine. When we dined together we discussed books or scientific matters."

"Any women you know of?"

"I doubt it. Father had been a clergyman and had very high principles. I am sure he had no improper relations with any woman."

"Well, you're not under arrest, but don't leave the house for a while. Somebody will be up from the district attorney's office, and the coroner is on his way."

"I'll return to my room. I can always find something to occupy me."

8

THE FINGER OF SUSPICION

WHEN ROGER HAD gone Horton looked at his assistant. "Cool bird," he remarked. "It's hard to believe a great scientist like him would kill his own father."

"Say, that feller has a cruel streak a yard wide. You ought to have seen him plug away at Maloney's eyes in that fight in Jersey. The crowd made the referee stop the fight. He hasn't got any heart, that guy."

"Well, we have no evidence against him. We've got to find a motive, establish a quarrel, see if the old man was going to disinherit him, find the weapon. Too bad he didn't finish that letter."

"The kid was first in the room. Why didn't he take away the sheet of paper? He could have."

"Lost his nerve."

"Don't you believe it. He's got an iron nerve."

"Well, let's have in the servants."

Mrs. Jardine and the cook and the butler were on the griddle for an hour before the officers were through with them, and by that time an assistant district attorney, James S. Quinlan, was on the scene while the coroner had come and examined the body.

Quinlan, who was an alert, good-looking young man

with prematurely gray hair, listened to the police theory but shook his head at the end of it.

"Won't hold," he said. "The coroner says the bullet penetrated the heart which means he wrote those words before he died, not afterward; so your theory that he was trying to identify the murderer falls to the ground. The servants confirm all Thule's statements about relations between him and his father, you say."

"Yes. They were a queer pair. Wrote notes to each other all the time."

"These were not ordinary people. Young Thule is supposed to be the greatest genius alive, and the old man was more his manager than his father. Roger dominated the father completely; I have heard that. They both probably went around in a brown study for weeks without speaking to each other. And if Thule wanted to commit a murder he would do it so cleverly we would never have a chance of pinning it on him. Assume the crime was committed by somebody else. Investigate the private life of the Rev. Thule. Did you find any clews?"

"It looks like an inside job," said Horton, somewhat crestfallen. "Doors and windows locked. The shot was fired from eight or ten feet away. Servants say that nobody had called, up to the time they went to bed. Not a darn thing to indicate anybody was in the room with him."

"Sure of that?"

"Positive."

"You are a pair of fine sleuths," said Mr. Quinlan. "Take a look at this." He took out of his vest pocket a small square of fine linen and extended it to Horton who inspected it in silence, smelled of it and returned it.

"Where the devil did you get that?" he demanded. "I swear it wasn't in the room."

"Mr. Thule was sitting on it," replied Quinlan.

Horton laughed in relief. "That let us out," he stated. "We didn't touch the body. That's the coroner's job."

"Find the lady and see what she has to say. In all probability she called on Thule last night, sat in his chair, and dropped her handkerchief when she changed her seat so that the old man could take it and write a note to his son. And it's possible she shot him while he was writing."

WHILE THE SLEUTHS were considering this, Quinlan pulled the bellcord and asked that Mr. Thule be sent for.

Roger entered in a moment and the assistant district attorney introduced himself after a cordial handshake.

"Please dismiss from your mind any notion that we suspect you, Mr. Thule," he said heartily. "We have already discovered enough to clear you. Your reputation is well known to me and I know you will help us in every way possible in our investigation."

"If you don't discover my father's murderer, I shall," said Roger firmly.

"Now I hate to disturb any impression you have of your father's—ahem—careful life, but it seems that he had a woman visitor last night."

"Indeed!" exclaimed Roger, really astonished.

"When the body was lifted from its chair we found a handkerchief beneath it, a woman's handkerchief. Do you know with what women he was acquainted?"

The young man smiled faintly. "I have no knowledge whatever of my father's private life. May I see the handkerchief?"

Quinlan took it from his pocket and passed it over. Roger inspected it, then put it to his nostrils. His eyes may have widened, but the others saw no change of expression.

"There is a very slight perfume," he observed as he returned it.

"Yes. I don't know what it is."

"Well, it may help you to trace the owner."

"You know of no woman of your father's acquaintance with a perfume like that?"

"If my father was acquainted with any woman I am ignorant of it," he replied.

"Well, I thank you very much. I'll keep you informed of our progress."

Roger shook hands, bowed to the policemen and went upstairs. He entered his room, passed into the bathroom and through it into a large chamber fitted up as a laboratory in which, of yore, he had made thousands of interesting experiments. Opening a cabinet he took down one small bottle, secured a second bottle, poured some of its contents into the first, shook it well, then emptied the fluid within into the sink, after which he poured into the sink some vile-smelling acid. He washed it all down the pipe with hot water, cleansed his hands very carefully and returned to his room. He was perspiring freely, and his face was very pale, but there was nobody to observe him.

"Oh, my God," he said slowly. Never before had he used that expression, because he did not believe in God.

Only a week ago he had surprised and delighted Eloise Lane with a vial of marvelous perfume of a sort she had never encountered before. Since the first meeting he had been giving her curious but apparently inexpensive presents, which she received with mockery as moves in his campaign.

This perfume he had manufactured himself by blending several of the rarest and most exquisite French perfumes with a chemical fluid of his own. He had just destroyed all evidence of its existence in his laboratory. There was only one woman in the world who had that perfume, Eloise; therefore the handkerchief beneath his father's body was the handkerchief of Eloise, and she must have been the nocturnal visitor whom the police suspected of the crime.

ROGER HAD BEEN pursuing Eloise calmly, methodically, cunningly and confidently, undaunted by her apparent indifference, assured by his book knowledge of the sex that in the end she would succumb. He had pursued her as cold-bloodily as a scientist with a net on the trail of a beautiful butterfly which he proposed to kill and place in his collection.

Acknowledging her beauty, her charm, her strength of character, her willfulness and her ingenuity, and being uninfluenced by personal emotion, he had no doubt whatever of the end of the game. Now, unexpectedly, horribly, he was shocked into the knowledge that he, Roger Thule, loved Eloise Lane. He was petrified with terror at her entanglement in this crime.

An apostle of selfishness he was, yet he knew now that he would lay down his life to save her. His own father lay dead below and his death had brought upon the youth the knowledge that he had loved him and misjudged him. He had determined to bring the murderer to justice—and the finger of suspicion pointed to Eloise.

Eloise, of course, must be innocent. She could not have

been the visitor since she had never seen his father and would not call on a man she did not know—but she was the only owner of that perfume and the bull-headed police would pounce upon her, if they found her, and drag her to jail. He had just had an example of the police talent for the obvious in the theory Horton had constructed out of nothing at all, which would have made him the criminal if it hadn't collapsed in the light of truth. They would enmesh Eloise. They must not.

His concern for her overshadowed, for a time, the astonishing fact that he loved her—that Roger Thule was capable of love like any college student or young clerk—that he had picked out one woman to be infatuated with even to the extent of shielding her if she had killed his father. Yes, he knew he would do that. If necessary he would shoulder the crime himself. Self-sacrifice! How he had sneered at that virtue! Yet for Eloise he would sacrifice himself.

He must get that perfume away from Eloise and destroy all traces of it as he had destroyed the portion of it which he had left in his laboratory, and he must warn her to be on her guard.

The phone? No. Undoubtedly the detectives still had him under observation and the wire was probably tapped. Call on her? He would be followed and attention attracted to her. At this moment her boudoir was likely to be delicately scented with the delicious perfume. Even a police nose was capable of identifying that, for it was like no other in the world.

He would go to Whiz's gymnasium this morning as usual; from there phone Dr. Marvin and send the doctor to warn Eloise. He had no desire for training, this morning;

he was saddened inexpressibly by his father's death and shocked by the intrusion of the perfume of Eloise. But the police knew he was a boxer and, while they would consider him hard-hearted to go about his work on the day of his father's death, they would not think it suspicious. And no time was to be lost in reaching Eloise Lane.

It was possible Eloise had lost her handkerchief and some other woman had picked it up. That scent, unless neutralized, would last indefinitely. That must be the explanation. He regretted now he had been so completely uninterested in his father's friends and acquaintances. One among them had slain him, and that person must pay the penalty.

While in theory he disdained the Hebrew doctrine of a life for a life, he wanted this especial murderer punished—unless it were Eloise.

IT WAS A very troubled young man who left the house at ten o'clock and who walked briskly to the Physical Culture Institute; but he was not so troubled that he was unaware of the fat shadow in his tracks. While Quinlan had assured him that no suspicion attached to him, he had not accepted that assertion, for he knew that everybody in the house would be a suspect until the murderer was found.

Roger had sat upon Olympus, immune to the vexations of spirit of the humans so far below, contemplating serenely the sum of mortal knowledge and gradually becoming engulfed in boredom to a point where he wanted to slip into oblivion. Now he was tingling with life and a prey to common emotions; full of ambitions, hopes and fears. He had, that morning, come into contact with tragedy and with love, and was for the first time in his life experiencing anxiety for some one else.

He entered the gymnasium, nodded curtly in response to the respectful greetings of the habitues who looked upon Tom Moore as a coming champion, and found Whiz thumbing a dirty ledger in the untidy office.

"Call up Dr. Marvin and ask him to come over at once. Something very important, but be careful not to mention me on the phone."

"Sure. What's on yer mind, doc?"

"I can't tell you all, but my father was murdered last night. Shot through the heart. While I am not under arrest I am suspected and a detective is probably waiting outside. I'm going to my locker and get into fight togs. Send Marvin into the gym when he comes. I'll talk with him in public."

"Gee, doc, I'm sorry. You must feel terrible. Murdered? Any idea who done it?"

"None whatever. Put in that phone call, please."

Whiz looked after the broad back and turned to the telephone.

"His old man murdered and he comes right over and gets into ring clothes," he muttered. "That guy ain't human."

He was wrong, however. Roger was human at last.

In a quarter of an hour Dr. Marvin came into the gymnasium and found Roger pummeling the punching bag ferociously.

"I left four patients in my office," said the specialist. "From Whiz I gathered that something very important required my presence here."

Roger left the punching bag and faced the physician with an expression of anxiety.

"Thank you, doctor. I appreciate your promptness. Last night my father was shot through the heart while sitting in his library. When they lifted the body they found a handkerchief, a woman's handkerchief, scented with a special perfume which I manufactured and presented to Eloise."

DR. MARVIN'S RUDDY face paled. "You don't think—"

"Certainly not. But there is no other person who owns this perfume and she will be arrested on suspicion if they find it on her. I am under observation myself, so I want you to go to Eloise, get the vial containing the perfume, have her fumigate all her clothes and handkerchiefs to destroy the scent, and thus avoid being dragged into the affair."

"But if no one except Eloise has this perfume—"

"I tell you I manufactured it myself."

"How did it get into your father's library?" the doctor finished.

"Eloise never met my father and certainly did not bring it there. It's possible she dropped her handkerchief, and somebody picked it up. In any event, she must be saved from annoyance. And please tell her that the idiotic police are shadowing me and I shall not call on her for a few days. Find out if she has any notion how she lost the handkerchief."

The doctor nodded. "Knowing how you regarded your father, I won't offer the usual expressions of sympathy."

"I've been a fool about that as well as other things," Roger said slowly. "I am very much cut up about it, doctor. It seems that I am not devoid of human feelings after all."

Marvin smiled as he grasped his hand. "I am sorry it took such a tragedy to convince you of that," he said. "I have known all along that you were very human, Roger. I'll go to Eloise immediately."

"No, go back to your office, and then, after at least half an hour, call on her. You may be followed if you have been seen talking to me. Don't communicate with me, either. I'll call you from a public pay station."

"Yes, yes. Let's take all precautions. Now, Roger, you will inherit your father's fortune. Drop this prize fighting business."

"On the contrary, I'm going at it harder than ever. To make an admission which I would not have confessed to myself until recently, I get a thrill out of it."

"You are a fantastic individual, Roger. *Au revoir.*"

While Roger punched the bag his mind was busy. He must discover as much as possible about the private life of his father. Doubtless there would be correspondence, papers in the safe, many ways of getting information. Discover all his acquaintances, eliminate each one who proved that it was impossible for him or her to commit the crime, and eventually discover the criminal. It ought to be fairly simple. Did Eloise know anything? Impossible!

9

RING BUSINESS

MR. STEVE HAVERTY was the kind of champion to bring joy to managerial hearts, and Tim Hearn, whose good fortune it was to handle his business affairs and act as guide, cicerone, and friend, was greatly envied by the profession.

For three years Steve had been on top of the heap. He had fought two big battles since winning the belt and disposed of his opponents with almost too much ease. But he had not yet needed to enlarge the size of his hat. He was docile, good-natured and amiable as a big Newfoundland dog, ready to take Tim's statement that anything was necessary, indifferent to the terms arranged for him, splitting his earnings fifty-fifty without the slightest objection that the business end of the partnership was getting more than he deserved; in fact, he was the ideal champion, and Tim loved him like a young brother.

If, during his career, anything shady had ever taken place in his contests, Steve knew nothing about it. He had pulled punches occasionally and let an opponent stay the limit, on Tim's say-so, because it would help his next match, but that was in the days when he was nobody in particular. Since he won the title he had gone into the ring for the purpose of knocking out the contender, and did so, neatly and picturesquely.

"He's nothing but a great big kid with a heart of gold," Tim used to tell the reporters.

Tim had been having a hard time keeping the women away from Steve during the past three years because the big fellow was susceptible, ingenuous, and a perfect mark for an adventuress. Tim's method was to buy the ladies off, taking the necessary heavy payments out of the common bankroll without bothering to consult the champion. He went at them without delay before they had time to make much impression upon the pugilist. Occasionally Steve would wonder why a certain girl had stopped calling him up, but he speedily forgot her, while the young woman had withdrawn from the field with five or ten thousand dollars, depending upon how good a huckster she happened to be.

Tim had no objection, now, to the marriage of the champion, who must marry sometime and might as well do it while the field of heavyweights was not dangerous, but he loved the boy and he was determined that no vampire should get her claws into him. So two cabaret singers, a little motion picture actress, and a musical comedy show girl had been pensioned and sent away. Eloise Lane was different. If Eloise would marry Steve, Tim Hearn would be very happy. She was one hundred per cent, that youngster.

TIM HEARN LOOKED a good deal like an undertaker, for he had a long, lugubrious face, was tall and spare, and usually wore black clothes. He fancied small, ready-made bow ties which slipped over the collar button. Somewhere he had managed to secure Congress shoes, an ancient type of footgear which had elastic sides and no buttons or laces.

Tim had begun life as a bartender, had graduated into following the races, done a little theater ticket speculating and finally found Steve, who was nineteen years old and fighting for a ten-dollar bill.

Tim Hearn was as honest as a bank president, though perhaps that isn't such a good simile; he was a bachelor, and a millionaire. His own profits and Steve's he had invested intelligently.

As a matchmaker he was a Shylock, as a watchdog he was a mastiff, and as a student of fighting he was a master.

Nothing happened in the game about which he didn't hear almost immediately, because he had a multitude of correspondents and his purpose in life was to keep Steve champion for more than twelve years, John L. Sullivan's record.

He had his bad habits: a sneering manner and a caustic tongue, and he would have barked himself out of his job with anybody save Steve Haverty. His bitter Irish wit centered upon the harmless foibles of the champion. The Jap valet, whom Steve had acquired a couple of years before, got on his nerves; and the fighter's rather flamboyant taste in clothes was a sore point with him. Steve indulged himself in this respect without regard for the jibes of his manager and even the pointed criticism of Eloise Lane could not subdue him.

Steve and Tim lived in a four-room suite in a small but expensive hotel in the Forties near Fifth Avenue, They were having breakfast there, two days after Steve's victory over

Lefty Murphy, and on the morning when Roger discovered that he had loved his father and did love Eloise.

"There's a good man comin' along, by the name of Tom Moore," said Tim, apropos of nothing. He had a very slight brogue, though he had been born in America.

"Yeh? Never heard of him," said the champion indifferently. "Who did he ever fight?"

"Nobody much yet, but he's matched with Rosenbaum."

"That big bum!"

"Oh, Rosenbaum ain't so terrible. He could never get into the front row, but it takes a good man to lick him."

Steve ate some of his egg. "Well, when he licks Rosenbaum, tell me about him."

Tim chewed on a piece of fried ham and answered with his mouth full.

"He'll lick Rosenbaum."

"Well, I hope he comes along. After I flatten Phil Crowe there isn't anybody else in sight, is there?"

"Nobody that could get a gate. Whiz Malone is managing this Moore and I hear from Whiz's gymnasium that this is a funny bird. Whiz always calls him doc, and he's an educated guy."

Steve grinned: "I'll finish his education maybe."

"It seems that Moore is a ring name, Steve. This bird is big and strong and is supposed to be the best educated kid in the world. Name of Thule."

"Him? I've met him! Say, he ain't actually winnin' fights, is he?" demanded Steve in astonishment.

"Licked a big beaner, name of Maloney, over in Jersey. Maloney knocked him down twice in the first round, and he got up and sailed in and they had to help Maloney out of the ring."

STEVE LAUGHED INCREDULOUSLY. "I met him at Eloise's. He's giving her a rush. Eloise told me he plans to take the championship away from me, but that girl is such a kidder I didn't pay any attention. Say, this Roger Thule used to be a lightning calculator when he was a kid. I seen him once. He's got a brain, he has, but how can he be a fighter?"

"Well," drawled Tim, "all he's got to do is to trim Rosenbaum and a couple of more and he may get into the ring with you at that."

"I don't like him much," said Steve. "Eloise says she don't like him either, but she lets him hang round just the same. He's one of those superior birds. You feel like poking him in the nose just for the way he looks at you."

"He isn't much of a hitter, but the boys in Whiz's place say he is awful hard to hit and when you do land on him you can't hurt him."

"Wait till he meets me!" boasted Steve. "I don't suppose there would be any gate, though, for a bimbo like that. They'd say it was a set-up."

"I don't know," replied Tim thoughtfully. "The way things are now, you can't get a big gate just for a fight. You're not the drawing card Dempsey was, kid, and these palookas in the heavyweight class can't even give you an argument and the public knows it. It's show business, these days. Now if this Moore was to knock over three or four pretty good men and if they built him up in the newspapers as a great scientific sharp going to show that muscle ain't any good without brains, he might be the biggest card we could get. Only—"

"Only what?"

Tim laughed. "I got to make darn sure he is your meat. I'm not puttin' you up against anybody that has a chance. You got nine years to go, kid, before you equal John L."

"You don't suppose this lightnin' calculator would stand a chance against me!"

"Listen, bo, you ain't any mental giant. If this feller is as big and strong as you are and knows how to fight, his brains will lick you."

"Say, I may not be strong on geography and geometry, but when they bring that stuff into the ring, where are they?"

"I'll tell you about this Moore after the Rosenbaum fight. I'm goin' to be right there."

"I hope he does turn out pretty good. I'd like to plaster him, with Eloise in a ringside seat. Get him for me, Tim."

Tim chuckled, "I'll get him for you if he's good for you."

If Roger had heard this conversation he would have realized how shrewd was Whiz Malone when he said he wanted his fighter "good, but not too good."

10

DREAM'S END

THE REVEREND THEOBALD Thule was buried two days after his murder, and his funeral was attended by a great many people, very few of whom were known to Roger. There were half a dozen clergymen, friends of long standing, officers of charitable societies to which he had been an important contributor for years, a dozen men and women of the lower walks of life, who informed the son with tears in their eyes how the father had gone out of his way to help them; there were a number of persons whose relations had been social, and several theatrical folks who remembered him ten years back.

There was a long and rather florid sermon in a church of the denomination in which the dead man had once preached, and Roger found himself grateful for the encomiums bestowed upon him, even though he knew that preachers always found plenty of pleasant things to say of the dead. Finally came the interment, the thud of clay clods falling upon the wooden box in which the coffin was incased.

His father's lawyer returned to the house with him, accompanied by the representative of the district attorney, Mr. Quinlan. The will was short. A few bequests to the servants, a donation of ten thousand to an East Side settlement house and the residue of the estate to the son of whom he had been so proud.

"Do you know how much your father was worth?" asked the lawyer, Mr. Ransome.

"I understood that he had in the neighborhood of a million dollars. I don't know how it was invested."

"Recently he realized a hundred thousand dollars which was deposited in the City National Bank and placed in escrow, to be paid to Dr. Thomas Marvin upon his assurance that a certain matter was carried out."

Roger nodded.

"He left no information with me about this matter. So far as I know he was accepting Dr. Marvin's say-so. Do you know just what this transaction is?"

"Yes."

"That's interesting," said Mr. Quinlan. "What is it?"

"A private matter between him and Dr. Marvin," Roger said coldly.

"Yes, but, in view of the circumstances connected with his death, I think I have the right to know."

"I am very sorry," said Roger. "It was a matter of which I have full knowledge. Dr. Marvin is a specialist of the highest character and when he tells me that it is time to pay over the money I shall make no objections."

Quinlan looked grave. "It won't do," he protested. "This may be behind the tragedy. I want the facts."

"You'll have to get along without them," the heir said curtly, "you must take my word, and that of Dr. Marvin, that there is no possible connection between this arrangement and father's death and the amount involved is only a tenth of his estate."

"I'm sorry," interposed Mr. Ransome, "but your father had hard work raising that money. I don't believe he was worth anything like a million dollars and I wouldn't be surprised if there was very little left after he had put that check in escrow. If there is any way of inducing Dr. Marvin to relinquish his claim on it, I should advice you to persuade him to do so."

"I SHALL TELL you this much," said Roger, "There is a prospect of the money being returned. I am very hopeful that it will be. The doctor is in the position of an umpire in this matter and the decision as to its disposition rests entirely with him. That was my father's wish and it is mine. However, you must be mistaken regarding his estate. A few years ago I know we had a million dollars because he told me so. It was the fruit of my years as a lecturer."

"Your father was a poor business man, Mr. Thule, and he made bad investments. He contributed heavily to charities, and you lived expensively."

"Am I to understand that Mr. Thule was a poor man?" demanded Quinlan.

"I doubt if there is more than enough left to pay these bequests," declared the lawyer.

"Humph! It was natural to suppose that this crime was connected in some way with money. Murders are usually due to one of two causes, money, or vengeance of some sort, and Mr. Thule appears to have been a very good man. If he had no money, what could have been the motive?" The assistant district attorney eyed Roger sharply.

"That is what we must discover," the young man said simply.

"And that makes it necessary for me to have the facts regarding this large sum in escrow."

"I have assured you it is in no way connected with my father's death," the young man said tartly.

"If you'll pardon me, that is for me to decide."

"I'll tell you this much, gentlemen. A short time ago I was sunk in a condition of lethargy which alarmed my father, who called in Dr. Marvin. Father was willing to pay any sum to restore me to a normal condition, and this amount was agreed upon."

"But it's the most outrageous fee I ever heard of," protested the lawyer.

"It's not a fee to a physician. It is payment of services of quite a different character. I have told you so much, won't it suffice?"

"No," declared Quinlan. "Your father's death was mysterious and there is a mystery here. You are now in excellent health. I am informed you are amusing yourself by boxing with professional pugilists. Why was the money not paid? Why is it still in escrow?"

Roger thought, "This is a dangerous man. I should not have told him anything. The trail leads straight to Eloise and it was Eloise's perfume on the handkerchief in father's chair." Aloud he said, "Because the conditions are not quite fulfilled. As I said, I am hopeful that it may not be necessary to pay over this fund. I am sorry I can say nothing more."

"Then I shall question Dr. Marvin."

"As you like. Why not?"

"Your father kept all his papers and whatever securities he owned in safety deposit boxes," said the lawyer. "I don't think you will find anything here."

"His house safe has been sealed by the police, and I have already gone over his papers," said Mr. Quinlan. "I found nothing helpful, but I shall be pleased to remove the seals in your presence."

ROGER ROSE. "I leave my interests in your hands, Mr. Ransome. I am unnerved by the events of the day and I should like to go to my room."

He left the two lawyers and went upstairs, feeling very tired and bewildered.

Money matters had never interested him in the slightest because he had known that he and his father were well-to-do and there was no necessity of earning his living; but now it appeared he was penniless. He had a marvelous education. His scholastic attainments were known all over the world, and without trouble he could secure a full professorship at any of a dozen colleges or universities, at a salary of five or six thousand a year.

Roger was not a specialist, his learning was broad and embraced many subjects. He was a splendid chemist, astronomer, linguist, psychologist, mathematician, physician, physicist, biologist, geologist—an expert in many "-ologies" and "-isms," capable of taking a chair at a university and handling a score or more of subjects; but he was not an inventor. As Dr. Marvin had asserted when he was trying to bring him back to an interest in life, he had been so busy acquiring universal knowledge that he had produced nothing in any line. He could write books upon a score of subjects, but scientific books rarely sell well.

He had no idea how much he had been spending, doubtless fifteen or twenty thousand a year. His personal library was worth thirty or forty thousand, but it wouldn't sell for a fifth of that and he would perish rather than part with it. The market value of his learning was five or six thousand a year. As a child, half-educated, he had earned a million because he was an intellectual freak; for the brain of the genius grown to manhood the world would pay five or six thousand a year.

There was a hundred thousand dollars in escrow to be paid to Eloise Lane when he was convinced that he could not make her fall in love with him, and the only way he could get it back would be to win her affections—in which case his only wealth would be the money she had forfeited by yielding.

Well, he loved her, he would marry her if she would have him, but with the realization of his love had vanished all his assurance. Eloise, until the other day, had been only a specimen to his crabbed scientist's mind, a pretty fluffy thing to be ensnared by an infallible method; now she was the most important person in the world and he was abased by his consciousness of his unworthiness.

Furthermore, he was mercenary if he pursued her; his financial interest demanded that he win her. Wouldn't she realize that and refuse to believe in his sincerity?

He had told her so often that it was impossible for him to love any woman that he must have made her believe it, so what would she think him now when he assured her that he was deeply in love with her? A liar, making another move in his chess game.

He had been a rich man's son, a millionaire, a prize to

be won by a shrewd young woman. Now the prize would go to her merely for the refusal of him. He did not think Eloise was mercenary but a hundred thousand dollars for refusing a man she did not like would be a temptation to any normal woman.

What an utterly preposterous idiot he had been! How he had befooled himself in supposing that his astute attentions, his monologues of an informatory character, would win a girl like Eloise! He had been a pedant delivering a lecture, instead of an ardent wooer. Of course she mocked him. He had never made the slightest impression on her.

Roger had had glimmerings during this past month of how he must appear to others, and now, to himself, he appeared the most consummate of imbeciles. His self-abasement was truly tragic. He sank upon his bed and buried his face in his arms, and presently he sobbed. He might be the scholastic marvel of the age, but he was only twenty-one years old.

HIS TELEPHONE RANG and it was Whiz on the line.

"Who do you think was just in to see me?" demanded the jubilant manager. "Tim Hearn."

"I don't know him," said Roger.

"You wouldn't. Tim Hearn is the manager of Steve Haverty."

"Well, what of it?"

"What of it? Kid, he's heard about you already. He's coming to see you fight Rosenbaum. He says, if you come right along, you might be worked up as a championship contender. What do you think of that?"

"I've just come from my father's funeral, Whiz," he said. "I really don't care anything about Tim Hearn."

"Criminy, I'm sorry," exclaimed Whiz. "I knew it was the day of the funeral, of course, but I thought this might cheer you up. Think you'll be in to-morrer?"

"I don't know. Perhaps."

"A good work-out will take yer mind off yer troubles, boy."

"All right. Thanks, Whiz," he said as he hung up. A moment later Roger brightened. He had gone over all his qualifications as a money maker, all his arts and sciences, but he had forgotten pugilism.

A professor earned six thousand a year, but Steve Haverty got half a million for a fight. Roger had entered the game without thought of money. Something Dr. Marvin said had piqued him, awakened his interest, and he had boasted he could beat the champion if he made the effort. Well, let him go on with the business, and beat the champion. Haverty was his chief rival with Eloise. If she did not admire brains she might love the combination of brains and brawn; and at worst he would rehabilitate his fortunes.

He would confess himself vanquished by Eloise and direct that Marvin pay over to her the hundred thousand dollars: then he would enter the lists again, humble, a different individual. He might have a chance.

As regards the perfume, all had gone well. Dr. Marvin had possessed himself of the vial and had personally arranged the fumigation of Eloise's clothing and her apartment. No suspicion had fallen upon the girl, no policeman had soiled her threshold, and she had sent word by Marvin that she had no notion how the handkerchief had come into his father's library, while she offered Roger her sympathy.

In a few days more he could safely present himself before Eloise and tell her that she had won, that he could not win her and the prize was hers. After that—look out, Steve Haverty.

Roger's depression fell from him. He picked up a scientific work and was speedily lost in its pages. In a day or two he would move into the country and, for the first time, subject himself to the kind of training that Whiz insisted was necessary for the bout with Rosenbaum: no time for literature there.

11

TOSSING AWAY A FORTUNE

"NOW, CHILDREN," SAID Dr. Marvin, "I invited you here to thresh things out."

Eloise Lane and Roger Thule were again in his little dining room. Eloise was again ravishing, but her color scheme upon this occasion was green instead of white, a shade which was even more effective in contrast to her bright yellow hair. Roger was in his evening black and white, with lines in his fine face which had not been there upon their first meeting. He interrupted the specialist.

"I think I know what you have on your mind," he said. "I want to say something first. Eloise, I issued you a challenge the first time we met. I must have seemed to you a disgustingly opinionated and conceited individual. I want to tell you now that I am quite satisfied that you do not love me and are not likely to, within the year or ever. Therefore I throw up the sponge, as we say in the prize ring. You win. I lose. I authorize Dr. Marvin to pay over to you the sum of one hundred thousand dollars which is in escrow at the bank. I congratulate you heartily."

Eloise turned very white and looked appealingly at Dr. Marvin.

"That's what I want to talk about," declared the doctor.

"Roger, you listen to me. I misjudged your father and I admit it. So did you. He was a good man, he loved you, and he was perfectly sincere when he said he would sacrifice his last cent to save you. However, he allowed me to suppose he was worth a million and I demanded that he put up a hundred thousand, partly to punish him and partly because I supposed he could afford it. From what your attorney tells me, there's only ten thousand dollars left after the bequests in the will are paid—

"That has nothing to do with this matter," said Roger sharply. "I instruct you to pay over the money to Miss Lane who has won it. There is nothing more to be said."

"Is that so?" snapped Eloise. "I won't take it, do you hear?"

"You have got to take it," he declared.

"Will you both listen to me!" pleaded the doctor. "Eloise accepted the proposition because she supposed, as I did, that your father was wealthy and could spare a hundred thousand dollars to get you out of your imbecile determination to die because there was nothing worth living for."

"Very well," answered Roger. "I am determined to live because I enjoy life and I have a lot of things to live for. The fee has been earned and must be paid."

"If you think I'll take your last cent," began Eloise indignantly, "you have an even poorer opinion of women than I supposed you had. I don't want the money, I haven't earned it, and I'll never touch it, so there."

"I admit in the presence of the doctor that you have resisted my suit successfully and that's all there is to it. Pay her the money, doctor."

The blue eyes of Eloise began to sparkle and she smiled dangerously.

"So you are a coward, after all," she taunted.

"A coward?"

"You are withdrawing, not because you haven't made me love you, but because you are afraid you will fall in love with me. After all your protestations of immunity, you are worried."

ROGER SMILED TENDERLY at her. "I'm not afraid. It's already happened, Eloise. Of course you won't believe me."

"Certainly not. That's just another of your moves. When all else fails, pretend to be mad about the girl. Fire and tow stuff." She smiled contemptuously.

"Since I have officially withdrawn and the money is yours, why should I pretend now?"

"I can't be expected to read the mind of a genius. But I won't take the money."

"In that case, doctor, you will have to give it to charity," he said firmly. "The transaction is finished."

Eloise regarded Dr. Marvin, who nodded. "I have to dispose of the money at Roger's command, since his father is dead. If he wants it to go to a rat hospital, there it must go."

"But this is preposterous," she protested. "The poor boy hasn't a cent. Roger Thule, you are the most exasperating person I ever met in my life."

His answer was a flash of his white teeth.

"I have a solution," said Dr. Marvin slowly. "Take the money, Eloise, marry him, and there you are."

Eloise jumped to her feet.

"I wouldn't marry him if he were the last man in the world," she declared. "I'll never marry any man I don't love."

She was very beautiful in her anger, Roger thought, very desirable, and quite unattainable.

"You have heard, doctor," he said quietly. "Dispose of the money in some manner. It doesn't belong to me."

"Sit down, Eloise," Dr. Marvin commanded. "There is no sense in getting excited. If you don't want to marry Roger, you don't have to. The money is yours, since Roger admits he has failed. He won't accept it back, and you need it yourself. Why give it to charity?"

"Please, Roger," pleaded Eloise, with another sudden change of mood, "forget this whole mad arrangement and take back your money. You need it—you need it more than I do, for I know how to earn my own living and you don't."

He thanked her with his eyes, but he shook his head. "I can earn my living better than most men. The matter is settled."

She was silent for a moment, then she flashed him a new kind of look.

"If I remember your challenge," she said, "it was for a year, You were to make me love you in a year. You have had only two months to try. I'm not entitled to my reward until the year is up. In the meantime—well, why not keep on trying?"

"Good girl, Eloise!" commented the umpire.

"DON'T YOU SEE?" asked Roger hesitatingly. "I can't go on. Before, it was a scientific experiment. Now I would be trying to win a hundred thousand dollars. You would think I was mercenary."

"I would rather think you mercenary than a cold-blooded fish. Besides, I wouldn't. You are entitled to your year, and I am not going to take the money until you have failed in the time limit you set yourself."

"She's right, Roger," declared Dr. Tom Marvin. "Only, if you win her love and fail to marry her, I'll personally murder you."

"Don't you worry about me," declared Eloise proudly. "I'll give Roger his chance, but I'm no more likely to fall in love with him than he is with me."

"If you want the truth," blurted Roger, "I'm in love with you, now, this minute."

Eloise glanced at him sharply, then laughed. "You are rushing things, Don Juan. Tell me that in six months and see if I believe you."

"It's true, though," he said.

"Well, the proposition has nothing to do with that. You must capture my affections, and you have strong competition."

"Let's drop the subject for now," proposed the doctor. "It is understood that the money remains in escrow until the year is up. Eloise, have you any idea that the police are on the trail of your perfume?"

"I don't think so, doctor. There is no trace of it in my apartment or on my things. I hated to give it up. Such a lovely perfume."

"And you haven't yet remembered how you lost that handkerchief?" asked Roger.

She shook her head. "Are you sure it was the same perfume?"

"As it was my own invention," he replied, "I am certain of it."

"It's very mysterious," commented the doctor.

Eloise rose and gave her hand to Roger. "Time for me to go to the theater. Please call me a taxi, doctor."

When he had gone, Roger drew close to her. "Will you please try to forget the money, Eloise, and believe, if I continue to seek you out, it is because of the pleasure I get from your company?" he asked earnestly.

"Beware," she mocked. "If you fall in love with me, it will serve you right."

"Eloise!"

She laughed and waved good-by.

12

THE ROSENBAUM BATTLE

THE TRAINING QUARTERS of a champion are apt to be elaborate and the champion's suite imposing, but an aspirant who is training for a purse of three hundred dollars must do with considerably less. Most of the fighters in that class make use of a gymnasium in town and continue to live in the lodging house or tenement for which they are regularly paying rent.

For Roger and his two sparring partners Whiz had rented a vacant shack on the Sound shore near the village of Searsmont, and within easy reaching distance of New York. He chose it chiefly because it was in a region of fields, woods, and dirt roads. Roger had never done much distance running, but his instructions were to jog a couple of miles the first day and increase it daily until he was doing at least five or six miles, for the benefit of his wind and his legs.

His sparring partners were a pair of chopping blocks, glad to get board and lodgings and twenty-five dollars per week, but Whiz figured that his assistant, Grogan, should go down one day and himself the next to give Roger real work-outs.

With premeditation Roger went to Searsmont without books, for he wished to concentrate upon the business he had entered upon a whim, but which had become so tremendously important to him. Success in pugilism meant a fortune in a very brief period, and he had to have money, much money.

He must prove to Eloise his ability to earn a very comfortable living, to show her that he would not need the fund in escrow which she had refused to touch until the year was out. Moreover, he needed money to engage the best detectives to track down his father's murderer, for he did not believe the police would find him. And last of all, he meant to demonstrate to himself his own worth in this line so alien to his education and his former aspirations.

He found the road work drudgery of the worst description, but he speedily recognized its value. He had not admitted it to Whiz, but in each of his three bouts he had found his legs weakening, and it was fortunate for him that the fights had all been short ones. As days passed, however, he was able to go six fast rounds with his sparring partner's without any shaking of the knees, and under Whiz's tuition he was hitting harder.

"The trouble with you, doc," said Whiz as they rested after four fast rounds and a cold shower, "is the trouble with all amachures. You are fast and clever, and you think the game is not gettin' hit. It ain't. You can't knock out a good man without setting yourself and putting every pound you've got behind your fist, and you can't do that while you're avoiding his wallops. You've got to take one to give one. You got to forget your defense, risk getting kayoed yourself, and plump it over.

"In all your fights you've only hit just as hard as you

dared without dropping your guard. You only use one fist at a time to sock with, but you can't be blockin' with the other one and still put the steam into the punch. The thing to do, when you are ready with the knock-out blow, is to forget that the other guy has got hands at all. You're quick enough to get it over before he lands on you, and you got to take the chance. All flashy boxers has this trouble. Land one and get away; that's their style, and that's why so few of them ever become champions.

"Dempsey, Jeffries, Fitzsimmons, and John L. were all sluggers; ready to take a stiff punch to plant one. Steve Haverty is like that. He'd take all you could give him for fifteen rounds, and then, when you were all tired out from poking him, he'd smack you down with just one old-fashioned haymaker." Whiz shook his head dolefully, then continued:

"Now, this Rosenbaum is a boxer. If he had a knock-out punch he'd be up in the big money. You and him will put on a rotten fight, but I think you can outpoint him. You'd have to take on five or six like him for small purses if it wasn't for Tim Hearn takin' an interest in you."

"WHAT DIFFERENCE DOES that make?" asked Roger.

"Why, if Tim likes your style and says the word, I can get you on in Madison Square Garden with a pretty good man in a semifinal, and after that you'll get a couple of main bouts at good clubs for good money."

"In view of the fact that he is Haverty's manager, I think that is very kind of him," Roger said naively. Whiz grinned. "The heck it is. Tim's looking for a set-up for Haverty that will draw a gate, and he's wise that you're the Lightning Calculator. He told me so. He thinks there is good publicity in that. But if he thought you had a chance with Steve, you'd never get into the ring with him. Tim wants Steve to beat John L.'s record of twelve years as champion."

"Have I got a chance with him?" Whiz scratched his head, then shook it.

"You ain't a real fighter, doc. Steve has been battlin' for eight years because he loves it; he fights by instinct, and that's quicker than thinkin'. He's ten pounds heavier than the best you can do, and he'll always be stronger. You got a lot of scientific tricks, but Steve will be on top of you, and you won't have time for them. He can box, too, but he knows nobody can hurt him much, and he's too anxious to knock out his man to waste time doing a Jim Corbett. You might keep away from him by footwork for a few rounds, but he'll get you in a corner and pound down your guard and then hit you so hard that no Hindustanee mesmeristic trick will save you."

Whiz was so earnest that a little of Roger's confidence oozed out of him. "You don't know yet all I have up my sleeve," he defended.

"It won't be good enough, kid. But the loser's end of a match with Haverty will be worth goin' after. Now maybe you think I hadn't ought to talk to you like this. I wouldn't if you was just an ordinary pug, but you're a very clever feller, and there ain't any use handin' you the bull. You'd know if I was lying. You know a heck of a lot more than most people. By the way, how did you know I was goin' to sidestep to the right and bring up a left uppercut when you rushed me in the third? You met me with your right just as I sidestepped and took all the wind out of my body."

"I read it in your eyes," said Roger with a smile. "So far I have always been able to read what my opponents intended to do by their eyes."

"Yeh? Then look out for a cockeyed scrapper," laughed Whiz. "I heard of that stuff before, but it's just guessin'. You can't really tell."

"That's what makes you all think I am so fast," declared the youth. "I am not really very fast, but I get ready when I see the warning signal."

Roger was first in the ring in the Phoenix Club in Long Island City, entered to the accompaniment of faint applause, and sat in his corner and inspected the house with some interest and more disgust. It was a concrete structure which seated about three thousand, and it was very nearly full and tainted with the aroma of the unwashed.

The full lights were not on in the ring, and he was able to discern faces in the first half dozen rows, which he likened to rings of animals with gleaming eyes. It was an entirely masculine audience, for which he was glad. In Jersey City there have been a few soprano shrieks amid the bass and barytone rumble of excited fans.

Rosenbaum entered, clad, like himself, in an old bathrobe. He squatted in his corner, unshorn and unshaved, his most prominent feature a large and as yet unbroken nose. Rosenbaum was a boxer and knew how to protect his nose, but a few smashes on it would give him grief.

ROGER THULE, PH.D., M.D., Fellow of half a dozen scientific societies, world-renowned scholar, and author of several brilliant scientific brochures, was crouching in a corner of a prize ring, prepared to fight with his fists against an ignorant brute with a prominent nose; his mind was centered on his chances of smashing that organ. It was

well his father had not lived to be aware of what his gifted
son had become, Roger thought, with sudden self-con-
tempt. What business had he in a place like this, in a business like this?

Clang! Automatically he rose and walked to the center
of the ring, where he touched gloves with his opponent,
who took occasion to lift his upper lip in a sneer. Then back
in his corner, off with the bathrobe, and into battle. *Clang!*
The beginning of the first round.

He threw off Roger Thule with the bathrobe and, as
Tom Moore, moved tigerishly toward Ed "Peaches" Rosenbaum, who had reached the center of the ring before him
and crouched defensively. He noted that the man's body
was almost as dark as that of a mulatto and that it was well
protected. His own position was upright, on his toes, left
hand outstretched, right glove against his chest.

He poked at the top of the black head with his left,
and immediately the enemy sprang at him, both arms like
piston-rods, his intentions being to plunge into a clinch
and see what he could do to Moore in the way of infighting. Tom Moore deftly side-stepped the rush and tried to
straighten the man up with an uppercut as he flashed by,
which landed against bulging biceps.

A second plunge, and this time he was in a clinch. Fortu-
nately he had plenty of experience in infighting, for Whiz
had insisted upon working with him in this way a large
part of the time, and he pinioned his opponent's arms so
he could not do much harm.

Separated by the referee, they sparred for a moment,
and the impatient crowd began to boo. Roger's power to
concentrate enabled him to ignore the rabble, but it stimu-

lated Rosenbaum to set himself and drive in a right, which Roger blocked neatly and countered with a hard right to the side of the jaw. The sock of the glove against the flesh drew a chorus of "Ahs" from the bloodthirsty, and for the first time the crowd began to approve of Moore. A stentorian voice bellowed, "You're there, Tommy, old boy!" and from the other side of the ring a pair of bull lungs suggested that he finish Rosy up now.

Rosenbaum was boring in, and Moore backed away, thereby losing the favor he had just gained, but the student was discovering that this was the first clever man he had encountered. He had boasted that he could read his opponents' intentions in their eyes, but Rosy's blows followed the warnings so rapidly that Roger was hard put to block them. He took a hard one in the stomach before he was ready for it, and it hurt him. The round ended with Rosenbaum aggressive and Moore strictly on the defensive. The judges gave it to Rosenbaum.

"Keep out of clinches and straighten up that crouch," whispered Whiz. "Set yourself and take a few swings at him if you don't think he can hurt you."

All Roger's instincts, however, were to thrust and defend, and he confined himself in the second round to jabbing cleverly, blocking swift drives, and retreating before the crouching menace. He started Rosenbaum's nose bleeding, but he took two heavy blows just above the belt, neither of which hurt him, as he assured Whiz when it was over. But the judges did not know that, and they gave the round to Rosenbaum.

They gave him the third and fourth also, while the angry

mob expressed itself fluently and picturesquely upon the subject of a fighter who wouldn't fight.

"HE'S A MILE ahead, kid," declared Whiz. "Tim Hearn's here, too. A couple more rounds like this, and you'll never meet Steve Haverty. Paralyze his arms the way you done Heffernan."

"He's too quick," replied the boxer. "I'm too busy keeping him away from me."

"If he wins another round you got to knock him out to win, and you can't knock him out."

The bell broke up the conference, and the conquering Rosenbaum came boring in, confidence gleaming in his eyeballs. Roger circled round him warily, jabbed at the nose, flattened it on the second jab, so that Rosy, whenever he was out of range, touched it consolingly with his right glove. And now he was plunging in again, both arms moving like parts of a machine. But instead of retreating, Roger set himself, neglecting to guard with his left as he marshaled all his strength behind his right.

Crash! In came Rosenbaum's right to his stomach; *crack!* came Rosy's left against the eye of the so-called Tom Moore; and then Roger's right fist, with all his weight behind it, drove terrifically against Rosenbaum's chin.

The swarthy man staggered back, crouched and instinctively covered up. He was out on his feet, but he was on his feet, and his arms protected his head like the quills of a porcupine. Again and again Roger was upon him, trying desperately to get at that chin, and a tattoo of blows rained upon the man who, for the moment, dared not hit back, and then the bell brought the round to a close.

"That was the stuff, kid!" exclaimed Whiz, whose hands

were trembling with excitement. "You had him goin'. You oughter ha' finished him, but he's a tough baby."

"I hit him with all I had," groaned Roger. "It wasn't enough."

"A few more like that will do the trick. You took two to land one. Did he hurt you?"

"You bet he did. I was setting myself for the punch, and that's all I thought of."

"Well, do it some more."

Rosenbaum came out cautiously. His nose had swollen enormously and his black eyes behind it looked like those of an animal. His instructions had been to keep away for this round; he was so far ahead he could afford it, and he followed instructions implicitly. Tom Moore had his turn at pursuing an elusive enemy, as, heedless of the crowd, Rosy actually ran away from him and the round ended without a blow having landed, while Roger's legs were tiring.

"Two rounds for you," encouraged Whiz. "Box him now. You got a chance to win on points."

"I've got to finish him. I won't last ten rounds. My legs."

"Then back away from him and watch yer chance," said Whiz mournfully. He figured the bout as lost.

Rosenbaum bounced out of his corner, fresh and full of vim, having fully recovered from the smash he had received in the fifth round; and it was evident to the crowd that he was through with running away. Roger stopped his rush by lightninglike jabs at the sore nose, took a dozen punches on the shoulders and upper arms, missed a right hook at Rosy's heart, and gave his opponent a chance to drive heavily at his own solar plexus. The blow apparently shocked him, for his shoulders drooped, his arms dropped to his sides, his head hung, and Rosenbaum did not notice that all his weight had shifted to the ball of his left foot.

Eager to finish it, the dark man tore in.

Up from his right knee came Roger's right fist with a hundred and eighty pounds of dynamite in it, and landed squarely upon the place on the chin known as the button. The evening's entertainment had come to an end, and they scraped Mr. Rosenbaum off the canvas.

ROGER STOOD FOR a second looking ruefully at the man who lay prone, then obeyed the referee's finger which pointed to the farthest corner, where he stood until Rosenbaum had been counted out. The man was already recovering consciousness, and he managed a grin when his conqueror came to him and helped his seconds lift him.

"I'm sorry," said the victor.

"'S all right," said Rosy. "I'd ha' done it to you."

For the first time the scientist got no thrill out of his victory, and the terrific bellowing of the crowd disgusted him. Whiz was dancing a jig in his own corner, and embraced him violently regardless of the fact that Roger was covered with sweat, and gore from Rosenbaum's broken nose. He slipped into his bathrobe and got out of the ring, and when enthusiastic fans patted him on the back as he passed he winced at their touch.

"What's the matter with you?" demanded Whiz, when they were in the dressing room. "You act like you got knocked out 'stead of winning a great fight. You dropped a mighty good man to-night, doc. You're on yer way up."

"It was so darned unfair," he replied. "Whiz, I'm like a knight in armor fighting unarmored men. I prepared for that blow in the chest, and it had no effect on me. By rights I should have been knocked out."

"Yah!" jeered Whiz. "You make me sick. Two things make a scrapper: ability to hit and get hit. Do you s'pose if this Rosy knew how to take a punch without gettin' hurt he wouldn't do it? I was watchin' yer legs, kid, and they was goin'. You wouldn't ha' lasted another round. Rosy's legs was O.K. He landed five blows to your one. You knew how to take a punch, and he didn't, and that's how you won. Forget it. If I knew how to give myself mental anaesthetics, as you call it, I'd have been champion, and you bet my conscience wouldn't ha' troubled me."

"Just the same, it's a rotten business."

"Oh, sure. So's politics and stock's and bonds. Lay down now and I'll give you a rub. Then the shower, and you'll feel like a new man.

"Come in!"

The door opened and the lugubrious Tim Hearn stood in the opening.

"Say!" exclaimed Whiz. "It's Tim Hearn, Haverty's manager! Come right in, Tim. What do you think of my boy, here?"

"Shake," said Tim, advancing; and Roger took his hand with mingled feelings.

"You're some tough baby," grinned Mr. Hearn. "That solar plexus ought to have sent you to dreamland, but you came right back. Pretty good boy, Whiz."

"You said it," replied the proud manager.

"Got a lot to learn, though, and his legs are bad. He ought to have more weight with his height. And he can't hit a hard blow without telegraphing it. A good man would have murdered you that time you set yourself in the fifth round, Moore."

"Rosy is a good man," protested Whiz.

Hearn laughed. "A fair boxer, but he's so cautious he'll never get anywhere. I think you can make something out of this kid, Whiz. I'm goin' to keep my eye on him. Say, Moore, the champ says he knows you. You're the Lightning Calculator."

Roger nodded.

"Well, Steve sent his regards. He likes to see a young feller get along. You do what Whiz tells you and you may be up with the good men yet. So long, Whiz."

Whiz was grinning like an triumphant Cheshire. "It's all right," he declared. "I was scared Tim would back off if you kayoed Rosy, but he thinks it was a lucky punch. He figures you're just a tough boy, and that's how you took that solar plexus. We're on our way, doc. The big money's comin'. I wonder how it'll feel to have all my bills paid!"

Roger had to smile.

"Remember, though, when I beat Haverty I'm going to retire."

A roar of laughter was his answer. "If you wait till then, kid, I don't have to worry. Got any idea how much money we'll make up to the time we get a match with Steve, if we do?"

"None whatever."

"We'll have at least a hundred grand in our jeans, maybe more. They pay big money for good scraps. I won't take a cent less than five thousand for your next bout, and the one after that ought to bring twenty-five thousand dollars, and after that fifty thousand dollars."

"Counting your chickens before they are hatched," warned Roger, but he was unable to resist his friend's enthusiasm. If he could make big money before he met Haverty, so much the better. He needed it.

"And the challenger's share of a championship match will be at least a hundred grand. Come on, kid. Get under the shower."

THE PRESENCE OF Tim Hearn at the Moore-Rosenbaum fight interested the reporters, and the contest occupied some space in the New York papers which usually ignored the bouts at the Phoenix Club. Here was a young heavyweight, the reporters pointed out, who had fought four times in less than three months, won all four fights, and three of them were knock-outs; while last night he had sent Rosenbaum to the carpet, a good boxer who had never taken the count before. Tom Moore was worthy of attention, and Tim Hearn was reported to have stated that he was coming along very fast.

The publicity got Whiz a five-thousand-dollar offer for a main bout in Brooklyn with Peter Powell, a tough Westerner who was already being touted as a coming champion.

Roger had a black eye and sore ribs the day after the Rosenbaum fracas, but on the whole he had escaped very well from a grueling contest. He also had a check for one hundred and fifty dollars, a pitiful sum for his weeks of training and the seven hard rounds before an audience. However, it was the end of his apprenticeship. From now on he would be well paid for his exertions.

Eloise called him on the phone in the morning to ask how he felt.

"I read in the papers that you fought a brutal fight and

knocked a poor fellow out" she said in her usual mocking tone.

"Just the same I appreciate your calling me up. It's kind of you."

"Are you presentable?" she demanded.

"I have a black eye."

"Oh. I was going to allow you to take me to tea, but that's out. Won't you get out of that terrible business now, Roger?"

"You don't seem to mind your friend Haverty's being in it," he said jealously.

Her tone changed. "He promises to retire when I marry him," she said blandly.

"I'll retire him," Roger declared fiercely.

Eloise Lane laughed and hung up on him.

13

TAKING A CHANCE

ROGER HAD BEEN aware from the first that, sooner or later, the news would leak out that he, the intellectual prodigy, had turned prize fighter, but he had not supposed that the humble fistic aspirant, Tom Moore, would be identified with him until he had fought some really important battles. However, Tim Hearn had mentioned to sporting reporters that Moore was a comer, and Detective Sergeant Jones, who had worked on the Thule murder case, had recognized Roger, and after the Rosenbaum fight he informed a police reporter who passed along the "story" for what it was worth.

The fact that a pug named Tom Moore had knocked out three or four pork-and-beaners was not news, but that Roger Thule, the boy marvel of the universities, was now demonstrating in the prize ring that a great mind was better than big muscles—that he had, in fact, already beaten four men, one of them considered a pretty good man—that made a great story.

The New York *Planet* got the story, dug out of its obituary department photographs of Roger as a child of five, a boy of ten, and a doctor of philosophy at fifteen, put a clever rewrite man to work, and turned out a whale of a tale.

Immediately the follow-ups began. The newspapers preferred to ignore the fact that Thule was a big, strong, clever boxer, and pictured him as a frail thinking machine who flattened the husky sluggers by science. Somebody remembered how he had opened up and permitted Moriaty to hit him in the stomach as hard as he wished, and they found out that Heffernan had been rendered helpless by pecking before Moore delivered the knock-out blow.

The Thule murder case had petered out because there seemed to be nothing to follow-up on it, but it was restored now to the front page and used as the motive for Roger's astonishing conduct. Being left penniless—to the perennially "broke" reporters, ten thousand dollars was the same as penury, when writing a story—the young scientist had entered the ring to earn a fortune so that he could return to his studies.

Roger refused to be interviewed, but that didn't prevent the reporters from publishing interviews with him in which he was made to say things that horrified him. There were also interviews with physical training experts who scoffed at the pretentions of a scientist in the ring; with college professors who stated that they were shocked and grieved that Mr. Thule should have entered upon such a career when great rewards awaited him in academic groves, and an interview with Steve Haverty, champion of the world, which is worth reprinting.

"Sure, I know Mr. Thule," said the champion. "When I was a kid I saw him in vaudeville as a lightning calculator and he was a marvel, take it from me. I met him socially a

"Bring around the papers," Whiz decided. "We'll sign!"

few months ago and he told me he was going to take the championship away from me. 'It's all right with me, Mr. Thule,' I told him. 'I meet all comers. You may be a great man in your line and I guess I've shown I'm pretty good in mine. You beat a few good men and show me you know how to fight, and I'm just as glad to meet you as anybody.'"

"But aren't you afraid of his scientific tactics? They say he beats men just by looking at them," slyly asked the reporter.

"If he can beat me by looking at me, I don't deserve to be champion," replied Haverty. "I'm not afraid of any man living when I step into the ring. From what I hear this fellow is a pretty good scrapper. My manager saw the Rosenbaum fight and tells me that he took a lacing and won by a lucky punch. I couldn't take on this Thule in an intellectual contest, I don't suppose, but when he steps into the ring with me, he'll find I'm just as scientific in my business as he is in his. Let this Thule get a 'rep' as a scrapper and let them put up the right kind of a purse and he can get a fight with me the same as anybody else. That's me, Steve Haverty."

LIKE MOST MEN of his type Roger hated the newspaper publicity, but Whiz reveled in it and even Dr. Marvin assured him it was a good thing.

"If you are in the game to make money," declared the physician, "you will find that advertising will do more for you than your fists. You are in wrong with the scholastic world already, and additional publicity won't hurt you any more."

Eloise phoned him and teased him in her customary manner, but, being a show woman herself, it was evident that she was impressed by his sudden elevation into the columns of newspapers.

The tall stories of his ring methods had one unlooked-for effect. The manager of Peter Powell forfeited his deposit of five hundred dollars and refused to permit his fighter to meet Roger Thule.

"Nothing doing," he declared. "I signed to meet a scrapper, not a magician. Pete can take any heavyweight in the business, but I'm not putting him up against a teller that don't fight fair."

Whiz was downhearted for a few days at the loss of a five-thousand-dollar purse, but his depression vanished when he was visited by a promoter whose arena was a ball park in Brooklyn. This astute individual agreed with Tim Hearn that the fight game was a circus nowadays instead of a boxing contest. A battle between a good heavyweight and a scholastic sharpshooter would be a box office attraction in his opinion. Thule was in the public eye already, and a quick match with a well-known fighter would keep him there.

He offered Whiz a guarantee of ten thousand or thirty per cent of the gross at Ebbets Field for a bout with Phil Crowe, a dangerous contender for the championship, and the offer was win, lose or draw.

"Here's my idea, Whiz," said Jake Fulbert, the promoter. "This boy of yours is a flash and Crowe will murder him, but so would this Peter Powell, whose fool manager ran out on the match. The thing to do is save him for a worth-while show. I don't care whether this Thule can scrap or not. If Crowe can knock him out in the first round, what of it? The crowd is there and we got its money. I'm gambling that the saps will pay ten dollars a seat to see Brains against Brawn. Maybe I'm wrong. If I am, you get ten thousand dollars. If I'm right we'll have a gate of at least a hundred fifty grand and you get forty-five thousand dollars for your end."

"You got Roger Thule wrong, Jake," said Whiz seriously. "You think he's just a bum with a few tricks. Now he had to be a good man to lick Rosenbaum, and you ask Tim Hearn if he showed any tricks. I want to nurse him along. He ain't ready yet for a great scrapper like Phil Crowe. I want him to have three or four fights under his belt before he goes up against that kind of fighter."

"And suppose one of them palookas flattens him."

"They won't."

"Well, suppose he licks them all in the next year. You can't get big money for a match for him then. Now's the time, while he's a novelty. And they'll be bettin' ten to one on Crowe if that's any inducement."

"It ain't," grinned Whiz. "I think Crowe will lick him.

I wouldn't bet a dollar on him myself. And it ain't fair to Roger."

"LET'S TALK WITH the boy," urged the promoter. "I feel it in my bones, Whiz, that he could pack the house. I'll set the fight for three months from now; that'll be July. I'll get the best press agent in New York to keep him before the public. Suppose he does get licked. Look at the money."

Roger, who was working out in the gym at the moment, was called into the office and Fulbert explained his proposition all over again. The promoter was studying the youth while he talked and his confidence was growing.

"I thought you was some big-headed curiosity," Fulbert said frankly, "but you look like a darn good scrapper."

"Good, but not good enough," declared Whiz, that curious manager.

Roger only smiled at the reflection upon his prowess. "I've fought four times and each time Whiz was sure I was going to be whipped," he said. "I've been a showman, Mr. Fulbert, and I know something of mob psychology. At the present moment I am a freak. I've been a freak before. I know one hundred times as much as I did when I was a child, but I can't cash in my learning for one per cent of what it brought in then. If I go on, as Whiz desires, and win my way to the top by beating one good man after another, the public will accept me as a first-class fighter, but it won't get excited about me. Just now, in the public mind, I am a side-show marvel; a man totally ignorant of the science of boxing, who is going into the ring against a great fighter with all the arrogance of a scholar. The public will think I shall be knocked out by the first punch, but it would rather see that punch than watch two evenly matched pugilists go fifteen rounds."

"You can't fight Crowe yet, Doc," protested Whiz.

"Think of the jack!" pleaded Fulbert. "Mr. Thule, you said something when you said you was a showman. I had a hunch, see, and I was willing to play it, but what you just said gives me nerve enough to go through. The capacity of the park at my prices is three hundred grand and I was figuring on half of that. Hanged if I don't believe we'll sell out. That's ninety thousand for your share, Whiz."

"And it eliminates all these disgusting preliminary bouts," urged Roger. "If I beat Crowe at Ebbets Field, Whiz, the champion will have to give me a match immediately, don't you see?"

"Say," exclaimed Fulbert, "you don't actually think you got a chance with Phil Crowe, do you, Mr. Thule? Why, he's got twenty-four knockouts to his credit. He stayed ten rounds against Steve Haverty, before Steve was the champ."

"I expect to beat him," replied Roger casually. "Whiz is my manager, Mr. Fulbert, and you have to sell him this proposition. If he says no, that settles it, but I hope he will say yes."

"Yes," said Whiz. "If they should be a sell-out and we got ninety grand, well, that's something. But this Crowe will take you, Doc, sure as you live."

"I'll risk it if you will."

"BRING AROUND THE papers, Jake," Whiz decided. "We'll sign. I can see your point about stacking the Doc against a big man right away while the fans are talking about him—only I hate to see my boy flattened when he might lick this Phil Crowe with more experience. If he only had had this fight with Powell."

"For a five-thousand-dollar gate you'd take a chance on a three-hundred-thousand-dollar attraction," scoffed Fulbert. "You're no showman, Whiz."

"I guess I'm just a has-been of a scrapper," sighed Whiz. "In my day the fans was wise. They wouldn't pay a nickel unless they was sure there was going to be a fight."

"Having seen your boy," said the jubilant promoter, "I think there is going to be a fight."

After Fulbert had departed, Whiz turned angrily upon his charge.

"You got your own way," he declared. "You'll get knocked into a cocked hat three months from now, but you might as well try to make a showing. Up to now you haven't ever really trained, the fights weren't worth it. Now I got to make you strong enough so this guy won't kill you. For the next six weeks you just eat hearty and have a good time, but every morning go on the road and jog six or eight miles. That's all you got to do. Six weeks before the fight I'll have training-quarters for you, some first-class sparring part-ners, and everything you need. I'll let Grogan run this joint while I train you myself. You been working pretty hard the last three months and you've gone through four fights. I don't want you to go stale, so that's why I say lay off. One thing we don't have to worry about is weight. The sky is the limit with heavyweights."

"I'm moving out of my house and I'm going to take an apartment somewhere," said Roger. "You think six weeks' training will be enough?"

"Oh, sure. That's all any man in good condition needs."

"Fine. They haven't found my father's murderer, Whiz. I'll round him up before it's time to start training."

"Now, don't you go taking any chances. If Fulbert's right, this bout will put us both on easy street."

"Don't worry about me. Worry about the murderer."

"Sa-ay! I wouldn't say you had a swelled head, Doc, but you certainly think a lot of yerself."

14

WINGED MONEY

THE NECESSITY OF preparing for the Rosenbaum bout had forced Roger to leave to the police the investigation of the murder of Theobald Thule. After several weeks' work they had made precisely no progress whatever. With six free weeks ahead of him, Roger thought he might have better success, and as a beginning, he walked from the locker room, wincing a little at Whiz's parting cut, and called up George Ransome, his father's lawyer.

Ransome he had accepted as his father's friend and confidant when he met him after the funeral. He turned over his affairs to him as a matter of course and had not questioned the statement of assets submitted to him, despite their alarming import.

His purpose in asking an appointment now was to go over his father's papers with the lawyer in the hope of getting a clew to the reason for the crime. The lawyer was cordial on the phone and invited him to call at any time, immediately if he wished, so Roger took him at his word. He had assumed the attorney for a man of large affairs like his father would be a member of a big law firm, but he found him in a single small office partitioned into two cubby-holes, one of which was Ransome's and the other that of a second lawyer who helped Ransome pay the rent.

Even this would not have made Roger suspicious had he not sensed that the lawyer was nervous. Then he turned his penetrating eye on him and saw through a smooth and amiable mask a small and cunning soul.

While Roger, like most scholars, found business details uninteresting, he could never have been a child lightning calculator had he not possessed a remarkable grasp of figures, and he understood bookkeeping.

"I have been hoping that you would come in to verify my statement," began Ransome. "I've had the papers ready for you for some days. It must have been a great shock to discover that your father left so little, though you will remember that I warned you when I read the will that such might be the case."

"I remember," the young man said evenly, as he seated himself and picked up the mass of papers which the attorney drew from a folio.

"How long have you known my father, Mr. Ransome?"

"About eight years."

"How do you happen to be his attorney?"

"Why, we met at a club and found certain things in common. We were both graduates of Atwater University in Ohio, though your father preceded me by ten years."

"Eight years ago. I was thirteen then and attending Harvard. My father was a rich man at the time, was he not?"

"Such was my impression," replied the attorney.

"Didn't you know?"

"No. He engaged me first upon a small suit against a

lecture manager who had canceled one of your dates. I forced the manager to pay two-thirds of your fee, a very satisfactory settlement. A few months later he handed me another small case. It was not for a couple of years that he placed all his legal affairs in my hands."

"YOU HAD CHARGE of his finances, did you not?"

"No," replied Ransome. "I never had charge of his finances. I occasionally advised him about investments. And I drew up his will five years ago."

"He told you then how much money he had, did he not?"

"Not exactly. He said he was worth around a million."

"And you continued to advise him about investments?"

"Yes; well, in a way." The rain of questions was beginning to disturb the equanimity of the attorney.

"In what way, please?"

"Well, I would tell him I considered a new issue of stock an excellent investment and he would tell me afterward he had invested, but he did not tell me how much."

"Have you any idea how he lost eight or nine hundred thousand in four or five years? The income from a million dollars should have been sufficient for both of us, as we lived."

"Mr. Thule, I don't like your tone," snapped Ransome. "You question me as though I were a witness in court"

"I am very sorry. It seems to me I have a right to ask these questions, though I do not wish to be rude. You were the friend and adviser of my father, who seems to have been so badly advised that he dropped nearly a million dollars in a few years. Since he consulted you, you must know what were those bad investments."

"Well, I don't," said Ransome hurriedly. "If he had

stuck to the securities I recommended, he would not have dropped his money."

"Do these papers contain the information I seek?"

"I am afraid they do not. You must remember, Mr. Thule, I only had his statement that he was worth a million. I confess I was surprised when he had so much difficulty raising a hundred thousand dollars. The papers before you show what securities were sold to raise the cash."

"Money does not vanish into thin air. If he bought worthless stocks he would still have them."

"There's about twenty thousand dollars worth of blue sky still in one of his deposit boxes," Ransome stated. "It's not worth five cents a pound as old paper."

"That accounts for twenty thousand, then. Including the money in escrow, the bequests, and what I have inherited, one hundred and fifty thousand more than covers it all. We have eight hundred and fifty thousand to be accounted for."

"Look here, young man, you must understand that I was your father's legal adviser, not his financial agent," Ransome said hotly.

"I understand," replied Roger blandly. "But I do not understand your heat. As his attorney and mine, it's your business to help me discover what became of his fortune."

Ransome managed an official smile. "I am trying to help you, Mr. Thule, but you shoot questions at me like a prosecuting attorney. I have told you your father said he was worth a million. So far as I actually know, he may never have owned more than a couple of hundred thousand."

"If he said so, he told you the truth. Who were his brokers?"

"Towle, Linder, and Madden acted for him on occasion."

"**THANK YOU. NOW,** this is a hard question to ask, but was my father blackmailed at any time, Mr. Ransome?"

Ransome looked surprised. "Not to my knowledge."

"A woman's handkerchief was found in the library the night he was murdered. Do you know if any woman ever thought she had a claim on him?"

"I don't know. He never mentioned anything of the sort to me."

"Have you any suspicion regarding his death? From your knowledge of my father, do you know of anybody who might think he had a reason for killing him?"

"Certainly not," said the lawyer testily. "I went all over that with the assistant district attorney."

"Thank you. Now I should like to go over these papers."

Ransome sighed with relief. "Take them into my colleague's office, if you want privacy," he said. "I'll be here to answer any question in regard to them."

Roger picked up the pile of documents and carried them into the partitioned-off space belonging to the absent lawyer. He spread them out on a table and went through them rapidly but methodically.

There were receipts for house rent, receipted household bills of every description, memoranda of no importance, personal letters, none which seemed significant, circulars, and the like, but no records or accounts save the details of the hundred-thousand-dollar transaction.

Roger had assumed that he would find, among his father's papers, account books which would explain his heavy losses of the past few years. Although his father might have been a poor business man, it would be impossible for him to handle many hundreds of thousands of dollars over a period of ten years without accumulating a mass of records of every sort, but there was no business paper in this lot which was more than three months old.

Roger had accepted the loss of his fortune and gone about the business of making one with his fists, and his interest now in the missing eight hundred thousand was whether it had a connection with his father's murder.

Although he was too intelligent to jump at conclusions, it had grown on Roger, as he talked with Ransome, that the lawyer knew very much more than he admitted about the affairs of Theobald Thule, and the inspection of Mr. Thule's papers sharpened his suspicion.

He was certain that money to the total of a million dollars had flowed into the hands of his father and only a hundred and fifty thousand of it was accounted for. If Theobald had lost a vast sum by speculation there would have been plenty of brokers' receipts and statements; if he had bought worthless stocks they would be on hand as evidence. There was no doubt that the outgoing herd of dollars would have left tracks behind it.

He had permitted Ransome to take charge of his father's effects and they had been in the possession of the lawyer for several weeks, time enough to enable him to destroy what he pleased; but the circumstances of his father's death had drawn in the district attorney's office, and Mr. Quinlan had also gone over the papers in his father's desk and house safe, so Ransome would not have dared to tamper with them for fear of discovery. That made it appear that his father's records and accounts disappeared before his death. Had he destroyed them himself?

No motive for the crime had been discovered by the

authorities, but Roger thought he had found one. The murder of Mr. Thule might have profited somebody to the amount of eight hundred and fifty thousand dollars or thereabouts.

HE CARRIED THE papers back to Mr. Ransome and laid them upon his desk.

"Don't you think it very curious that there is no record here of any transaction previous to three months ago?" he asked.

"Yes," replied Ransome. "For reasons of his own, I presume your father destroyed everything."

"You think he may have disposed of a large part of his fortune and did not wish anybody to know what he had done with it."

"If he had as much money as you suppose, that is possible."

"In that case, there would be canceled checks."

"They could have been burned."

"But the banks have records."

"Many modern banks keep no records of the persons to whom checks are paid. They record the payment on their books and their customers' statements, give him the canceled checks for his own information, and that's the end of it."

"Very well. I want copies of all bank statements sent to my father for the last five years. I presume you know where he banked."

"I know three or four banks in which he had checking accounts."

"Will you be kind enough to visit these banks and ask them to supply me with statements?"

"Certainly. I think I can have them for you in a few days."

"How well do you know Mr. Quinlan of the district attorney's office?"

"I met him for the first time on the day of your father's funeral. Why do you ask?"

"I thought you might get him to help you if the banks object to supplying statements."

"They won't. They are always glad to aid in a case like this."

"Well, I am sorry to have had to take up so much of your time."

"You may have as much of my time as you desire, Mr. Thule," said Ransome, with professional heartiness.

His cordial smile faded when the door closed on his client.

"Damned young cub," he muttered." He's too wise for this world."

He closed the door of his little office so that his stenographer might not hear him, and softly called a telephone number.

"Ransome talking," he said after a moment's wait. "Young Thule has just been in. He's clever as hell and he smells a rat. Look out."

The person on the other end of the line evidently demanded a personal conference, for Ransome said, "Very well, I'll be right over." Then he put on his hat, told the girl he would be out for an hour, and departed.

JAKE FULBERT HAD the signatures of Phil Crowe and Roger Thule, alias Tom Moore, upon his contracts the very next day. When he made his announcement to the papers, it caused a bigger sensation than even he had anticipated.

The sporting writers seized upon it for extended discussion, the news editors displayed it upon the front page, and the editorial writers grasped the opportunity to comment upon such an unusual match. The New York boxing commissioners immediately ordered Roger to call upon them and show cause why such an apparently preposterous meeting should be permitted.

Roger astonished the triumvirate by his personal appearance, for they had the popular impression of what a great scientist must resemble. When he had stripped, stepped upon the scales and submitted to an examination by the official physician, they were still more astonished, for his physical condition was perfect.

"You are as big as Crowe and you seem to be as strong," said the chairman of the board. "Just the same, you have only been in the ring a few months and you haven't the experiences necessary to meet a man like Crowe. I confess I'm surprised that you shape up like this. How long have you been boxing?"

"It has been my chief recreation since I was a child," replied Roger. "Whiz Malone will tell you that I was a pretty good boxer at sixteen when I was at Harvard and he was boxing instructor at the Heminway Gymnasium. I never entered amateur boxing contests, but I have always kept in training and I can refer you to a half dozen good boxing instructors who have had the gloves on with me the past five or six years. I have beaten four men since I entered the professional ring and that ought to convince you I am not a weakling."

"Look here," said one of the commissioners. "There's been a lot of talk about you licking those fellows by scientific trickery. I had an idea you were a little scrawny chap with spectacles and no physique at all, but you're big enough to put up a good fight without any funny business."

"I don't know what you mean by funny business. If you will ask people who saw my four fights, you'll find I took some hard punishment and won by beating or knocking out my men."

The chairman laughed. "This fellow Maloney has been telling people you made yourself invisible in the fight against him. Of course that's all bull, but how about it?"

"I was invisible to him all right," laughed Roger, "because I closed both his eyes, but I did it by jabbing at them, which, I believe, is permissible."

"Sure," said the third commissioner. "I got a report on that fight. Maloney knocked him down twice in the first round and gave him an awful beating, then he came back and out-boxed Maloney, jabbed him until he was blinded, and the referee stopped the fight."

"Well," said the chairman. "Mr. Thule is of age, he's a big, strong fellow that seems to know how to box, and I don't think Phil Crowe can permanently injure him if he survived a walloping by Maloney. Some of these third-raters hit just as hard as Steve Haverty, but they are shy on science. Our business is to prevent unfair matching. If Mr. Thule was nothing but a skinny college professor who thought he could meet a heavyweight and beat him with flubdubbery, I'd refuse to license the contest, but I don't see why we should interfere if Whiz Malone thinks his man is good enough to meet Crowe. Whiz is no fool."

"Do you think you have a chance, Mr. Thule?" asked one of the commissioners curiously.

"I do," said Roger coolly.

"Why?"

"Because I think I can outbox, outhit, and outgeneral my opponent, and I think I can stand more punishment than he can."

"You're a cocky rooster," laughed the chairman. "All right, go to it. We'll license the bout."

The statement of the commission that the bout was licensed because they were convinced that Roger Thule was as big and as strong as his opponent and capable of putting up a good fight was practically ignored by the newspapers, which were cartooning Roger as "Little Johnny Boston Beans" with enormous spectacles and arms like toothpicks. It was David and Goliath to the columnists, which was very unfair to Phil Crowe, who only weighed three pounds more than Roger and was half an inch shorter. Fulbert began to get orders for seats the instant the fight was licensed, and joyously he called up Whiz and assured him that they were going to have a sell out.

15

BUCKETS OF GOLD

AMONG THOSE WHO read the news-paper accounts of the match between Roger Thule, the Mental Marvel, and Phil Crowe, the Cave Man, was a gentleman whose name was E.H. Mason. His first name was Ethelbert, but, embarking in the show business early in life, he had found it highly desirable to conceal that fact.

E.H. Mason had been a lecturer with a medicine show some thirty years back, and he had been ballyhoo man with a circus, and a vaudeville press agent, from which he rose to become a theatrical producer of turkey shows—which may require explanation. Mason's turkeys were productions of Broadway musical comedies which had failed and which he revived to take into the sticks.

He could usually buy the production for a song after it had gone to the storehouse, cast it with inexperienced actors and chorus people, bill it as the original New York cast and play one-night stands in the Middle West. These were the days before the actors invented Equity, and Mason was frequently able to run a turkey five or six weeks without paying the actors anything but "eat money" and then abandon them in a remote village, to get back to New York as best they could.

Some of Mason's performers had to settle in such places and in the course of time got acclimated and became prominent citizens. He prospered, if his companies did not, and eventually set up in business as a manager of lecture tours. It was E.H. Mason who made the late Theobald Thule an offer for a tour by the Mental Marvel, Roger, at the age of eight, and he made so much money he was able to keep his agreement with Mr. Thule, which was the first honest piece of business of his career.

The show business was abandoned by him after that, and some time later he turned up as a partner in the brokerage house of Evans & Mason in the financial district of New York. After a few years Mr. Evans, a young man, sold out his interest to the junior partner in return for a very small sum of money. He had speculated unwisely.

The firm name remained unchanged and the business grew enormously. Evans had purchased a seat on the stock exchange which remained with the firm when he withdrew, and it became known as a very substantial and rather conservative house.

In the old days E.H. Mason had been rather a flamboyant person who wore checked suits and a large imitation diamond in his necktie, but as he went up in the world he had toned himself down and now dressed quietly, spoke softly, and exuded respectability. E.H. had gone to a dentist and had several prominent gold fillings replaced with porcelain.

There was nothing he could do about his face, which was large, broad and rather flat, with an undershot jaw which gave him a pugnacious appearance, and a pair of hard gray eyes; But he smiled much and was always merry and bright, and he impressed people as being strong and determined. **BUSINESS WAS NOT** good just now with E.H. Mason. It is an axiom in Wall Street that the sucker is always wrong and any man who coppers his bets is sure to win. Mason had believed that so powerfully that he based his business career upon it and, in the past, had been amply rewarded. When some gentle lambkin ordered him to buy on the exchange a few hundred shares of some security which he thought was due for a rise, Mason took it for granted that he was mistaken and didn't bother to buy it. So, when it dropped, he put all the lamb's money in his pocket instead of getting only the broker's share of it, which is a half of one per cent. This is what is known as bucketing, and it's against the law, but he didn't bother about that.

He was careful to do enough business upon the exchange to make people think he was a legitimate broker, but the bulk of his profits were of the bucket variety.

For the past two or three years, however, things have not been as they should be. The outsider in Wall Street rarely sells short, he buys, which is all right too; but the market had not been fluctuating properly for Mason's benefit, it had been rising steadily like an ocean tide. When things happened, like a war in the Balkans or a flood in the Middle West, which should cause the market to drop, it didn't even notice them. All the bucket-shop men were caught in this continual bull market, and among them was E.H. Mason.

All that kept his firm afloat was his ability to persuade his sap customers who made a killing to buy something else instead of cashing in, and he owed, at the moment he was lunching with George Ransome, something like five million dollars. His assets were a couple of diamond shirt studs.

"This is a very serious situation, Ransome," he declared. "You've got to handle this kid with great diplomacy. Here we had everything nicely covered up and he comes nosing around. It's a sharp nose too. I remember that youngster used to astonish me when he was eight years old."

"I don't see how he can find out anything," replied the attorney. "I'm getting bank statements for him as he asked, but I was careful what banks to mention. He admitted to me that he didn't know anything about his father's business affairs. I mentioned a broker who did a little business now and then for old Thule. He may find a few five thousand dollar transactions. I think he'll decide the old man was never worth more than a couple of hundred thousand and forget it. He stands to make a lot of money out of this crazy match with Phil Crowe and that will probably satisfy him."

"I haven't seen him for years, but I can still remember that head of his and that eye he's got, Boy, he could sling figures in those days. Lightning calculator was right. But supposing he got talking with the old man and he happened to mention my name and he found out I was a broker."

"I am sure he had no idea who were his father's brokers."

"How do I know there's no scrap of paper lying around his house with a transaction on it?"

"I tell you there wasn't a thing. I went over the library and the old man's bedroom with a fine-tooth comb. Quinlan was watching me, but your name wouldn't have meant anything to him if I had found something. Everything was eliminated before I got into the house."

"It was a clean job, I guess. Just the same, Thule might have talked to somebody who will mention me to the kid. The way things are, Ransome, I couldn't stand the slightest suspicion."

"How involved are we?"

"So involved that you'll never get a nickel of your money if I crash. You and I are tied fast together, Ransome, and don't forget it."

"ARE YOU GOING to pull out?"

"Certainly. I stopped bucketing three months ago. I'm a bull now, Ransome. I believe the market will hit the ceiling."

"I get half of eight hundred thousand. I need twenty-five thousand cash now," stated the lawyer.

"So do I," replied Mason with a mirthless laugh. "I had to raise fifty thousand yesterday to settle up with a bimbo who got cold feet. I impressed him, though, by paying; and I gave him a tip that ought to bring him back to-morrow."

"How much did you owe Thule when he died?" demanded the attorney.

"I might as well tell you. I owed him two and a half million dollars."

"Won't it show on the books?"

"Those books vanished the night he died," replied the broker. "He was a tough baby, Ransome. I never could persuade him to buy anything on margin. He bought outright, that bird, but he was so convinced of my integrity that he was content to let the securities lie in my vault and take my receipts. Say, when he demanded a hundred thousand dollars' worth of his securities I had to go on the floor of the exchange and pay cash for them. It cramped me. I don't mind telling you."

"If you crash you'll go to jail for about ten years. Have you anything laid aside?"

"A year ago I had a million and, like a sap, I kept putting it into the pot. I'm in on a couple of good things, though, and I'm getting quite a few lambs to sell short because of the coming election, which will clean them, because nobody's afraid of this election. I'll pull through unless this Mental Marvel comes down on me. I can't allow that. I hope Phil Crowe murders him."

"The fight is three months off. The fellow can't find out anything, but I admit he alarms me."

"If he gets on my trail it will be the worse for him," snarled Mason. "Do you suppose I'd let a twenty-one-year-old kid push me over and send me to jail? Old Thule would be alive if he hadn't made up his mind to cash in on everything."

Ransome drummed on the table. "The worst thing about killing is that one has to keep on doing it," he said softly.

"I've got my back against the wall," declared Mason. "I'm no timid gazelle. I've been tough in my time. You keep your eye on that kid. Put somebody on his trail. Is he interested in some woman?"

"I've seen him at the theater with a girl called Eloise Lane. She is appearing now in a play at the Fairmount Theater. It's curious, by the way, that he should be traveling around with her, for she goes out a good deal with Steve Haverty."

"The champion? Say, that's something. Woman stuff.

Get them jealous and maybe Haverty will beat him to death."

"Haverty is no fool. He does his beating in the ring."

"Yeah?" He considered a few seconds. "Just the same, it's a break for us that he's a fighter. A bad gang follows the fights. Gamblers. Thugs. Gunmen. Say, if Thule was bumped off it would be laid to fight followers. Get me?"

Ransome turned pale. "I don't care to get you," he replied, "I don't know anything about the death of Theobald Thule, and I should certainly regret to have anything happen to young Roger."

Mason thrust forward his premonitory of a jaw. "You have the liver of a chicken. Better go back to your office and we'd better not lunch in public again. That Marvel, if he happened to see us together, might start making inquiries, and he's going to need his health and strength for Phil Crowe. Pay the check, will you? I'm, ahem, financially embarrassed."

"Oh, no, you're just a stingy millionaire," laughed Ransome.

"Yeah? Can you imagine me if Thule came around and demanded his eight hundred thousand?"

16

THE TRAIL OF WEALTH

AS RANSOME HAD anticipated, Roger Thule called upon
the brokers which the lawyer had enumerated, and was
informed by them that his father had done small trading
with them in the past, but that for several years he had
transacted no business with them. The bank statements
aided Roger little, indicating that the depositor had not
been a man of very large means.

If it had not been for the poor impression made upon
him by Ransome, it is possible Roger would have dropped
the matter, but his knowledge of psychology was something
the attorney had not counted upon. Roger was certain that
Ransome was untrustworthy, probably dishonest, and that
he was unquestionably concealing something. There was no
doubt that either his father or somebody else had destroyed
his father's records. If they had been destroyed by somebody else, that person had a hand in his murder.

Among the items upon a statement supplied by the
Leffinwell Bank was the certification of a check for one
hundred thousand dollars and a deposit, two days previous to the certification, of one hundred thousand dollars
against which the check was drawn. The banking house
of Towle, Linder & Madden had not handled the sale

of the securities which realized this sum, and it occurred immediately to Roger that the check which his father had deposited must have been drawn by another broker. That broker was a person he needed to consult.

While banks usually do not keep a record of the signature upon checks which pass through their hands and are paid promptly, it seemed to him that the clerk who handled this particular check might remember something about it because of its size, and he called at the Leffinwell Bank and asked to see the president. He was referred to a vice president, to whom he stated his purpose.

"You'd be surprised how many checks for over one hundred thousand dollars are deposited and collected," replied the official. "We handle the accounts of some of the biggest firms in New York. However, I'll call the clerk who looked after your father's account and see what he knows. I doubt very much if he recalls a check which went through smoothly over three months ago."

The clerk appeared promptly and the question was put to him. He wrinkled his brow. "Thule is an uncommon name," he said at last. "I remember that deposit. There was something about that check. A few days before, a check from the same party, on the Grandison National, was sent back on account of uncollected funds, and Mr. Thule wanted to draw against the hundred thousand check for the full amount. The cashier called me up and I told him it would have to go through the clearing house before we could honor it. What the deuce was the concern—oh, yes, Evans & Mason. That was it."

"Evans & Mason," repeated Roger. "What is their business?"

"It's a brokerage house; has a seat on the stock exchange."

"Indeed. What is their standing?"

"It's considered a good house. We never had much trouble with their checks, and this one was paid all right."

"Are you sure of this?"

"Give me five minutes," said the clerk. "We keep a record of checks that don't go through smoothly."

In a couple of minutes he was back. "Evans & Mason had a check for eighteen thousand dollars returned for uncollected deposits, and the next day this hundred thousand check came in. Both checks were eventually paid, but that's how I happen to remember it."

"I'm very much obliged," said Roger and departed.

RANSOME HAD GIVEN him a list of securities sold to raise the hundred thousand dollars placed in escrow. It was an honest and straightforward transaction, and he did not dream that Roger in his investigation would go behind it. The lawyer supposed that Theobald's transactions with E.H. Mason had been perfectly covered up, for he was not aware that the wrigglings of the bucketeer in his effort to meet his checks and satisfy his customers had attracted the attention of some of the banks. If the smaller check had been returned because it arrived at the bank upon which it was drawn before Mason was able to make deposits to cover, it is very unlikely that the bookkeeper of the Leffinwell Bank would have remembered the signature upon the check made out to Theobald Thule.

One hour later Roger was sending in his card to E.H. Mason, and the pink face of that well known banker and broker turned gray. He helped himself to a drink from a locker in his private office and kept Roger waiting five minutes until he pulled himself together. What did the fellow want? Did he know anything?

"I'm sorry to have kept you waiting. An important client was with me," he explained when the son of Theobald Thule was ushered into the office.

"That's quite all right, sir. I'm glad you were able to give me a few moments." His penetrating eye rested upon the face of the broker. "I have met you before," he said sharply.

Mason broke into a hearty, if artificial, laugh. "I'll say you have, Roger," he declared. "I was wondering if you would remember me. You've grown into a great big fellow."

"You were the manager of one of my early lecture tours."

"That's right, my boy. Sit down. Have a cigar?"

"No, thanks, I don't smoke." He was studying the impressive and prosperous person opposite him. "You remember my father, of course."

"Naturally. I had the greatest admiration for your father, Roger. I used to call you Roger when you were a small boy. You don't mind?"

"Not at all. Did you see him during recent years?"

"Now and then. We reminisced a little when we met."

"I am surprised to find you in the banking business."

"Then your father never mentioned me to you?" Mason asked in surprise.

"Father and I were a strange pair, Mr. Mason. We never discussed persons, only books."

Mason beamed. This was good news. "Well, we didn't meet much. What can I do for you, young man? Want a tip on the market?"

"No, thank you. I am seeking information regarding my father's affairs. My father was supposed to have left a million dollars, Mr. Mason, but the sum of one hundred and fifty thousand dollars seems to cover the estate."

"Well, that's a tidy sum," declared the broker.

"It is my opinion that he was worth a million and I am trying to find out what became of the balance."

"If he had it, he most likely lost it on the market."

"If I can be assured of that I shall be satisfied but I cannot find a broker who bought and sold for him to any large extent."

"It ought to be simple. He would have plenty of broker's statements among his papers."

"All his papers, save unimportant ones, have disappeared."

"Well, then he didn't want anybody to know he had been speculating, and he destroyed them. Why not let it go at that?"

Roger smiled faintly. "Because I am not satisfied. I want to get from his broker, if he was playing the market, a list of his transactions."

"I see."

"DID YOU HAVE any business relations with him?" asked the young man with apparent casualness.

Mason hesitated. How had the fellow found him? Why had he called on him? Was it safest to deny everything or make a cautious admission?

"Very little," he said finally.

"You did not buy or sell for him anything running into large sums?"

"Oh, no."

"But you sold securities amounting to a hundred thousand and gave him a check for them!" the youth said sharply. Mason stooped to the bottom drawer of his desk, pulled it open, lifted the cover of a box of cigars, fumbled among them, and drew out one. He needed a few seconds to digest this. When he came up he was ready.

"That is true," he said blandly. "He asked me not to mention the affair but since you know about it I don't see why I shouldn't tell you." To himself he was saying, "How in hell did he find that out?"

"What were the details of the transaction, please?"

"Oh, the usual thing. He brought me a batch of stocks and bonds and told me to sell them and realize a hundred thousand dollars. I sold them and gave him the firm check. That's all."

He had a sensation that the eyes of the young man were penetrating his soul.

"What previous transactions had you had with him, please?"

"None. Oh, about four or five years ago I bought five thousand dollars' worth of something. I forget what it was."

"I wonder why he came to you instead of his regular broker," said Roger.

"You can search me. Wasn't there something unusual about that transaction? He asked me to say nothing."

"Do you know his attorney, Mr. Ransome?"

"Ransome? Yes, I know him, not well, just a casual acquaintance."

Roger didn't see why his father should have made a mystery about the sale of those securities, but it was possible he had done so. Ransome knew that the money was in escrow for some mysterious purpose and might have told Mason. It appeared that they were acquaintances.

"Were you under the impression that my father was a rich man?"

This was Mason's opportunity. "On the contrary, he told me that he was straining all his resources to get the cash. I had to sacrifice one or two of his stocks, but he insisted."

The young man rose, to the intense relief of the broker, for he had the same uneasy feeling that Ransome had experienced—that young Thule could not be deceived.

"Will you kindly make inquiries and let me know who was in the habit of handling the bulk of my father's transactions?"

"Why certainly, but it's possible he wasn't in the market much. I know he had some of those securities for five or six years, all of them had been purchased two or three years ago."

"How do you know that?"

"He told me so."

"It's very curious," mused Roger. "I have a list of those securities and every one of them has risen from ten to fifty points in the last few years."

MASON CURSED HIMSELF for making a rash, unconsidered statement, which was intended to convince the boy that his father had not been in the market, but had acted as a boomerang.

"Maybe you are right," he stammered. "He told me so at the time, though, I'll look them up."

"Which of the securities were sold at a sacrifice?" persisted the relentless cross-examiner.

"My dear Roger, I buy and sell hundreds of thousands of securities every day, sometimes millions, and I can't be expected to remember something which took place more than three months ago. It's possible that when I told him he was sacrificing them I meant that they would go much higher if he held on."

"I see," said Roger coldly.

"How did you learn that I handled this deal?" he asked. "From Ransome?"

Roger's eyes bored through him. "Did Ransome know of it?"

"I—I don't know."

"I traced the check to the Leffinwell Bank and a bookkeeper happened to remember that it was signed by your firm."

"Oh, I see."

"Thank you and good afternoon, Mr. Mason."

"Good afternoon," he ejaculated. Never in his life had this wily buccaneer been so glad to see the back of a visitor. When the door closed on Roger he wilted, took another drink and sat down to reconstruct the conversation.

The impression that Roger had made on him was terrifying. He saw clearly that he had made several damaging admissions and had been caught in one outright lie. He had admitted that Ransome knew he had handled the hundred-thousand-dollar deal, although he knew that Ransome had referred the boy to another broker. Young Thule, as yet, had not traced the missing eight hundred thousand to Mason's office, but he was hot on the trail.

Some five years before, Mason had renewed acquaintance with Theobald Thule and persuaded him that he was a fool to keep his fortune in gilt-edged, but low-interest-bearing securities. He showed him how he could double his money in a few years by the outright purchase of good industrial and railroad stocks selling at a low price, but which were bound to go much higher.

The ex-clergyman had confidence in Mason because he had been honestly treated by the promoter during their showman days, and he had gradually turned over to him his entire fortune. Mason had sold the gilt-edged securities, purchased others, displayed them to Thule, and then persuaded him to leave them in his charge, in exchange for receipts. These securities Mason had promptly sold and pocketed the proceeds. Later it wasn't even necessary to show the certificates to the victim. He sent him statements which Thule filed away in his safety deposit box to which he was persuaded to give his broker a key. Mason had Thule's power of attorney, as a matter of course, for he was buying and selling upon his own judgment.

Every now and then he sent the ex-minister a statement of profits, which showed that his fortune was rapidly increasing, and he received and banked the dividends from what few stocks remained in the name of Theobald Thule, sending Thule his personal check for them and for dividends of stock Thule supposed he owned, but which the broker had sold.

It's possible Mason might have acted with a certain degree of fairness to his client if the perpetual bull market had not ruined the bucketshop business. And then Thule had unexpectedly demanded the sale of certain securities which he supposed belonged to him, and conditions forced Mason to spend a hundred thousand dollars to buy them in the market.

The existence of Thule who had his receipts for stock of a supposed value of two and a half millions became a terrible menace, and Thule had conveniently ceased to exist. The indebtedness of Evans & Mason to the Thule estate had been obliterated with him, so far as Mason and Ransome had been able to manage it. Nevertheless they were playing a desperate game, for a great sum of money cannot vanish and leave no trace and there were plenty of traces for those who knew how to find them.

They had expected that Roger would accept the statement of his father's lawyer with only perfunctory checking up, but the Mental Marvel was on the trail with a nose like a hawk. Already he was suspicious. The fact that he had checked the prices of all the securities involved in the hundred-thousand-dollar transaction proved that.

"Something will have to be done about this young fellow," muttered Mason. "And soon."

ROGER WAS VERY suspicious. His recognition of Mason as the showman of the past intensified the bad impression made upon him by the man's personality. As a child he had never liked Mason, although his father had assured him that the man was entirely reliable. He had the face of a hard, pitiless and unscrupulous person who would only be honest because he considered it the best policy. He found the old showman wearing habiliments of respectability, but he had divined, the instant he entered, that Mason was afraid of him.

He was convinced that the hundred-thousand-dollar deal was only one of many handled for his father by Mason, and the admission of the broker that he knew Ransome persuaded him that Ransome must know of this business relation, yet Ransome had steered him toward a broking house which had not handled much business for Mr. Thule at any time.

If Mr. Thule had played the market upon the advice of Ransome and through the house of Evans & Mason and had lost the greater part of his fortune thereby, there was no reason for the pair to conceal the fact; the records could be immediately produced to show where the money had legitimately gone. But they were concealing it, and there were no records.

Why?

Obviously because Mr. Thule's money had not been lost on the market. Perhaps he had played the market and won, and Ransome and Mason had taken advantage of his death to sequester his winnings. That would account for their attitude, but a banker buys for his client and in his name and scores of corporations would have Mr. Thule's name on their books and would be sending him dividends.

Then was it possible that they had sold Mr. Thule out without his knowing it and were hiding the cash?

Roger was going at the thing like a problem in mathematics, coldly, logically and directly.

His father had been murdered and he had no known enemies. He was a kindly, well-intentioned man who had never injured anybody. There was no motive, apparently, for slaying him.

But suppose Mr. Thule knew that these men held a vast sum of money which belonged to him, and demanded it, and they could not or would not pay. If he had the proofs he could put them in jail. Money and revenge, according to the police, covered the motives of nine-tenths of all murders. Here was some eight hundred thousand dollars, motive enough for a score of murders.

If Thule lived, he would either get his money or jail those who were refusing to give it up. If he died and they succeeded in destroying the proof of indebtedness, they won a fortune and stayed out of prison. Ransome, in Roger's opinion, was a fox, but Mason was a wolf. Mason would not hesitate to kill for his interest.

Mr. E.H. Mason had murdered Theobald Thule for eight hundred thousand or more dollars. Q.E.D.

Roger's problem resolved itself like this, but as yet he was not prepared to act upon his result. There was a possibility that some other had slain his father and the two crooks had hastened to take advantage of their opportunity to possess themselves of his estate. There was still the handkerchief to be explained, the handkerchief upon which his father had been sitting when he was slain, and which was scented with the unique perfume Roger had manufactured for Eloise Lane. If Mason had killed Theobald Thule, where had he possessed himself of the handkerchief of Eloise?

17

A NEW ADMIRER

BUSINESS HAD BEEN dropping for several weeks at the theater where Eloise Lane was playing a bit in a society comedy, and she was not surprised upon reporting at seven thirty one evening—it was shortly after Roger's interview with E.H. Mason—to find a notice upon the bulletin board that the show would close four nights later, on Saturday.

She had been earning seventy-five dollars a week and saving very little of it because, in New York City, a young actress has to live in a decent place and wear good clothes and eat occasionally. It was late spring and shows were closing on all sides and the prospects of a new job within three months were very slight.

Her lower lip quivered a bit as she read the notice and her eyes grew misty, but she managed to laugh when a fellow actor came along and made a wise crack about the demise of their drama.

Eloise had good friends, of course. There was Dr. Marvin, and Steve Haverty, and Roger Thule. All she had to do was to notify Dr. Marvin and receive one hundred thousand dollars in cash upon which she could live in comfort for the rest of her life; and she need only telephone to Steve

Haverty and receive great wealth and the champion of the world as her husband. Oh, yes, she had friends, but Eloise had no intention of appealing to any of them.

Steve Haverty was getting hard to handle. Having begun by despising Roger Thule, he was now jealous of him. He was confident that Eloise would have agreed to become Mrs. Haverty long ago if the Mental Marvel had not appeared on the scene, though he was wrong to be confident of this for Eloise had never seriously considered marrying the pugilist although she liked him a lot. Maybe she had dallied with the idea now and then before Roger entered her life, but she had not taken it to her bosom, and now it was impossible.

She could not marry Roger. In the first place he did not love her, and in the next place she had placed herself on record so strongly as hating him that it would be difficult to destroy the record. Roger interested her, of course. He attracted her. His prowess in the ring appealed to her even more than his intellect because it seemed a greater thing in Roger than it did in Steve Haverty, who had nothing else to recommend him. He intrigued her, held her interest, fascinated her. Perhaps she loved him, but she didn't like him. Her list of the things about him she didn't like was as long as her arm.

His arrogance was annoying, his assumption that she was inferior mentally was infuriating. Of course she was, but he didn't have to make it so evident. He was pedantic, preposterously opinionated, confident he could make her, or any other woman for that matter, love him. He was positive that all he had to do was to put his mighty brain to work to unravel any mystery. He had declared he would find and bring to justice his father's murderer and he hadn't discovered a thing. He hadn't found out what her handkerchief was doing in his father's chair the night he was murdered. And he hadn't the faintest suspicion in the world that she knew his father and had visited him the night he died.

There were nice things about Roger. Despite his great knowledge he was naive, and he didn't know the world at all.

Eloise Lane had far more experience in life than he. And he was handsome and big and strong; and he was generous. He had refused to accept the money in escrow, although she had offered to give up her claim on it and though he was almost without resources. That was fine of him.

If Roger got some terribly big bump, if it was demonstrated to him in some very decided manner that he didn't know so much, he might be a much nicer person. If this Phil Crowe beat him badly in the fight which was to take place, it would show him that he wasn't the superman in every line of endeavor that he considered himself. And then—well, if he actually did fall in love with Eloise and wanted her to marry him—she would think it over.

In the meantime she was out of work and had only a couple of hundred in the bank, and she had to get some kind of a job.

SHE GAVE A good performance that night despite her depression. While she was changing and removing her make-up, the stage door man knocked upon her dressing room door to announce that Mr. Steve Haverty was below with a friend and wished permission to come up.

"Tell them they can come in five minutes," she instructed.

Steve was nice and she was feeling blue, and he was sure to want her to go to supper with him and his friend.

Steve in full evening attire was a spectacle worth going miles to see. He patronized the best tailors, his clothes fitted perfectly his superb torso; his shirt was the best quality and swankiest linen weave, his vest was in good taste, his diamond shirt studs a bit garish, but no worse than those of many men about town. No important criticism could be made of his attire, yet the effect, upon him, was bizarre.

The face which rose above the gleaming white shirt front did not belong, nor did the huge red hairy hands; and when the shining black silk hat rested upon the bullet head the effect was dumfounding. His broad smile and very white teeth prevented him from being terrifying, but it took a girl like Eloise to appreciate the sterling worth that was muffled in the stiff shirt.

Eloise, long ago, had decided there was nothing to be done about Steve's appearance, and he was less gaudy in evening clothes than in his afternoon attire, being limited in color choice to black and white.

Behind him was another sort of man, also a big fellow although dwarfed by Steve. He wore dress clothes with distinction—Steve was best-looking when he was stripped for the ring. The other's manner was refined, the air of humorous apology for his intrusion perfect, and instinctively Eloise distrusted him as much as she trusted Steve.

The hard eyes, the protruding jaw, the shape of the mouth, all meant to the girl of the theater a predatory male and, to her, he suggested an old-fashioned road showman putting on a front.

"Want you to meet a frien' o' mine, Eloise," said Steve.

"Great pal of my manager, Tim Hearn. Name of E.H. Mason."

"How do you do, Mr. Mason?" she said politely, but she ignored the hand which he was preparing to extend.

Steve flopped upon a wooden chair, his weight causing it to creak ominously.

"Mr. Mason's a big broker downtown. Him and Tim handle my business affairs, and it's a lucky thing for me. They've made a barrel of money for me."

"That is very kind of Mr. Mason," she said coolly.

"Oh, I get mine," laughed Mason. "I take off my broker's commission on every deal. It's a pleasure to meet you, Miss Lane. Steve took me to see the show to-night and insisted upon bringing me back with him."

"You certainly were great, kid," declared the champion. "You had it all over the leading woman. I was telling Mr. Mason that it would be good business for him and me to put up the money and make a star out of you."

"Thanks," she said dryly. "I lack the experience necessary for stardom."

"I REMEMBER WHEN you danced in the Follies," said Mason. "I saw your act several times and you were marvelous. It's queer to see you playing a bit in a little show."

Eloise sighed. "I strained my heart and had to stop dancing. Now I must take what I can get."

"Will you come to supper with us, Eloise" asked Steve.

"I'm wearing old clothes. If you will take me to some cheap, quiet place."

"I suppose you couldn't dig up another girl," Steve hazarded.

"I assure you," Mason said hastily, "I shall be quite

content to be along with you and Miss Lane. Do you think my presence will be *de trop*, Miss Lane?"

"Not at all," she said perfunctorily. "I have no girl friends, Steve. You ought to know that."

He waved a big hand carelessly. "Well, I just asked."

They took a taxi to a quiet sidestreet café which was almost empty, and the appearance of the world's champion created the usual commotion among the cooks and waiters.

Steve and Eloise chattered in their usual bantering fashion, while Mason was content to study the girl and wonder how to bring up the subject which was on his mind. Steve brought it up for him.

"Seen the Lightning Calculator lately?" he demanded.

"No," said Eloise. "Not for some days."

The champion laughed. "Take a good look at him, because when Phil Crowe gets through with him he'll never look like the same bozo. Imagine Whiz Malone being sap enough to sign articles for a match with a great scrapper like Phil!"

"Then you don't think Roger Thule has a chance?" asked Mason.

"How could he? He don't know the game. He's only licked a few palookas who would have fallen down by themselves if he hadn't pushed them over, and right away he gets a swelled head and thinks he can take on a first-class man. I'll hand you a laugh, Mason. He thinks he can lick me!"

"No," exclaimed Mason, and laughed heartily.

"Sure. I met him once at Eloise's place before he had a single fight under his belt and he told me he was going to take the championship away from me. Can you beat that?"

"No!" exclaimed Mason once again.

"Sure. Eloise heard him, didn't you, Eloise? How's that for a swelled head?"

"Roger is very conceited," said Eloise rather tartly, "but you are no shrinking violet, Steve."

"I'm talking about my own game. I don't think I could buck this guy in his. That's what I call conceit."

"Do you know Mr. Thule quite well, Miss Lane?" asked Mason.

"Quite well. We are good friends."

"How can a girl like Eloise stand for a walking encyclopedia?" marveled Steve.

"I am interested in him for a curious reason," said Mason with much candor. "Years ago I was a concert manager—"

"I knew it," laughed Eloise. "When you entered my dressing room I was sure you had been in the show business. It's impossible to conceal it."

"I thought I concealed it very well. You are the first who has not been surprised when I told them. Anyway, I booked a lecture tour for young Roger Thule, and became very well acquainted with his father."

"Indeed," exclaimed the girl, her eyes sharpening.

"WELL, MR. THULE and I continued our acquaintance and after some years I went into the Wall Street game and he occasionally asked my advice upon investments. Some time ago he came to me and asked me to sell for him a hundred thousand dollars' worth of securities, pretty nearly all the property he had in the world. I sold them and gave him the money and he put it in escrow for some transaction which seemed very mysterious."

"Yes?" she commented blandly.

"I wondered if you had any idea what this transaction might be, since you are a friend of young Roger. I understand the money is still in escrow."

"Mr. Thule has not discussed the matter with me," she said mendaciously.

"You are a close friend of Dr. Thomas Marvin, too," he continued.

"Really, Mr. Mason," she laughed, "I am flattered to learn that you were sufficiently interested in me to find out the names of my friends. Yes, I know and like Dr. Marvin."

"He's a great scout, that old boy," declared the champion.

"Dr. Marvin, as I understand it, is the umpire in this matter."

"I'm afraid I can't tell you anything about that."

"Well, it's of no consequence," said the baffled investigator.

"You will be in an embarrassing situation if your two good friends, Roger Thule and Steve, here, ever enter the ring together," Mason continued, with a change of attack.

"I don't think there is any chance of that," she said evenly.

"Not a chance in the world," declared Steve. "He's a set-up for Phil Crowe. The only way you can get to the top of the fight game, Mason, is to start at the bottom and step on all the rungs of the ladder, see. This smart-aleck takes a few pork-and-beaners and thinks he can fly up. Phil has forgot more than he'll ever learn about boxing."

"But think of the young man's amazing learning. The papers intimate he brings other things besides a pair of boxing gloves into the ring."

"Phil's manager will have him searched before he steps in," grinned Steve. "Here it is, Mason. A five-year-old boy can spell cat and so can you. You know a thousand times as much as the kid, but you can't spell cat any better. This is a fight, not a contest in trigonometry,"

"Take me home," commanded Eloise. "I'm bored."

Both men hastened to apologize for discussing a distasteful subject and Mason thought of another one.

"You reminded me of some one, Miss Lane," he declared. "I've been trying to think. You can't be more than twenty-one or so and this was fifteen years ago. There was a girl—did you ever hear of Hester Price?"

Eloise looked astonished. "Yes. She was my mother. Her married name was Lane."

"Think of that now! I knew her well," he exclaimed heartily. "She had your eyes and hair and that little trick you've got of cocking your head to one side like a bird. She was one of the principals in a musical comedy which I produced and took on the road, it must be eighteen years ago, maybe twenty."

"Mason," exclaimed Eloise. "I've heard her speak of you."

"Say," exclaimed Steve. "Ain't that a coincidence now. E.H. and your mother were friends."

"I wouldn't exactly say that," said Eloise dryly. "Mr. Mason was the owner and manager of the company and he skipped out of town in Eelsville, Indiana, leaving the company stranded. He took the receipts of the engagement with him."

Mason looked shocked and was cursing himself inwardly for his lack of judgment in opening up the past. "I assure you that you are mistaken," he stammered. "I was the owner and I was not present. It was the company manager who left Eelsville."

"I'm not mistaken," said Eloise. "No doubt you discovered that honesty is the best policy after that event."

"Look here, Eloise," protested Steve. "E.H. is one of the biggest brokers in New York and he never would have done a thing like that. You must be mistaken."

She shrugged. "Maybe I am. I want to go home. Good night, Mr. Mason."

"AW, SAY, ELOISE," protested Steve when they were in the taxicab, "that was an awful dirty crack you made to E.H. Say, he's the squarest guy in the world. Him and Tim Hearn are great friends, and it's through him that Tim has been investing our money for years. Say, he's made us a million profit on our investments in a few years. Is that being crooked?"

"Well," said Eloise, "I don't like him. I didn't like him when he came into the dressing room. He's too smooth and polished, but I could see the wolf behind it. I bet he started in life with a circus, operating the game that has three shells and a little-pea in it, and it's his own fault that I found out he was the crooked manager who skipped and left mother without a cent, and with a two-year-old daughter to take care of, in a dreadful hole called Eelsville, Indiana. If he has turned honest and made a million dollars for you and Tim, I bet he made two million for himself out of your money."

"I tell you he's an all-right guy," said Steve doggedly.

"Steve, it's lucky you can fight," she said shrewdly. "You'd starve to death if you had to live by your wits. I'm surprised at Tim. Send him around to see me."

Steve had a bright thought. "Sure, and I'll come with him."

Eloise laughed. "Furthermore, Mr. Mason wasn't asking those questions about Roger Thule out of curiosity. He had a motive."

"If I ever get this Thule in the ring," said Steve savagely, "I'll batter him into a cruller. That guy is a swellheaded stiff and I'm getting sick of his chasing around with you."

"You're getting sick?" she demanded. "And who appointed you to dictate to me about my friends? Climb down, Mr. Champion, climb down before you fall."

Steve promptly climbed down. "Aw, gee, I didn't mean to get your goat. Can I come in for a while?"

"At one o'clock in the morning, Steve? I'm afraid your other lady friends are spoiling you. Good night."

Just before she fell asleep, she said aloud.

"I wonder why that big crook was anxious to find out about the hundred thousand dollars."

18

ON THE TRAIL

IT DID NOT occur to Roger Thule to take the assistant district attorney into his confidence regarding the progress he had made in unveiling a motive for the murder of his father, because he had never asked aid in solving a problem of any sort, and his old assurance died hard. Anything which baffled Roger Thule was not likely to be clear to a police official.

E.H. Mason was the logical murderer; motive, the theft of the Thule estate. He was hard, brutal, without morals or scruples, and entirely capable of killing a man for gain. However, the Thule mansion had been locked on the night of the crime, and the servants had declared that no person had called upon Mr. Thule up to the time they retired at eleven o'clock. The coroner had fixed the time of the crime at midnight or before, and Roger had agreed with him.

It was possible that Mason might have called by appointment, been admitted by his father, had slain him and departed, as he had entered, through the front door. Or it was possible that Mason had sent a woman to commit the crime—the woman who had left behind her the handkerchief with Eloise's perfume on it. But Roger thought a man of Mason's type was too shrewd to have a woman confederate who might betray him any time he offended her, even though she implicated herself thereby.

It would be necessary not only to prove that Mason had stolen a vast sum of money from his father, but to prove that he had either visited the house and committed the crime in person or was the instigator of the murder.

Roger began by questioning the servants, describing Mason and asking them if such a man had ever called upon his father, but they assured him that they had never seen a person who answered to his description. Handicapped in his investigation by his lack of acquaintances in the business district who might have given him a line upon the character of Mason, and despising, as he did, the intelligence and honesty of private detectives, Roger set himself to construct the motive for the crime in full details, and by his remarkable reasoning power he evolved a theory so close to the facts that Mason would have been dumfounded if he heard it expounded.

According to the logician, a man who has sequestered a vast sum of money belonging to another, and who has established himself as a prominent and successful member of the community, would prefer to return part of the funds and give promises to pay the rest, rather than commit a crime for which he might go to the electric chair. If, however, he had not possessed the money which the rightful owner had demanded, and had been threatened with exposure and criminal procedure unless he returned it, he would have been rendered so desperate by the situation that he would have killed to save himself from financial ruin and risk capture and punishment for murder.

In what way could Mason have possessed himself of

"Who was you goin' to croak? This gent?"

and lost the fortune of Roger Thule? Well, if Mr. Thule
had brought him securities to sell, Mason must have been
his regular broker; at least he had had dealings with him
before.

Most likely Mr. Thule had been investing through
Mason for some years, and perhaps had permitted his
securities to remain in the broker's keeping, with authority to buy and sell according to his judgment. Mason had
betrayed his friend's confidence, used the stocks and bonds
in his own speculations, and so faced ruin if Mr. Thule
demanded their return.

No matter how bad a business man his poor father
might have been, he would surely have had among his
papers plenty of evidence that Mason was caring for his
property. Mason, in order to conceal his stewardship of the
securities, had to recover all his letters and receipts, otherwise he would gain nothing by the murder of his victim.

Once they were in Mason's possession, there would be no evidence to implicate him in Thule's business.

THIS WOULD EXPLAIN why there had been no papers discovered among his father's effects which related to business affairs more than three or four months back. Mason or his agent had killed Theobald Thule and destroyed all documents which might bring a demand upon him from the heir. Roger's father, however, had possessed safety-deposit boxes in bank vaults, and in these boxes certain receipts and papers showing business relations with Mr. Mason might be found. No good to destroy what documents were in the house, if the contents of the vault would betray him. And Mason knew very well that these vaults would be inspected by a representative of the district attorney in case of the murder of their lessee. Did he have a key to the vault? Had he stolen the key from Thule's body? It happened that Roger Thule had neglected to include methods of management of bank vaults among his manifold studies; but he knew how to find out what he wanted to know. He telephoned to the Leffinwell Bank and asked for the manager.

"If a man has a key to a friend's safety-deposit vault, will he have any difficulty in entering?" he demanded.

"I'll say so," replied the banker. "He must have a written order from the lessee of the box, and also sign an acknowledgment that he had admittance."

This theory of Roger's was not constructed in half an hour of intense thinking. It built itself slowly as a result of several days' devotion to the subject, but the information received from the bank gave him a chance to try it out.

He set out immediately for the Leffinwell Bank, sought

the manager of the vaults and got a setback. His father's box had not been opened for a year, and upon that occasion it was by Mr. Thule in person. He sought the other two banks in which his father had possessed vaults and was given the same statement. Up against a blank wall. He considered, returned to the Leffinwell Bank, and asked for the clerk who had told him about the business of certifying his father's check for $100,000.

"You mentioned a bank the other day upon which was drawn the N.S.F. check by Evans & Mason which held up their check for $100,000 made out to my late father?"

"Did I? I don't remember." The clerk went to his filing cabinet and dug up the information.

"That was the Grandison Bank on Fifth Avenue," he said. "Glad to oblige."

Roger took a taxi to the Grandison Bank and descended to the vaults.

"I am the son of the late Theobald Thule," he said. "Did my father have a safety deposit box here?" The inquiry was purely speculative, a forlorn hope.

"Don't think so," replied the manager. "Don't remember the name. I've only been in charge here a month, though."

He looked it up. "Yes, there was a Theobald Thule who had a big box but he closed it out and gave up the keys a little over four weeks ago."

"Had the lease run out?"

"No. It had six months to run."

"What formality is connected with giving up a box?"

"Oh, you turn the keys in and get a receipt and fill out a form."

"Would you mind letting me see that withdrawal blank? I presume it is on file."

"Certainly." He rummaged in a cabinet and produced a printed form.

ROGER INSPECTED IT. It was signed by Theobald Thule, per E.H. Mason.

"Is this regular?" he demanded.

"No. Wait a minute." He delved again and produced an order signed by Mr. Thule authorizing the bank to permit E.H. Mason access to his box at any time.

"It's a power of attorney addressed to this bank, and we took it when he ceased to transact business here," the clerk explained.

Roger looked at the date of the withdrawal blank. March 8th. It was the day of his father's murder.

"Is there any prospect of these papers being lost or destroyed?"

"No, sir. Back they go in the cabinet. They belong to us."

"I am very much obliged." So these two criminals, Ransome and Mason, had not covered up their tracks so cleverly!

His father had permitted Mason to go to his most important deposit box whenever he pleased; for the boxes at the other banks were of the smallest size. Mason had withdrawn the contents of the box and turned it back to the bank six months before the rent was due, and upon the very day Theobald Thule was murdered. Ransome, the other conspirator, was able to tell the district attorney that the three small boxes in other banks belonged to the murdered man because he knew their contents were of no importance.

However, they couldn't destroy the receipts in possession of the Grandison Bank. They had to take a chance on these and assume that the heir of the murdered man would never make inquiries there. Because Roger was a scholar they supposed they could pull the wool over his eyes in a matter of business. He thought he could put the pair in jail upon a conspiracy charge on what evidence he had turned up.

He, Roger Thule, had told Ransome that eight hundred thousand odd dollars could not vanish without a trace, and Ransome and Mason, shrewd business men, had supposed they were able to make it do just that thing. They had failed.

They must have known that there were clews pointing in the direction in which the money went, but they were desperate, took chances, and hoped the young man they were cheating would not be keen enough to find these traces of his father's fortune. That they had been desperate, that Mason had been bold enough to rifle the safety deposit box in the Grandison Bank and that Ransome had tried to conceal from the heir that his father had ever had a box there, told Roger that they were covering up a loss, not concealing a treasure.

He might find and punish his father's murderer, but the prospects of getting back his fortune were nil.

He regretted this, not so much because he wanted the money, but because with it there was no possibility that Eloise could consider his continued pursuit of her as mercenary. She had assured him she did not think him mercenary; it was at her insistence that the hundred thousand dollars was still in escrow instead of back in his own possession, yet he was afraid that she might suspect his motives and this fear came because he really loved her.

For the same reason he had hesitated to call on her since their interview at the house of Dr. Marvin. So, when Eloise called him on the phone the morning after his discovery at the Grandison Bank his heart leaped joyously.

"Good morning, quitter," she said.

"Hello, Eloise. Why quitter?"

"You seem to have thrown up the sponge. Here I am and you haven't made me love you, yet."

"Please, can't you forget that nonsense? If we could only meet as friends and not think about the confounded money—"

"I assure you I'm not thinking about it. So far as I am concerned it doesn't exist. I just wondered if you didn't want to come to dinner to-night and tell me how you're going to outfight Phil Crowe."

"I'll promise not to talk about myself at all if you'll let me come."

"Better yet," laughed Eloise. "I'm losing my job Saturday night and I must graft all the meals possible. Come early because I have to be at the theater at half past eight."

Eloise vetoed expensive restaurants on the ground that she was not dressed for them, and six-thirty found them in an Italian *table d'hôte* basement where the wine was red and cheap.

19

SHADOWED

"**I SUPPOSE YOU** thought I was falling for you when I was bold enough to call you up," Eloise teased. "My real motive was curiosity. I wanted to ask you about some one."

"I'm sorry. I hoped it was because you really wanted to see me."

"Well, I can stand seeing you once in a while," she admitted. "But I met a man last night who was unduly curious about you and was anxious to know why your last hundred thousand dollars was in escrow. He is a broker by the name of Mason."

"Mason! How did you meet him?" he demanded.

"Steve Haverty brought him round. It seems he handles the finances of Steve and his manager, Tim Hearn, and he saw me in the play and thought I was wonderful."

"So you are."

"You don't say! I twigged him for an old-fashioned showman as soon as I laid eyes on him, and this very smooth gentleman proceeded to betray himself and it developed that he managed a troupe once, stole the receipts, and left the troupe and my poor mother stranded in a village in Indiana."

"Do you know, you've never told me anything about

yourself before, Eloise. I never knew that your mother was an actress."

"Our chatter never got as far as discussion of our ancestors. Mother was on the stage. She is living up-State."

"I am not surprised to learn that Mason is a crook. He managed one of my early lecture tours, and gained my father's confidence. It is my opinion that he stole most of father's fortune."

"Ah! That explains why he was asking questions about you. Imagine his asking me if I knew why the money was in escrow! Probably he would like to get his claws on that."

"I learned the other day that father got him to sell the stocks which supplied the money he put in the hands of Dr. Marvin."

"Then perhaps you can force him to give back the rest of your money," she exclaimed. "Oh, Roger, wouldn't that be wonderful!"

"The only reason I would like it would be to come to you and say, 'Eloise, I am rich again and don't need that hundred thousand dollars. Now will you believe I really love you and want to marry you?'"

"Stop," protested Eloise. "You know you couldn't love any girl. You know there isn't any such thing as love. You can prove it by a mathematical formula."

"I'm afraid I couldn't prove it now. I'm losing confidence in science, Eloise. Science can't explain to me why I get a thrill when I touch your hand."

He laid his hand on hers and she snatched it away as though it burned her, "No fair," she laughed. "Anyway, if you want me, you know how to make me love you. It's as simple as playing checkers to a great scientist, isn't it?"

"Hang it, no," he declared. "I'm not the same man I was when you first knew me. I'm getting more and more primitive every day. Dr. Marvin found me trying to will myself out of this world because it was so stupid and uninteresting. Now I think the world is a wonderful place, chiefly because you are in it."

"Stop talking about me," she demanded. "When do you begin training for your match with Phil Crowe?"

"I open a training quarters in a couple of weeks, but I am preparing for it now."

"How?"

"AS YOU KNOW, I am a physician as well as a doctor of philosophy, and I have a much greater knowledge of anatomy and the possibilities of the human body than these people who call themselves physical trainers. I have always kept myself in good physical condition because it was necessary for clear thinking, but I have never needed abnormal strength and stamina. However, I have always known how to get it. Since I entered the ring I have been following a diet to give the best results in this direction, and have worked out a series of exercises which build muscles in quick time.

"For example, I found that five or six rounds in the ring place an extraordinary strain upon the legs. Most prize fighters who have reached the age of thirty are beaten because their legs weaken under this strain. I paid no especial attention to my legs in my early contests, and found that they did not stand up as they should. My manager and trainer thinks the way to build them up is long-distance running, and overlooks the effect of this upon kidneys and the heart. I am using a system of leg exercises of my own invention that has improved them enormously already, and I do not think they will betray me when I meet Phil Crowe."

She studied him. "You are a very, very extraordinary person. You have the face of an intellectual; it's hard to conceive how one boy could ever learn so much about so many things. But the most mystifying thing about you is your strain of brutality. How can a man of your type engage in the business of prize fighting? No matter how much profit there is in it, I should think you would shrink from beating your fellow man."

Roger laughed. "Science is cruel and merciless, Eloise, and a true scientist possesses little benevolence toward his fellow man. Peace and love are Christian qualities which are utterly at variance with the laws of the universe. The first protoplasm that crawled out of the mud millions of years ago was belligerent and cannibalistic, and all living things have fought with and devoured other living things since life began. Science believes that man has been on earth half a million years while the philosophy of love is only a few thousand years old. Not only man and the animal kingdom, but all forms of nature are savage; the fittest survives.

"Let the law of love be sincerely practiced for a few centuries and man would vanish completely from the earth. War has always served a great natural purpose as well as a purely evil one, for it has prevented overpopulation. You probably do not know that the Roman Empire about seventeen hundred years ago included some two hundred million human beings. Had Christianity been sincerely practiced and war abolished and this population multiplied according to the normal rate there would be forty or fifty billion beings on earth at the present time, which is ten times as many as it can support."

"What have these statistics to do with prize fighting?" she demanded shrewdly.

He spread out his hands in a gesture of apology. "I merely wished to show why I, as a scientist, have no moral scruples about beating or even killing my fellow man. I will admit that it offends my sense of good taste to step into a ring and exchange blows with a moron for the amusement of other morons. That's just ultra-fastidiousness; for deep in me, as in all other normal human beings, is a fierce and brutal instinct which loves battle. After a round or two I think only of conquering my opponent; the nasty surroundings don't bother me, and the character of the crowd doesn't disgust me. And, after all, I need the money I am fighting for."

"YOU'RE JUST A brute after all," she declared, "and I hate brutes."

"No," he denied. "That's modern education. Women always have loved brutes. The most beautiful women belonged to the most savage brute who won her in battle and carried her off to his cave. She loved him and bore him children. If you like me at all, I venture to say that you like me more because I am a fighter as well as a scholar, than if I were just a puny scholar with pacifist principles. When I beat Haverty I wouldn't be surprised if you loved me."

"That would have nothing to do with it," she denied.

Roger smiled. "You admit you like Haverty. Why? He is a big hulking, ignorant brute whose only decent quality seems to be good nature, which he checks outside when he steps into the ring. If he were a longshoreman or a truck driver you wouldn't give a man of his appearance and low order of intelligence a glance. You find likable qualities in him because he is the champion of the world as a result of knocking senseless a number of equally savage brutes. Be honest: don't you?"

"Why," Eloise blushed unaccountably, "I never thought of it that way. I suppose I get some satisfaction out of having the champion of the world eating out of my hand, and lying down and rolling over when I tell him so. Just the same, it's a poor business for a man like you."

"When I have knocked your idol off his pedestal I'll retire," said Roger with a smile.

"Oh, yes? Speaking of Steve, it appears that Mr. Mason has been handling his investments and those of his manager and has made an enormous sum of money for them. You think he stole most of your father's fortune, and I know that he was dishonest in the old days. Isn't it strange he should play straight with Steve?"

"Perhaps he enjoys the friendship of the champion and wants to earn his gratitude. Though he doesn't seem the type to me."

"You can't tell Steve anything about his friend, but I am going to tell Tim Hearn what I know about Mason. Do you mind if I mention what you have told me?"

Roger shook his head decisively. "I had rather you wouldn't. I have nothing against Haverty and his manager, but it might get back to Mason that I suspect him. I am not through with him yet, and I don't want him warned."

"Very well. Now it's time to go to the theater."

He called a taxi and delivered her at the stage door in

the Forties west of Eighth Avenue. Dismissing the taxi, he walked toward Eighth Avenue. He had not told Eloise that he suspected Mason of having had a hand in his father's murder, and he had not credited Mason with sufficient acumen to suspect that he was suspected of making away with his father's property. And he had no premonition that Mason had concluded to put him out of the way.

In one of Shakespeare's plays there are three characters referred to as *First, Second* and *Third Murderer*, because their profession was killing people for hire. Murder as a vocation seems to have died out for a few centuries and then to have revived in the United States in the past decade. In New York and Chicago has arisen a type of criminal known as "gunman" because he carries a gun on his hip and earns his living by using it.

Three men had followed Roger and Eloise to the Italian café, and when they came out and stepped into a taxi they had taken another cab and trailed them to the theater. The three had stepped into a doorway while he said good-by to the young actress, and were close on his heels as he walked toward Eighth Avenue. A taxicab, moving very slowly, kept close to the curb just behind them.

20

MARKED FOR DEATH

THE STREET WAS dark, the theater crowds had already assembled; Roger had passed beyond the radiance of the illuminated theater marquee, and was going by a small cigar store when the man in the center of the trio, who were only six feet behind the victim, drew a revolver from his pocket and pointed it at his unsuspecting back. Young Thule knew more than any man of his age in the world, but he didn't know that a hired gunman was about to empty his weapon into his back, and in another second he would have dropped dead upon the sidewalk if luck had not been with him.

A drunken man was violently ejected from the cigar store, catapulting out upon the sidewalk, arms swinging. He crashed against the gun holder, threw his arms around him in a clumsy effort to preserve his equilibrium, and fell with him to the pavement. The killer's finger had pressed upon the trigger and a cartridge exploded, but the bullet flew wild.

Roger turned like a flash, saw the struggle on the sidewalk, and assumed that the gunman was trying to shoot the other man. He swooped on the fallen pair and tore the weapon from the hand of the killer just as the two assistant murderers leaped into the waiting taxi, which immediately darted forward, turned the corner of Eighth Avenue on two wheels and vanished from the scene.

A crowd appeared as though sprung out of the ground, and the heavy hand of a policeman descended upon Roger's shoulder.

"Gimme that gun," he demanded, and Roger handed it over.

Half a dozen persons began to tell the officer conflicting stories about what had happened, and during the excitement the gunman succeeded in extricating himself from the embrace of the drunk, scrambled to his feet and ran a few yards into the clutches of a second patrolman.

Roger was saved from embarrassment by the proprietor of the cigar store, who called Roger's captor by his first name.

"I seen it all, Dan," he declared. "This souse was in my store and making trouble so I gave him the bum's rush through the door. He slammed into the guy that the other policeman's holding and they went down. He had a rod in his hand, and I guess the bum saved this gent you've got from bein' drilled, for the gun went off when they fell and there wasn't anybody in sight except your man. He swings round and jumps on the pair on the ground and dragged the gun away. I seen it all, I tell you."

"I know this yegg," the second policeman, who had captured the gunman, declared. "He hangs out near Ninth Avenue and Forty-Sixth Street. Who was you going to croak? This gent here?"

He shook his prisoner like the rat he resembled, for

the gunman was a swarthy, undersized, low-browed alien whose slouch hat had fallen off during the struggle.

"I ain't sayin' nothing, see" snarled the prisoner.

"Maybe you'll talk to the lieutenant," retorted the policeman. "Help me get him to the wagon, Dan."

"You come with us, mister," the policeman called Dan said to Roger. "Lucky Tom Giddings here saw you. Want to take along the drunk, Bill?"

"Got to. He don't know nothing, though. Look at him."

The drunken man had passed out on the sidewalk and was now snoring.

Two more policemen came through the crowd and the party adjourned to a police telephone box, with Roger standing most uncomfortably in the oddly assorted group of four policemen, a gunman and a drunk who was out on his feet.

AT THE STATION house Roger presented his card to the sergeant at the desk without suspicion that it would create a sensation.

"You're the Mental Marvel that's going to fight Phil Crowe," exclaimed the lieutenant, looking over the desk man's shoulder. "Say, I'm glad to meet you, Mr. Thule."

"Yes, I'm matched with Phil Crowe," he said with a smile.

"But you're a big, strong feller! From the papers I thought you was a Peewee. Now don't you worry about this affair, Mr. Thule. This egg was out to kill some one and he mistook you for the guy. The drunk whanged against him, the gun went off and you took it away from him. Nobody hurt, but we'll send this gunman up the river for a stretch for violating the Sullivan law. You don't have to be a witness. You don't want to have anything on your mind to interfere with your training."

The solicitude of the lieutenant was amusing, and convenient for Roger, but before he left the station house he had to meet and shake hands with all the reserves and assure them he expected to win his battle.

He returned home fully conscious that he had a narrow escape from being murdered by mistake. Except for the fact that the cigar store owner had chosen as the proper time to throw out the drunk the exact second when the gunman was pointing his weapon at Roger's back, he would have been either dead or mortally wounded, and the fact that the killing was an error would not be of any earthly consequence to him.

While Roger was astonishingly learned he was not omniscient, and his study of psychology had not been along the line of criminal research. Consequently he was not aware that his interview with Mason had convinced that worried criminal that his acumen was so great he would soon uncover the whole plot and throw the broker in jail for murder and conspiracy unless he was speedily disposed of.

Roger was not yet convinced that Mason had personally slain his father, although the man was capable of violence if pushed too far; there was the owner of the handkerchief to be considered, for she might have fired the shot for reasons of her own or might be a tool of the lawyer and the broker. That the pair had taken advantage of his father's death to hide their possession of most of his property Roger was sure.

So he did not now jump immediately to the conclusion that the man with the gun who had almost dropped him was an agent of Mason's, but he thought it strange indeed that a person sent out to kill a certain individual should be so unfamiliar with the appearance of his victim that he would fire at somebody else. It was possible, of course, because of the low mentality and drugged minds of modern gunmen; so Roger accepted the police explanation because he knew of no reason why any one should wish him assassinated.

A man who lived in New York was always in danger of being killed by a brick falling from a high building under construction, being blown up by an explosion, or hit by a stray bullet; and no amount of precaution could save him from chance casualty. Nevertheless he resolved to pay more attention to his surroundings when next he walked down a dark street, instead of being in a brown study over the inexplicable attraction of one particular girl above all the others.

Despite the police lieutenant's good intentions, Roger did not escape annoyance as a result of the incident. As a pugilist he was big news, and a reporter got the story from the police station. In the morning papers Roger discovered that while he was walking down a dark street a gunman was stealing up behind him with the intention of murdering him; by mental telepathy the Intellectual Marvel had realized his danger, turned suddenly, grappled and overpowered the killer and handed him over to the police.

The part played by Fate, the cigar storeman, and the drunk were ignored by the newsmongers because of the chance this gave them to exploit the alleged mental magic of the young pugilist. The sporting writers seized it to ask what chance Phil Crowe had to land a blow upon a man who could turn his back and know exactly what his opponent was doing. There had been no betting on Roger Thule up to this time, but the paper odds of ten to one dropped to five to one at once and a good many bets were made at that figure.

E.H. MASON READ the newspaper explanation of Roger's escape, which was confirmed by the cowardly confederates of the captured assassin as an elegant let-out, and he was almost credulous enough to believe it. Eloise read it and didn't believe it, but trembled for the safety of the young man who interested her more than she would admit to herself; and Phil Crowe read it and began to worry.

"What the heck am I up against?" he demanded of his manager. "I only got two fists, but this guy, 'cording to what I hear, is a good scrapper, can take a lot of punishment, and he's a mind-reader besides. Can we duck out of this fight?"

"Go on, you big sap," snorted the manager. "It's goin' to be a sell-out, and even if you get licked you're rich. You can knock the mind-readin' out of him with the first punch."

Roger called on Dr. Marvin next day and told him what he had discovered about the broker Mason and the attorney Ransome.

"What I can't figure out," he said, "is how a man who is a broker and knows the market could possibly lose so much money."

The doctor smiled quizzically. "You're a bright boy, Roger, but you're not well acquainted with Wall Street. Most likely Mason runs a bucket shop. Do you know what that is?"

"Certainly I do, but you're wrong. Mason has a seat on the Stock Exchange."

"And so have all our best bucketeers. They do considerable buying and selling on 'Change, but they make their big money by bucketing orders when they think the purchaser has made a mistake. What your father probably did was give him buying orders which were never filled."

"But in that case he would have my father's money. I assumed it had been lost. I have been looking up the market for a couple of years back, and find that the whole list had advanced from twenty to a hundred points. It's a fact, isn't it, that outsiders rarely sell short?"

"Yes, that's true enough. Now, Roger, I am willing to take my oath that your father, when he put up a hundred thousand dollars to win you back to health and an interest in life, thought he was worth a million at least. You can tell by a man's manner if he is putting up his last dollar. He would have made some protest, would have asked if twenty-five thousand or fifty thousand wasn't enough; but he made no objections whatever to the sum I named. I remember asking him if he thought it was too much. He replied that he would spend his last dollar for you, but he certainly didn't act as though he were doing it."

"But in that case—"

"HOW COULD IT happen? Well, you say, Mason had authority to go to your father's strong box. That meant he trusted him implicitly. It's possible that all his securities were in charge of Mason, or, at least, Mason was entitled to take them when he wanted them. That's often done. Many persons who play the market depend entirely upon the judgment of their broker and give him authority to buy and sell as he pleases. Most likely, when Mason bought fifty thousand dollars' worth of stuff for your father he held the stock and gave him a receipt. He might have sold the stock next day without notifying him. Now if he was bucketing and the market kept rising despite his own judgment, your father's statements would make him think he was gaining huge profits when he didn't actually own a share of stock. Of course Mason was responsible to him, and sooner or later there might come a reckoning day. Suppose Mr. Thule decided he had cleaned up enough and instructed Mason to deliver him his securities; and assume it would cost the broker half a million or more to buy them in at the market price and deliver them to him; that demand of Mr. Thule's might have been his death warrant. It all depends upon the caliber of Mason. Is he a potential murderer, in your judgment?"

"Indubitably."

"Then he killed Mr. Thule or had him killed. What are you going to do now?"

"Frankly, I am at a loss. I think I have evidence enough of conspiracy to clap them both in jail."

"Yes, but no proof that they were connected with the killing. It's possible somebody else killed your father and they took advantage of it. Ransome was left alone with your father's papers; he might have destroyed the receipts."

"No, the assistant district attorney, Mr. Quinlan, went over them with him."

"It's certain your father would not have destroyed statements and receipts that were worth eight or nine hundred thousand to his son and heir. That makes it evident that they were destroyed by those who would benefit from their destruction. Let me make a suggestion."

"Please do."

"A lot of bucket shops are insolvent as a result of this bull market, but carry on because they persuade their customers to reinvest instead of cashing in. A smash in the market would wipe the slate clean for them. If you have Mason arrested now it would cause his firm to crash, but if the bears get control, it's possible he will pull through and can be forced to return your father's money."

"I don't care anything about that. I want him punished for the murder of my father."

"But you have no evidence, just now. I suggest that you let me put detectives on Mason. Let's dig into his past and get his complete record. From what Eloise told you it must be a very shady one. It may give us a line upon possible confederates. A few weeks won't make any difference. Roger, what do you make of the attack on you last night?"

"I SUPPOSE I look like somebody who was scheduled to be shot."

Roger smiled.

"Humph. Roger, the world is full of people who believe in fairies. You have a great reputation as a scholar and people give you credit for being even more clever than you are. Now you bearded the wolf in his den. You forced Mason to make damaging admissions and you probably scared him half to death. You were so intent upon what you were getting out of him that you forgot that all-seeing eye of yours. Perhaps Mason thinks you know already that he killed your father."

"You mean he set the gunmen on me?"

"I think that kind of man is capable of it."

"By George, I believe you're right. With me out of the way it would be to nobody's interest to pursue the investigation. And that means that there will be other attempts on me."

"I shouldn't be surprised."

Roger smiled. "I don't think its on the cards for him to murder me."

"There's your old arrogance. Your overweening confidence is your greatest danger."

"No, no, I'll be on my guard. I assure you that I can pick out a dangerous man at a glance if I am forewarned. I now assume that Mason is after me. Don't worry, doctor."

"It may not be a gunman this time."

"I tell you I'm warned. If you know a good firm of detectives, will you set them on Mason?"

"Leave that to me. How are you getting along with Eloise?"

Roger's face clouded. "I don't know. She baffles me. I can usually look into a person's mind, but not hers."

"You understood her well enough the first few times you met her."

"Certainly. She thought I was an opinionated ass, lacking in every human quality and she was determined to get the hundred thousand dollars."

"And then you fell in love with her and she became a mystery. Is she in love with you?"

"I told you I can't tell you any more. I know she liked Steve Haverty a lot."

"He's a pretty decent chap, Roger, but not for Eloise. That girl had very little education and from the age of sixteen she has been on the stage, but she has the best mind I ever found in a woman; she does the right thing by instinct, and she is as well read as any girl of her age can possibly be. I don't think she will marry Steve and she won't marry you until you have learned to be humble instead of arrogant."

"Am I not learning?"

The doctor laughed. "You have a long way to go yet."

21

A CLEVER PLOT

WHIZ MALONE HAD had a brief and fairly glorious career as a welterweight, during which he "spent his money like a good fellow," as they say in the business. But he found himself, in his early thirties, written off as an old man with no more prospects of being in the "big money."

He had no other qualifications for earning a livelihood save use of his fists, and for several years had found it hard work to make enough to board and lodge him. He had been a clever boxer, however, and he gradually established himself as a teacher of boxing and a physical trainer, but lost two college jobs by taking too much to drink in a conspicuous manner. Since that he had been a total abstainer.

By getting a hundred dollars down at five to one upon a middleweight bout which was supposed to be one-sided but wasn't, he got a stake, and he boosted the roll into a couple of thousand by a streak of lucky betting which had enabled him to open his Physical Culture Institute. He had not had much luck in getting wealthy men to improve their physical culture, but he had made a fair living by permitting second- and third-rate boxers to train in the place. It had looked to Whiz, when Roger Thule appeared upon the scene, as though he would probably die poor; now, he was manager of a fighter who was in the big money and he had a fifty-fifty split. It just didn't seem true.

Until the Phil Crowe match Roger hadn't earned enough to pay his fees at the gymnasium, but the way the tickets were going, two months in advance, it was evident that the boy's share of the gate would run far above his guarantee. It was up to Whiz to prepare his man in the best possible way. They must have first-class training quarters, really good sparring partners, cooks, rubbers and all the appurtenances of a potential champion in training. It would go far beyond the bank roll of the little manager.

He was forced to tell his predicament to Roger, who laughed and asked how much it would cost to do things in the regular way.

"We can't get out of it under four or five thousand dollars, doc, if we get good sparring partners and settle down in a decent place."

"Go ahead. I've eight or nine thousand cash and we're sure of a lot more than that, even if I lose."

"I hate to take your money, Doc, but I'm pretty near broke and you can take my half of the expenses out of my share of our cut."

"That's quite all right. I am engaging my own masseur, though. I have invented a system—"

"Look here, doc. You got to do as I tell you. There's only one way to rub a fighter."

"You know a lot about fighting, but very little about muscular action and less about anatomy, Whiz. Do you forget I am a physician?"

"What ain't yer?" demanded the little man in despair.

"When Phil knocks you cookoo, remember you wouldn't listen to me."

Roger laughed and clapped him on the big shoulder. "You think he's going to do it anyway, so I prefer to use my methods instead of yours. I'll give you a check for a thousand for preliminary expenses. I am going to be busy for a few days. Moving out of the house into an apartment and I've got to box up my library. About half of it has to go to storage."

"Now ain't that too bad," said Whiz with mock sympathy.

Roger's library had been the thing dearest to him in the world until Eloise had swum into his life, and it still held second place. He had to divide it with the greatest care lest he send to storage a volume which he might want under his hand, and he was already in possession of a number of big book crates which he was filling slowly. It was especially slow work because Roger would take a volume from the shelf, open it, and a sentence or a paragraph would catch his eye, whereupon he would drop into a chair and become absorbed in the book for hours.

HE WAS WORKING in the library, the room in which his father had met his death, one evening a week or so after his interview with Doctor Marvin. Before dinner he had called Eloise, to be told that she was engaged for that evening, which probably meant Steve Haverty.

Roger set about his packing in no good humor. However, a passage in Racine attracted him and he read an entire play before he closed the book and placed it tenderly in a crate.

Next to it upon the shelf was Tacitus, his father's favorite historian, and he lifted the book and opened it, saw nothing interesting and was about to close it when something gray fluttered to the floor, a sheet of note paper. He picked it up and read the following lines:

DEAR MR. THULE:

I'll come to your house after the theater to-morrow night, but I assure you that nothing you may say can influence me or affect my decision.

E.

The handwriting was unknown to him, the initial might mean anything, but it was dated the day of his father's murder, and his nostrils were quivering, for, from the paper, was wafted a subtle but unmistakable perfume, the perfume of Eloise. And the initial "E"—hers!

He never had received a letter from Eloise, but it would be easy to identify the handwriting if it were hers. Dr. Marvin knew it. But dared he let Dr. Marvin in on this?

Eloise had declared that she had no notion of how the handkerchief had come to be upon his father's chair and she was not aware of having lost a handkerchief scented with her unique perfume.

She did not know his father and, therefore, could not have written him and paid him a visit—after the theater, too—upon the night of his death.

Could not—unless she were lying to Roger. The writer of this letter must have called because she had left the handkerchief, and both letter and handkerchief had the same scent.

He sat down and mopped his brow, for he was shocked and startled and his usual fluent reasoning failed him.

When the letter came, Theobald Thule had been reading Tacitus, had perhaps used the note as a book marker, which made it fairly evident that this was not a letter which perturbed him. Undoubtedly he knew the writer. Eloise was playing in a show and would have arrived at eleven or a little after, while Mr. Thule was murdered before midnight. Of course, it was absurd to think that Eloise had written the letter or called on his father, but it was curious that both handkerchief and epistle bore that damning perfume. Any other perfume in the world might be the property of others as well as Eloise, but this was unique, his own blend after many experiments upon a day when he was in the laboratory in a frivolous mood.

He read the letter again. Mr. Thule knew the writer so well that he was endeavoring to change her decision in some matter, and she warned him that his arguments would be useless. This meant that they had relations of some sort and at present were not in agreement.

But what could Eloise and his father have to discuss? What decision of the pretty little actress provoked the opposition of his father? And how did she get in and out without attracting attention?

The discovery of the handkerchief had revealed to Roger that he loved Eloise, and the letter, again pointing suspicion toward her, confirmed it, to his acute distress.

FOR THE PRESENT he decided to assume that some other woman, mysteriously possessing the same perfume, had called upon his father before his murder. It must have been before, because Theobald Thule had been sitting on the handkerchief when he was shot. There were strained relations between them—were they strained enough to cause this woman to bring a revolver with her to the interview? A woman with a gun in her possession he knew to be a menace, for in hysteria she might fire for trivial reasons, reasons which would not move a man to violence.

If the unknown woman, who simply must not be Eloise, had killed his father, it was because of a situation between them which seemed to have no connection with the financial imbroglio which affected E.H. Mason. In that case Ransome and Mason were innocent of the crime, but had been quick to take advantage of it. And yet Roger had a feeling amounting almost to a conviction that it was Mason who had killed his father.

It was impossible to discuss this letter with Dr. Marvin, but he could write a note to Eloise which would draw an answer and thus compare the two specimens of handwriting. He hated to entrap Eloise; it was a cruel trick, and an indication that he lacked faith in her; but could he stand this doubt? Her handwriting must be so different that it would wipe away suspicion. But if it happened to be the same handwriting? Even then, she was innocent. She would give him an explanation if he asked for it.

He walked the floor for five minutes in his chaotic state of mind, then snatched a sheet of writing paper and scribbled the following:

DEAR ELOISE:

Won't you give me the evening after to-morrow? There is something I want to tell you. Please send me an answer by return mail.

ROGER THULE.

He felt like a felon when he slipped it in an envelope and addressed it. But he had to know.

The philosophy of Roger was naturally deductive, reasoning from certain assumptions, instead of empirical, reasoning from facts, for the latter is based upon experience of life and he had little.

Roger Thule thought he was an aloof philosopher; but he was just a boy who was frightfully worried about a girl. He did not sleep much that night and when he tried to read he discovered that for the first time in his life he couldn't concentrate.

Eloise would get the letter in the morning mail and he might expect an answer by afternoon. The handwriting would not be that of the woman who had written to his father, he was sure of it, but it would be a great relief to have the evidence that it wasn't.

About eleven o'clock while he was packing in desultory fashion; he had omitted his customary strengthening and developing exercises, he was handed a telegram from Eloise.

"Why so formal?" it demanded. "Come get me at seven."

The cordial tone of the telegram almost compensated for her failure to write a letter. She must be as eager to see him as he to see her when she took the trouble to telegraph instead of to post him his reply. But that proved nothing about her handwriting.

AT DR. MARVIN'S suggestion a private investigator was not only digging up the past of E.H. Mason, but a bank detective was at work trying to trace his father's financial transactions for the past five years. Marvin was certain, since Mason and Ransome had already demonstrated lack of thoroughness, that other evidence leading from Mr. Thule's checking accounts straight into the office of Evans & Mason would be found.

An investigation into his own father's past life seemed also in order, but Roger shrank from that. He almost wished he had never started any inquiries since the trail seemed to lead back to Eloise. Well, to-morrow night he would ask her point-blank. She wouldn't lie.

And that afternoon E.H. Mason telephoned to him.

"May I come to see you, Mr. Thule?" he asked. "I've been thinking over some things you said when you were in my office and I think you are entitled to all the facts."

"When would you like to come?" asked Roger, who managed to keep his astonishment out of his voice.

"I can be up in an hour."

"I shall be waiting for you."

He considered when he had hung up the telephone whether he should ask Dr. Marvin to be an unseen witness to this interview, and then called up the doctor to find he had been called out of town for a consultation.

Was Mason bold enough to contemplate killing him in his own house at mid-afternoon? He did not think so, but he was at a loss to know what the man could have to say to him. Perhaps he and the doctor were all wrong in suspecting the fellow of setting the gunmen on him, while Mason had no full intent, but still thought he could pull the wool over the young man's eyes.

He awaited the broker impatiently, but the man was late; three o'clock came without him. At five minutes past three the housekeeper notified him that a Mr. Mason was on the telephone in the library.

"I'm sorry to have kept you waiting," began the broker, "but circumstances have come up which make it impossible for me to get away to-day. Suppose I call you again and make another appointment."

"As you please," said Roger, and hung up abruptly, just as the glass crashed and splintered behind him. He swung about to see a great hole in a window pane. A cone-shaped metal object was rolling on the floor.

Had it not been for the gun incident of the other night Roger might have required several seconds to comprehend that he was looking at a bomb which had been hurled through the window with murderous intent; and had he not been familiar with the character of such weapons it is probable he would have taken to his heels. The instinct of self-preservation causes people to try to run from a bomb, although evidence shows that a victim rarely saves himself that way.

Roger's coordination of thought and action was perfect. He swooped on the "pineapple" and pitched it through the broken window through which it had come, and then he ran out of the room.

There was an explosion like a thunderclap, the house shook and rattled, and all the windows were broken. The tinkle of splintering glass continued for several seconds after the report of the bomb had died away. Roger was thrown to the floor in the front hall, but picked himself up uninjured.

The library window through which the bomb had been thrown looked upon a twelve foot areaway, and the window was some ten feet above the passageway. The explosion had shattered the basement wall of the Thule house and also the wall of the house on the opposite side of the areaway, and had torn a great round hole in the brick paving upon which it had fallen. Aside from broken windows and the destruction of bric-a-brac, it had done no other damage within the houses, but fragments of a man were found by the police near the head of the areaway, and the supposition was that it was the dismembered bomb-thrower.

HAD ROGER OBEYED the ordinary urge to run from the bomb, it would have exploded in the library and destroyed most of the house and its master as well. But in the fraction of a second he had to think he realized that this could not be a concussion bomb, since the thrower knew he had to hurl it through a closed window, in which case it might explode from the slight resistance of the glass; it was probably a bomb which contained a time fuse to explode it a few seconds from the time it left the thrower's hand.

In those few seconds Roger could not escape. It was probable that it would explode in his hand as he picked it up, but there was a faint possibility that he had time to pick it up and throw it out the window before the explosion came. As it happened, he had a second left after he threw it through the broken pane into the areaway, during which time he made the front hall. Even there he had been thrown upon his face by the vibrations from the explosion.

The person who had thrown the bomb had evidently tarried a second too long in the areaway, secure in the knowledge that the bomb was inside the house. He was hoist on his own petard when it bounced back into the alley.

Of course the explosion drew a crowd and the police, but Roger went to his own room, telling the housekeeper to say

she knew nothing about it. All windows in his house and
the house next door had been broken by the explosion, so
the library pane, through which it had originally entered,
was no clew. There was no sense in telling the police that a
bomb had been thrown into his house, because they would
not know who was responsible for the outrage, and he did.

Roger was in marvelous physical condition, but he was
not without nerves, and he was experiencing the reaction
from the terrific strain of those two seconds between the
discovery of the bomb, his disposal of it, and the explosion. His nervousness took the form of an outburst of
rage against E.H. Mason. He cursed him and threatened
him, and drove his big fists into the pillows of his bed as
he would have liked to drive them against the body of the
broker at that minute.

That Mason had instigated the bomb outrage was
perfectly obvious to him, and proved that Mason was also
responsible for the gun attack that had failed. Mason had
no communication to make to Roger, but had called him
upon the phone to discover if he were at home, and made
an appointment for an hour later to make sure he stayed
there.

Then, at five minutes after three, having waited until his
hired assassin was planted with his bomb under the library
window, he phoned again, aware that the phone was in the
library. His purpose was to have Roger at the phone when
the metal bomb came crashing through the window. He
had expected that the young man would ask him when he
would like to make another appointment, and he probably
intended to keep him in conversation until the explosion
of the bomb informed him that his plans had not failed

this time; but Roger had hung up on him in disgust, and this action had saved Roger's life.

When he grew more calm he realized that he had no proof whatever that Mason was responsible for the bombing. The man was sitting in his office down town, had called him as he probably had called thirty people that day, had made an appointment and broken it. By a strange coincidence he had called to break the appointment a moment before some unknown person threw a bomb at the person uptown with whom he was talking. If Roger had been killed, the fact that Mason had an appointment with him would probably not have come out.

22

INTO HIDING

IN MORE PRIMITIVE times men who were enemies went gunning for each other, and whoever slew the other was acquitted upon the ground of self-defense by a frontier jury; but modern civilization claims to be able to protect good citizens so skillfully that they do not have to guard themselves against their enemies. That this claim was unjustifiable was evident by the two attempts made by Mason against Roger Thule. From the first he had escaped by accident, from the second by quick thinking and a stout heart.

Roger realized that Mason was determined to get him, and that the authorities, under the circumstances, could not protect him. In the first place he could not convince them that he had any ground for his suspicion against Mason, and in the next place it would take more than an indifferent bodyguard supplied by the police department to save a man marked down for death by the criminal element with which Mason appeared to be closely affiliated.

If he wanted to remain alive, then it was up to Roger to get Mason, and he had no doubt that he could concoct a neat, safe, fool proof manner of slaughtering his enemy, but he didn't want to kill Mason, because he wanted Society to do it legally. In Roger's opinion Mason deserved the electric chair for his connection with the assassination of Theobald Thule, and he wanted him tried and convicted. If he was forced to kill Mason to save his own life he might have difficulty in convincing the authorities that he acted in self-defense, and he had no desire to go to the chair for slaying a murderer.

There was only one thing to do, then, since he would not take the offensive against Mason just at present; get out of a city where killing is a matter of such extreme simplicity.

In a couple of months he was matched to meet Phil Crowe, and he would probably earn upon that occasion a sum of money which would make him independent. A wound or injury of any sort would do him out of these prospects, and he could not expect to escape scot-free from Mason's thrusts much longer. First beat Crowe, get the money, and then go after his mortal enemy.

In his own training camp, surrounded by persons in his pay and devoted to him, he would be safer, and he could depend upon Whiz to keep suspicious strangers at a distance. He would start training in a couple of days instead of in a couple of weeks. Give Mason plenty of rope. In two months Roger would be financially well-upholstered and far better equipped to trail his father's murderer.

He learned from the police who had insisted upon talking with him that a man had been killed in the areaway. He was convinced that the victim had intended to be his own murderer, but he did not supply the officers with this information. Until he was ready to strike back he did not wish Mason to think that he was aware his life was being attempted.

Whiz Malone made no objections when Roger dropped into the gym an hour later to tell him to open up training quarters the day after to-morrow.

"Sure I can get ready," he declared. "You can do light work for a couple of weeks."

"Have you given out the location of our quarters?"

"Haven't even told you, yet," grinned Whiz. "I only rented the place day before yesterday."

"**DON'T TELL ANYBODY** for a couple of weeks. I have reasons for getting out of town, and I don't want anybody to know where I am. Where is this place?"

"It's a little farmhouse in Douglas County. The farmer and his wife will cook and do the chores for us."

"Then I can run up there without attracting any attention. I'll let the servants finish my packing and close the house. Don't tell anybody around the gym where I am until we're ready to start hard work in a fortnight."

"Who are you hiding from?" asked Whiz shrewdly. "Some dame?"

"I have reason to think that the unknown person who murdered my father has made two attempts on my life, the second by throwing a bomb through my library window only an hour and a half ago. As I would like to keep our mutual engagement, Whiz, I am taking precautions."

"Whew! Get out of town tonight!" said the manager, much impressed.

"No. I've an engagement to-morrow night which I must keep."

"Well, get out of the house tonight. Put up at a hotel. Say, doc, we can't take any chances. The tickets are selling wonderful."

"I'll take no chances that I can help," said Roger grimly. "You notify these people in Douglas County to expect me."

THE INCIDENT OF the bomb had not driven from Roger's mind the necessity of having a showdown with Eloise about the letter and the perfume, but it had enabled him to await his engagement with more patience than he otherwise would have displayed. The savage daring of his enemy put him on his mettle, and he felt now toward Mason as he had felt when he stepped into the ring against the clever Rosenbaum—a battle to be fought, an opponent to be laid low.

As repairs were not completed to the windows of his house, he decided to take Whiz Malone's advice and spend the night at a hotel, and lest he be followed there by minions of the deadly Mason, he changed taxicabs twice before he entered a small, select East Side caravansary.

This action of his was responsible for his missing Eloise, who read of the bomb outrage in the evening newspapers and called him several times during the early evening. When he returned to the house in the morning he found a letter from her, the first he had ever received, and he tore it open eagerly, to read:

DEAR ROGER:

I am frightfully sorry to break our engagement to-morrow night, but you understand that my resources are slender and the chance came to jump into a good part in a show in Chicago. I have extricated myself from the final performances of the dying drama in which I have been playing here, and at six to-morrow morning I shall leave in an airplane. I have to learn my part in the plane and jump into the show to-morrow night.

I called your house three times tonight and your house-keeper finally admitted you would not be home. I was much distressed to hear of the bomb explosion. Following on the heels of the gunman affair, it looks as though you were in danger from some source. Please, Roger, take care of yourself. Forget you are a superman and take ordinary precautions. I'll write you from Chicago and I hope you'll keep me informed of everything that has happened.

ELOISE.

It was not until he had read this letter from beginning to end that Roger remembered that he had schemed unsuccessfully to draw an epistle from Eloise. He was bitterly disappointed at her unexpected departure, but he knew that things happened suddenly in the show business, and it was his fault that they had not talked last night; he had neglected to tell the housekeeper what hotel he was going.

Well, it would be easier to bury himself in a training camp for a couple of months if Eloise would not be in New York so near as to be tempting. And after thinking all these loverlike thoughts, he scrutinized the handwriting, scowled incredulously, and took from his pocket the other letter.

It was not only the same handwriting, but the same stationery. Eloise had written the letter to his father. Eloise had called upon his father the night he was shot, and it was her handkerchief which was found in Mr. Thule's chair despite her denial of it!

AT THE MOMENT the assurance of this drove home in his brain, his heart grew stout and demanded, "What of it?"

Eloise most certainly had not killed his father. For

reasons of her own, which were undoubtedly good reasons, the girl had concealed her acquaintance with Theobald Thule, and the fact that she had called on Mr. Thule that night. In time she would explain.

If she had had any information which would aid in bringing the murderer to justice, she would not have refused to divulge it to Dr. Marvin and himself. Her visit on that night was a coincidence, that was all. Why, it completely cleared things up. He had hesitated to determine upon Mason as the killer until he had discovered the owner of the handkerchief. Since it was Eloise, and she was innocent, Mason was guilty and Mason would have to pay the penalty. But, in his own interests, Roger thought he would give the criminal rope. His own future depended upon the engagement with Phil Crowe, and Mason would be allowed to live until that battle was over.

It is a tradition that a pugilist must go into training for a match, a tradition based upon the fact that the old-fashioned pugilists were upon a continual spree except during these training periods. A few months of abstinence from liquor and from over indulgence in fatty foods, with plenty of good, healthy exercise would bring the old-timers to fair condition.

The modern pugilist, who is a total abstainer, and who takes pretty good care of himself for twelve months every year, finds the old extremes of training unnecessary, but he yields to custom, goes into the country and permits visiting journalists to see him punch the bag, skip the rope, and go a few rounds with his sparring partners.

Whiz, during Roger's slight training for Rosenbaum, had tried to induce him to go to bed at nine o'clock in the evening and arise at five thirty, having the ignorant man's delusion that early to bed and early to rise makes a better fighter, and Roger had been so bored without his books that he usually yielded.

Whiz had heard of the Swains from a fighter who had trained at their home four or five years ago, and he had chosen it. Though the house was small, the barn was unusually large, and could be fitted up without difficulty as a gymnasium.

On the place was a pond and pine woods, and in the vicinity were many miles of narrow country roads, very little traveled and ideal for long-distance running.

"**I'M PAYING ONLY** fifty dollars a month for the rent of the farm," said Whiz, "and I supply all the grub we use, and give Mrs. Swain twelve dollars a week to act as cook for as many as come. Her old man eats free. I think it's a pretty good deal, doc."

"Don't these people farm at all?"

"Naw, they're too lazy. They raise a little garden truck. Old man Swain is a corner grocery store loafer, one of them guys that sits on a cracker barrel and discusses how to run the country. Mrs. Swain is a nice old lady and a good worker. I think they got a small income, but they're tickled to death to rent the place for training quarters. They'll probably live a couple of years on what they get out of us."

During the trip up from the city, Roger had taken Whiz somewhat into his confidence, and he made him realize how desirable it was that his whereabouts be kept secret for a while.

"I was wondering if we couldn't charge admission to your training quarters, the way Dempsey and Tunney used to do," admitted Whiz; "but if you've got people gunning for you, we can't afford to let the public in."

They reached the Swain homestead late in the afternoon and found both husband and wife waiting to greet them. Mrs. Swain was a round-faced, bespectacled, dumpy, motherly soul of about fifty, who looked like the good cook she undoubtedly was.

Mr. Swain was a stringy individual with a very long nose, long, lean lips, and a nondescript chin which was perpetually in motion because there was always gum in his mouth; and when the chin moved, so did the mouth and nose. Whiz usually referred to him as "Old Rubber Face."

"I'm going back to town in the morning, Mrs. Swain," Whiz told her, "The camp doesn't open officially for a couple of weeks yet; and we don't want it known that Mr. Thule is here. So keep it dark. That means you, Swain."

Mr. Swain's small, greenish eyes snapped angrily.

"WHEN YOU SET up the ring," Roger told Whiz, "I want you to paint lines on the floor canvas three feet apart and crisscross like a checkerboard."

Whiz gaped at him. "For the love of Mike, what for?" he demanded.

"Just experimenting in footwork."

"Next thing you know Phil Crowe's people will hear of it."

Roger laughed. "I hope they do," he declared. "I'll try to think of other novelties for their entertainment. In your opinion, Whiz, I'm going up against a man who is my superior in every department of the boxing game. Perhaps I can even up by what is known as propaganda. I'll see if I can't worry him. The newspapers can be depended upon to make a mystery out of everything I do. Probably Phil and his manager will waste a lot of valuable time wondering why I have the floor of my ring painted like a checkerboard."

"Yeah? It'll do you more harm than it will him, because you'll be looking for the lines when you get in the ring in the ball park and they won't be there."

"Don't worry so far ahead."

Roger thought that Mr. Crowe, who had come up from the logging business, might be superstitious and very credulous. Therefore, there would be weird and mysterious doings at the Thule training quarters.

If worry over a lawsuit had sent Jack Dempsey into the Philadelphia ring against Gene Tunney in no condition to wage a championship fight, Phil Crowe ought to be sufficiently bewildered at the reports he would receive from the camp of his opponent.

He was conscious of a wonderful sense of well-being, as he sat in that plain little country dining room that evening, after his second piece of apple pie; and he regarded the homely countenance of Whiz and the unbeautiful faces of the Swains with benevolence.

The old world was a thrilling place when a fellow shinned down from his mountain top and mingled. Here he was in love with a beautiful and mysterious girl, engaged in trying to discover who had slain his father, and in danger of death at the hands of assassins who had already tried guns and bombs on him. If this was not enough to keep occupied a young man of twenty-one, he was about to go into training to fight the second best boxer in the world.

23

SHOW BUSINESS

WHEN JAKE FULBERT, the promoter, assured Whiz
Malone that boxing had turned into show business
and the way to draw a crowd was to put on a circus, he
only repeated what the late Tex Rickard had discovered
several years before when he staged the first "Battle of the
Century" between Georges Carpentier and Jack Dempsey.
The Frenchman was only a few pounds above the middleweight limit and had never fought a man in the class of the
champion of the world. All boxing authorities were agreed
that he had as much chance as a jackrabbit with a bulldog;
that there wouldn't be a fight at all.

Against that, press agents averred that Carpentier was
handsome, that he had a very blond skin, that he had served
France faithfully in four years of war, that he was dauntless
and as champion of France and England would fight to
the last against the savage American champion. They were
all good arguments for a theatrical entertainment, though
not for a boxing contest. It turned out to be a theatrical
entertainment, attended by a hundred thousand people
and turning in a million and a half gate.

Mr. Rickard staged other theatrical entertainments after
that: Dempsey's go with the Mad Bull of the Pampas,

Firpo, and his two affrays with Gene Tunney, all possessing every element of theatrical exploitation.

On the afternoon of July 10, the last piece of pasteboard for the fight at Ebbets Field between Roger Thule and Phil Crowe passed into the hands of a purchaser. Fifty thousand spectators—three hundred and thirty thousand dollars in the box office—and Jake Fulbert was tearing his hair because he hadn't charged twice as much for his seats.

Popular interest in the battle between Brains and Brawn had been ingeniously aroused and skillfully nursed until it reached white heat upon the day of the fight. The meeting of the two men had an irresistible appeal, not only for the thoughtless, but for the boxing connoisseurs.

The wiser fight fans, the canny sporting writers, the hard-boiled managers, the gamblers and the sophisticated hangers-on of the game were sure that Roger Thule would be lucky to last one round against the mighty Phil Crowe.

They knew that his little basket of tricks would not avail him much against a first-class tornado like Phil, and for weeks they had been telling all and sundry that there was nothing to it; yet wild horses could not have kept them away from the ball park. It was something you knew all about, but you had to see, as one wisenheimer, who gave up fifteen dollars for a ringside seat, expressed it.

ROGER HAD STATED to Fulbert that at present he was a freak in the public mind, something weird and marvelous and worth seeing; and the event had proved him right. In the multitude of fifty thousand ticket-holders were thirty or forty people who were not fight fans in the ordinary sense and knew little about the boxing game, but who had been drawn in by the ballyhoo. This was what the promoter had hoped might happen, but what particularly amused him was that his net had drawn in all the wise ones, too.

With the aid of the encyclopaedias and works of popular science, Mr. Fulbert's press agents had concocted fight propaganda of new and picturesque character. They dripped polysyllabic words; psychological reactions, coordinations, autosuggestion, psychoanalysis, anatomical efficiency, and other expressions which had no business in pugilism.

They published preposterous anecdotes of Roger's acumen as a child and even more preposterous yarns of how he had befuddled and scientifically demolished his four ring opponents. No matter how fantastic the statements made regarding these fights, the opponents of the Marvel hastened to corroborate them while Maloney of Jersey stuck stoutly to his story that Roger, after having been soundly beaten by him in the first round, made himself invisible, and won the fight in that way.

And from the training camp in Douglas County came tales that aided to whet public interest. The Brain Champion worked in a practice ring which was marked off like a checkerboard. He had a Japanese masseur whose work was done behind closed doors. He had an automatic sparring partner, a stuffed dummy which moved about the ring by some sort of clockwork and righted itself every time it was knocked down by the boxer. He had a book of life-size charts of the human body and would explain the gruesome things to any of his visitors who could stand to look at human internal organs. Understanding anatomy as he did, he had found three or four more vulnerable spots on the body where a knock-out punch could be delivered.

When asked to point out these vulnerable spots he

There was a flash of fire from a ringside seat

laughed and said he would demonstrate them on Phil Crowe.

A discharged sparring partner accused him of having his body filled with electricity which knocked a man down when touched by the fist of the scientist and this tale was widely published and received wide credence among the public. The real facts in this case were as follows:

Roger had gone three rounds each with two sparring partners and Whiz sent into the ring the third, one Dick Feurst, a hulking third-rater who occasionally patronized the Malone gymnasium in New York City.

Roger had boxed with the fellow several times, but upon this occasion he had been attracted by his manner, threw a penetrating glance at him and shouted for Whiz.

"I've had enough; no more boxing to-day," he said loudly. "Whiz, get that fellow's gloves. There is mischief in his eye."

Whiz swooped upon Feurst as he was secreting the

gloves and found a half pound of lead in the right glove. The little manager personally beat up the scoundrel and drove him out of the camp. In supposed revenge he concocted the electricity yarn.

This was the only move against Roger which might have been made by Mason during his period of training. Apparently the fact that the young man had settled down to train for his battle with Crowe had reassured Mason regarding his intentions toward himself, or else the defensive cordon around the training camp thwarted other murderous efforts. Roger was not even sure that Feurst's treachery was inspired by Mason. He might have been an emissary of the other training camp; in any event the crook had an imagination and unwittingly helped the ticket sale.

THE MAIN BOUT was scheduled to go on between nine and ten in the evening, depending upon whether the preliminary contests ended abruptly by knockouts or went the limit.

At three in the afternoon, Roger Thule and Phil Crowe met for the first time, the place being the New York office of Jake Fulbert, the purpose, to weigh in.

Crowe was in the West when his manager signed the fight articles and so had missed his chance to inspect the young man known as the Mental Marvel. It was unfortunate for him that he had no mental picture of Roger Thule to set against the preposterous stories which drifted down to his training camp and reached his ears despite the effort of Marty Green, his manager.

Phil was sitting in a straight back chair in a corner of the office while Marty went over the box office advance sale reports with the promoter when Whiz Malone and

Roger Thule entered. Jake almost knocked over a table
in his eagerness to shake the hand of the young pugilist.
While, in his opinion, Phil Crowe was the great fighter, it
was the Mental Marvel who had drawn a three hundred
and fifty thousand dollar gate.

"Guess you boys haven't met," said Fulbert. "Phil, this is
Roger Thule. Roger, mitt Phil Crowe."

Crowe was a blond young man of twenty-six or so, long
of arms and legs, broad-shouldered, and physically splendid. His yellow hair was parted in the middle and grew
low upon a broad forehead. He had overhanging brows
and small deep-set blue eyes, a snub nose, a long upper lip,
a grim mouth and a heavy chin. He looked like a Scan-
dinavian lumberjack from the Michigan woods and from
those woods he had come three or four years ago to burn
up the heavyweight division.

He got on his feet as Roger advanced toward him with
outstretched hand, and his heavy lids lifted as he stared
curiously at his opponent. His hand went out mechanically,
for he was studying Roger's handsome highbred face, and
after several seconds he drew a deep breath then expelled
it in a contemptuous "Huh!"

"Delighted to make your acquaintance," said Roger.

"Sure," Crowe said in a heavy bass rumble. "Me, too,
mister, you don't look so much. I been hearin' a lot o' bunk
about you."

"All I have heard of you has been very complimentary,"
replied Roger.

"Sure. I've done pretty good. I'm not afraid of you, feller,
and you try any funny biz on me to-night—"

"Snap out of it, Phil," commanded his manager. "Treat a gent like a gent."

Phil Crowe grinned, revealing a lot of bridgework which would undoubtedly be taken out of harm's way before the fight. "I'm only warnin' him," he apologized. "But I can tell this guy's all right. We been listenin' to a lot of bunk."

"If it wasn't for what you call the bunk," said Fulbert tartly, "you'd be fighting for ten thousand dollars tonight, Phil, instead of something like ninety grand. Remember that, my boy, and don't try to wind the fight up in a round."

Crowe laughed. "I'll let him stay a round or two, but he's got to behave."

"Look here, Mr. Crowe," said Roger hotly, "I bet you my stake to-night against yours that you don't knock me out in a round, or two, or five!"

"Nix! Nix," Managers Marty Green and Whiz Malone quickly vetoed this suggestion with delightful harmony.

"Come, come, weigh in," commanded Fulbert. Roger weighed one hundred and eighty-seven and one-half pounds and Phil Crowe weighed one hundred and eighty-nine.

"What do you think of him?" demanded Whiz when the pair were in a taxi on the way to their hotel.

"I think he has been worrying a lot," said Roger. "He is as nervous as a cat. He expected me to have horns and a tail and his outburst was due to relief that I wasn't as terrible as he supposed."

"I saw three of his fights," Whiz declared. "The boy is there. He's faster than Rosenbaum, packs a big wallop and it's impossible to hurt him. You won't be able to keep away from him and you can't stand up to him. I give you three rounds, honest, doc."

"Yet you admit that I can hit very much harder than I could three months ago and you have marveled at the development of my legs, and neither you nor anybody at camp can lay a glove on me when I don't want it to touch me."

"Oh, you're good, but this feller is elegant. Haven't you got any nerves at all, doc?"

"Yes," admitted Roger. "I am full of pleasurable anticipation. I have never been so thrilled in my life."

Whiz patted the big biceps of Roger's right arm. "You sure have a great disposition. And Phil was worried all right, only he probably thinks now that everything he heard was so much boloney and he'll tear in at you as though he was up against a palooka."

"If he does," said the Mental Marvel, "he will speedily regret it."

24

INTO THE RING

A PRIZE FIGHT in the open air is always more picturesque than a battle within an inclosure, and the presence of pure atmosphere is an advantage both to contestants and spectators. The ball park was dimly lighted—it was constructed for daylight rather than evening festivities; there was great confusion in seating the multitude which began to storm its entrances about eight thirty, and upon the field where many thousand chairs had been placed the confusion was greatest.

The ring had been set up between the pitcher's box and second base, and overhead lights threw upon it a radiance brilliant in contrast to the rest of the inclosure. In the ring a pair of unknowns were industriously pummeling each other without attracting the slightest attention from those who were assembling to see the destruction of the Mental Marvel.

Roger sat in his dressing room trying to make himself deaf to the chatter of the well-meaning Whiz Malone and Dick Grogan who would be in his corner. Roger had worked out his own plan of battle and it was as different from that Whiz was outlining to him as flying from diving.

Roger had come along marvelously during his training

period but, in the opinion of Whiz, he was still far from being the equal of Phil Crowe. He was urging that his fighter use all his skill to keep away from Phil for three or four rounds and thus avoid an early knockout. Whiz considered this evening as the climax and also the finish of the doc's ring career. They would carry away a hundred thousand dollars as their share and all they had to do was to prevent the contest from being too much of a massacre.

As he sat on his cot with half-closed eyes, Roger was wondering if Haverty would be there and if the destruction of Phil Crowe would frighten the champion from giving him a match. He wondered if Eloise would be present with Haverty. She had written from Chicago that her show was closing and she wished to attend the match. Roger had asked her not to come, but he was afraid she might not pay attention to his wishes.

He didn't want Eloise to see him stripped in the ring, gory perhaps, bruised and battered. Even now he was so ignorant of the true instincts of a woman that he supposed he would appear repulsive to her.

"SEMI-FINAL IS ON," said Jake Fulbert, sticking his head in the door. "How's your nerve, Roger?"

"I'm quite all right," smiled the pugilist.

"Just so long as he gets into the ring and puts up his dukes," the promoter said to Whiz. "After that we're safe. I've been talking to Marty Green, Whiz. If Roger is willing to box for a few rounds, Phil will carry him. He wants it to look like a fight. We don't want this to smell too bad."

"I been telling him to keep away for a couple of rounds anyway," Whiz said in an aggrieved tone. "Maybe he'll pay some attention to you. What's the gate, Jake?"

"Three hundred and forty-eight thousand," said Fulbert in an awed tone. "And it's ours as soon as Roger gets into the ring. Even if he goes out on the first punch it's our legally, but there might be a riot. I didn't know there were so many suckers in the world."

Roger had to laugh. "It's lucky I'm not a coward," he declared, "or you two would have me crawling under the grandstand to get away from Crowe. Get out of here, both of you. I want to think."

Fulbert looked dubiously at Whiz who nodded glumly, and gave the high sign to Grogan. The three left the dressing room. Roger lay down on the cot and relaxed. The promoter was petrified with fear, he saw that. Most likely he had spent every dollar he had in the world in putting on this show and the failure of the Mental Marvel to appear would ruin him.

He could hear the murmur of the multitude, occasional sharp cries as one or the other of the semi-final boxers scored, and he could hear the gong which marked the end and beginning of the rounds. He discovered that he was beginning to tremble and he calmed his nerves by a method invented two thousand years ago by a Hindu *fakir*.

"Time to go in, Roger," Whiz shouted from outside.

The boy swung his feet out upon the floor and stretched. "Very good, Whiz," he replied. "Ready when you are."

In came his seconds who pushed him into his bathrobe. He had been lying clad only in his trunks for it was a hot, muggy night. Then he was conducted by an underground passage out through the baseball players' pit and upon the field. The nearest spectators caught sight of him and emitted a roar which swelled to terrifying proportions as he moved down a narrow aisle into the section erroneously styled "Ringside," though they extended a hundred and fifty feet from the ring.

He climbed through the ropes while pandemonium broke loose and coolly inspected the arena. As far as the eye could see there were people packed like sardines, people sitting in semi-darkness, people by the tens of thousands; and all of them seemed to be yelling.

He began to pick phrases out of the din and realized that this crowd was not cheering him, it was razzing him. In the contest of brains against brawn, the mob was very much for brawn. Several thousand leather-lunged brutes were trying to tell him what Phil Crowe was about to do to him. They were savage about it and sometimes funny, but the humor escaped Roger Thule.

If they had known it, there was no man alive less likely to be affected by a hostile mob, no man who was so gifted in concentrating upon the business before him. Roger knew mob psychology and had taken it for granted that the crowd would be with the fighter against the man of science. He was not distressed, but contemptuous, as he sat there. He sat for five minutes before Phil Crowe came across the field accompanied by applause that was thunderous.

"It would serve them right," Roger thought, "if I dove to the canvas at the first punch. No, most likely they would think they had received their money's worth to see science go out so quickly."

THE REFEREE, BARNEY Madden, was in the ring now, and who but Steve Haverty was climbing through the ropes! Now the roar of the crowd was tremendous; the champion was very popular. Steve went first to Phil Crowe and patted him on the shoulder, then he came to Roger, grinned good-naturedly and thrust out his hand.

"Think of you in this ring, Mr. Thule," he said. "You're up against a tough boy, but there's somebody outside pulling for you. Eloise Lane is here."

"I'm sorry to hear that," said Roger.

"I didn't want to bring her. I hate women at a fight, but she made me do it."

"Will you take her away if it's a mussy fight?"

Steve laughed. "I'll try."

They spoke in very low tones because thousands were eager to hear what the champion had to say to the Mental Marvel. Then the referee went through the formality of introducing the champion of the world. When the applause died out Steve held up his hand for silence.

"Much obliged," he said in his jerky fashion. "Just want to say that the man that wins this fight will be good enough to meet the champion, and the champion is willing. That's me, Steve Haverty."

"Phil Crowe!" shouted a man with a fog horn voice. Thousands of voices picked it up and told Steve who would be his next opponent. Crowe leaned on the ropes in his corner and grinned contentedly.

And now the ring was cleared. The newspaper photographers had snapped the fighters, the champion, the referee and other notables and it was time for business to begin. The announcer unnecessarily stated that it was a fifteen-round contest under Marquis of Queensberry rules. While he talked Roger discovered Eloise in the fourth row sitting between Steve Haverty and Tim Hearn. She waved her hand at him encouragingly.

The lights were turned on full, the men were called to the center of the ring for final instruction and touched gloves. Roger returned to his corner and stripped, and a murmur of astonishment went up. These people who had bought tickets to see a prize fight were astounded to discover that one of the fighters was a big strong fellow. They must have known he could not be a weakling, but they had expected a curious physique.

25

THE BATTLE

CLANG WENT THE bell. The gladiators moved swiftly to the meeting and the crowd noted that the Marvel advanced confidently and easily, and that it was Phil Crowe who was bouncing up and down, bobbing, weaving and circling.

Like a darting rattlesnake, Crowe's right arm shot at Roger's jaw and Roger avoided it by a slight bend of the head to the left, a movement that started with the punch, while a right hook landed with a thud on Phil's ribs and the crowd howled in surprise.

Crowe drew off and began circling on tiptoes like a great tawny panther. Roger turned slowly, facing him, alert but at ease. In his contemplation of this contest he had assumed that Crowe was quite as strong and clever as was reputed and might be unhurt by his blows, in which case the contest would go the full fifteen rounds. He had charted his practice ring and studied it for economy of effort while he had computed that ninety per cent of the energy spent in a boxing contest is dissipated uselessly.

Crowe, he saw, was a bundle of nervous energy without the least idea of conserving his resources. He was capering now, darting in and out, bobbing, bouncing and occasionally thrusting with left and right. Roger read his intentions clearly in his eyes and blocked and evaded the preliminary barrage of blows with ease.

Aware that the pair were experimenting with each other, trying their respective metal, the audience was silent for the most part, though a man on the upper level of seats kept up a steady stream of vituperation at the Mental Marvel.

Crowe was dancing in and out and Roger saw that he was coming to the conclusion that he was up against a good boxer, nothing more. He began to creep in, flat-footed, to grasp an opening and let go with his man-killing right, swaying from the hips with intent to confuse, and Roger determined to take the blow on the stomach for the sake of getting him off guard and off balance. He called upon his astonishing muscular control, guarded clumsily against a left feint exposing his body and the right of Phil Crowe hooked into it. It came with such force that it would have finished a battle against anybody else.

Roger had constructed partial immunity against it, but he hadn't counted upon its sheer battering effect—the push of it. Crowe threw himself completely off balance by the blow; he was a free target for a few seconds, but Roger went flying backward and landed upon the canvas in a sitting posture, a look of astonishment upon his face.

From the multitude went up a bellow of barbarous joy. The referee motioned Crowe to the farthest corner and the time-keeper began his count. Roger was surprised, however, not hurt, and his head was as clear as a bell. This was no opponent to permit to land upon the body; the punch had the kick of a mule. Probably nobody in the audience, not even Whiz, expected him to get up. Crowe thought the fight was over. He was grinning widely.

The count reached seven, then eight, and Roger scrambled to his feet and threw himself into a position of defense. There was a gasp from the multitude and then a cheer which burst spontaneously from thirty thousand throats; just like the cheer which had broken forth some years before when Firpo, after being smashed to the ground seven times in succession by the terrible Dempsey, sprang up and with one furious swipe sent Dempsey, the killer, flying out of the ring. It was a testimonial from a savage mob to the courage of a man it had assumed was all head and no nerve.

CROWE'S SECONDS, HOWEVER, were practical, not chivalrous.

"You've got him. Finish him! Finish him!" they yelled. The big man came tearing in wide open, contemptuous of a man who he supposed was tottering from the hardest blow he had ever struck.

"Keep away, keep away!" screamed Whiz, almost beside himself with alarm. Roger stood in a curious position, right knee bent a little, left foot at right angles to his right, right glove extended, left against his chest, the pose of a left-handed fighter. Then as Crowe bore down Thule's body was driven forward on the left leg, head guarded by the left glove, right arm extended full length; the position of a fencer who had thrust with a foil, and the right glove embedded itself in the base of the throat of the charging mammoth.

The speed of the thrust defied any attempt at defense, the rush of Crowe quadrupled the force of the blow, and it had landed upon the most sensitive spot upon the human body above the belt, a spot, by the way, which is rarely hit because it is usually protected by the bent head of the fighter. It brought Crowe up standing; his arms fell to his sides and Roger was upon him and hit him five times with right and left hooks to stomach and jaw while he was momentarily paralyzed. Phil Crowe began to totter; the anguish of the blow in the throat was written on his face, but the bell jangled before he toppled off his pins.

And now the shrieking and roaring and stamping and whistling and yip-yip of the throng was beyond conception. Crowe staggered to his corner and fell into the hands of his seconds while Roger walked coolly to his stool and submitted to the ministrations of his seconds with indifference.

Whiz was weeping with excitement. "You'd have had him in a couple of seconds more," he sobbed hysterically. "That was wonderful. Only don't do it again. Nine times out of ten he'd have murdered you when you drove in like that. Box him, will you!"

Roger could see that Phil Crowe's throat was functioning properly again, though for a few seconds the man had been strangling.

The bell!

Somebody had begun to chant, "Brains, brains, brains, brains," and accompanied it by stamping feet as the two fighters approached each other once more. Roger wasn't in the least fatigued, and Crowe's marvelous resiliency was evident in his buoyant approach. He knew as well as Whiz that the fencing thrust would work only once this evening.

Phil's little blue eyes glittered venomously. In his whole career he had never been so badly hurt as by that smash below his Adam's apple, and he promised himself to cut the

Mental Marvel to ribbons in revenge. Of course he would knock him out if he could, but a knock-out blow would be too merciful. He wanted to get him down and stamp on his face with his feet, as they used to do in the lumber camps where he had learned to fight.

Crowe's fury worked in the interest of his opponent for he was in no mood to box. He tore in, his upper lip curled back in a snarl, his great arms swinging murderously, but Roger exasperated him by the ease with which he evaded his rushes, and maddened him by his way of parrying his hooks and swings and tapping him heavily upon the biceps in retaliation. He could not keep out of a clinch, however, and he found Crowe a terrific infighter.

RABBIT PUNCHES WERE forbidden in this fight, but Crowe banged away at the Marvel's kidneys, while Roger seemingly was wasting punches against the concrete skull of his opponent. Many a man's hand has been broken by hitting a fighter upon the bony structure of the head, but there is a certain sensitive bone on the side of the head between the forehead and the ear and in this clinch he tapped away at this spot until Crowe, his face twisted with pain, stopped struggling and permitted the referee to break them.

When Crowe broke loose he staggered as though intoxicated and took two hard lefts in the face before he recovered and again started to carry the battle to his opponent.

Tim Hearn, sitting beside Steve Haverty, grasped his champion by the arm so tightly that his nails cut the flesh.

"Thule will lick him," he declared, "unless Crowe lands a lucky punch."

"Go on," retorted Steve, "he don't know how to fight. Did you see him busting his hand on Phil's coco?"

"Do you think he can possibly win?" demanded Eloise whose eyes were glittering feverishly.

"Got an elegant chance," said Tim. "He has brains, that lad."

The attack of Phil Crowe now was so furious that Roger gave ground slowly and his uncanny skill at judging the intentions of his opponent did not save him from two or three hard body blows and one on the side of the jaw which caused his whole nervous system to jangle.

He was perfectly cool. He had learned already that he was quicker than Phil Crowe and he had not yet begun to tire. He weathered the attack and began to sharpshoot effectively with his left, closing one of Crowe's eyes and cutting his right cheek. He was not even breathing heavily when the round was over and he had been sufficiently self-possessed to notice that Crowe had taken at least ten steps to his one and had thrown five or six heavy and fruitless blows to every one of his own which had missed.

"I think you can wear him down, doc," encouraged Whiz as he sponged his man. "He's fit to be tied and using up his energy like a crazy man. But that was his round, all right."

"He may have it," grinned Roger. "Stop dousing me, Whiz."

There were no fireworks in the third round. Roger, having tested Phil Crowe in the first round, had no further intention of taking a hard blow for the sake of giving one. He could mentally anaesthetize his chin or his stomach so that the blow did not disable him, but he still ached from that pile driver that had struck him, during the first round; and he did not think he could hit his opponent hard enough to knock him out at this stage of the fight. If he could gradually weaken and slow up Phil Crowe, the man's exhaustion would work for Roger and, perhaps, in the eighth or tenth round, he might be able to knock him down, provided he still had his own health and strength.

He boxed with Phil, contented himself with tapping steadily at his biceps and in clinches continued his work on those bones in the side of the head. Phil Crowe skillfully avoided his efforts to shut his other eye and he kept Roger very busy avoiding haymakers, uppercuts, and hooks that spelt dreamland. As Crowe landed lightly several times and Roger not at all, that round went to Phil along with the second.

So far there was no evidence that Crowe was slowing up and Roger was no longer fresh, despite his careful conservation of resources.

Whiz was satisfied already with the fight. Roger had lasted three rounds with a tornado, given as good as he got and demonstrated that he was a first-class man, which was more than the manager had hoped would happen. He continued to advise him from his encyclopaedia of ring lore, and his judgment always was to keep away and last as long as possible.

ROUND FOUR WAS a repetition of round three except that Roger thought that the blows to the head were affecting his opponent's coordination and the muscle blows were making his arms very tired.

Whiz had a tip from a pal who looked over the shoulder of one of the two judges that he had given rounds two, three and four to Phil Crowe, and only given Roger an even break on round one; but Whiz didn't tell Roger that, lest he get reckless and depart via the knock-out route.

Crowe was no fool, and it was dawning on him that, so far, he had received the most punishment, and the Mental Marvel was gradually wearing him down. His head ached frightfully from the blows upon those sensitive side bones and the muscles of his big arms were paining him. He had heard that Thule had disposed of a pork-and-beaner named Heffernan by tapping him on the biceps, and he began to be afraid. No more clinches for him; it made him shudder to think of those head taps, and he'd have to finish Thule in the next round or so if he were going to do it at all.

At the bell he plunged across the ring, no longer boxing, but swinging like a windmill and wide open. Rightly he had figured that Thule couldn't hit him hard enough to knock him out, while all he needed was to land one of those terrific swings. In a few seconds Roger was fighting for his life. He dared not set himself to slug with Crowe; he couldn't always be ready for a blow, and what Phil was throwing at him would knock him out of the ring.

He jabbed and retreated, whipped over a hard right-hander, straightened him up with a swift uppercut; but he couldn't stop the charge this time. He had to retire before the whirlwind, and he was driven toward his own corner battling desperately; and then, high above the rumble and mutter and chatter of the crowd, came a woman's scream; the scream of the only woman in the world who meant anything to Roger Thule.

"Roger! Look out! He's shooting at you! Oh!"

Roger, obeying an uncontrollable impulse, looked into the audience, and as he did so a terrific left swing caught him on the side of the head and toppled him to the canvas. At the same moment there was a staccato bark, a flash of fire from one of the ringside seats, and a bullet pinged its way across the ring and over the spot where Roger had stood a fraction of a second before when Phil Crowe had planted one of his wild ones.

Shrieking and commotion in the crowd; a man with a gun in his hand was running up the aisle toward the grand stand, and because there was a gun in his hand nobody interfered with him. Policemen were pushing toward him, but the crowd drew away and let him pass; he vanished in the darkness.

Eloise had observed the man because he occupied the seat in front of her and had arrived late, forcing her to take her wrap from the back of the seat. She had seen him draw a shining steel tube from his pocket and, secure in the intense concentration of the audience about him upon the battle, take aim at Roger Thule. She had shrilled her warning, Roger had looked, Crowe had struck, and he lay now on the canvas, unconscious perhaps, but unwounded.

The hue and cry after the fugitive, the enormity of the attempt to murder one of the boxers, had disorganized everything. Roger was down, Crowe was standing over him, the referee was looking after the fleeing gunman, and the timekeeper was standing up, forgetting to start the count. Six or seven immensely valuable seconds were lost before the yelling of Phil Crowe's seconds recalled the officials to their job.

Crowe had retreated to a neutral corner and come out of it; now the referee led him back, and the count started. Life was returning to the man lying prone on the canvas.

The blow had caught him completely off guard, and he was unconscious for fully ten seconds.

He came to at the count of three, and immediately drew upon his reserves.

Part of the big crowd was howling curses at the officials for failing to start the count, others were demanding that the fight be stopped because of the attempt at murder. One might say pandemonium reigned; but at the count of nine Roger was on his feet, and he was saved by the bell at the end of the round, just as Phil had been saved in the first round. Roger was too groggy for a few seconds after reaching his corner to understand what had happened, but it came to him quickly that Eloise had screamed a warning; he had glanced toward the girl's seat, and been hit by a thunderbolt.

"A GUY FIRED a shot at you, doc," Whiz told him as he worked frantically over him. "He got away. Crowe hit you when you wan't looking. Keep away now. He'll come out to kill you."

"So that's his idea of fair play," said the young man grimly. "Just for that—"

Now, Phil Crowe had knocked Roger down before it penetrated the head ringing from those persistent skull-blows that a man was pointing a gun into the ring, and that the bullet which whizzed past him might just as well be meant for him as his opponent. He was a brave boxfighter, but he had no stomach for bullets, and he lay in his corner in the intermission, trembling at his narrow escape.

"I might ha' been killed!" he muttered to one of his seconds.

"Go on; it was Thule they were after. Go out there now and finish him. You got him going. Slam right at him."

The jangle of the bell. The stamp of Phil Crowe's feet as he plunged at his opponent, the smack of glove against glove, and a clinch. And in the clinch Roger did a strange thing. He pushed his glove under Crowe's chin and lifted his head, and the two sweating savage faces were a couple of inches apart. Black eyes bored into Crowe's shallow blue ones. And they compelled his gaze as the referee broke them.

Something told Phil Crowe that a man with a gun was behind him and going to shoot. He threw a startled glance over his shoulders, and then the right fist of Roger Thule, with every ounce of the vitality which remained to him, struck against the point of his jaw and laid him low.

The finish came so unexpectedly that the audience was voiceless for a second, and then a roar like that of ten thousand lions went up toward the starlit sky.

Brains had beaten brawn. Roger Thule, the Mental Marvel, after having been saved from a knock-out by the bell a couple of minutes before, after the shock of having a gunman fire at him as he fought in the ring, had turned on his opponent and sent him down for the count.

How the thing had happened nobody, not even the referee, could tell. They had been in a clinch, the referee had broken it, and Thule had uppercut Phil Crowe so swiftly that he had no chance to guard himself.

Crowe came out of his trance in a few seconds to find Roger bending over him and ready to aid his seconds to carry him to his corner.

"What happened?" he demanded.

"You're knocked out," the referee informed him.

Crowe looked stupidly at the official, scowled ferociously at his conqueror, refused his hand, and got upon his feet unaided. For this he was roundly hissed by the crowd, which then returned to cheering Roger.

"What did you do to him?" demanded Whiz as he wrapped Roger in his bathrobe.

"Uppercut him."

"But before that?"

Roger smiled grimly. "You said he hit me when I wasn't looking. Why be fair with a man like that?"

"But what did you do?"

"I taught him what fear was. That is as good an explanation as any."

26

"WOMEN!"

ROGER WAS IN danger of being torn to pieces by his admirers now. The throng which had come to see the scientist massacred by the conventional pugilist was now wildly enthusiastic, and all sorts of queer persons insisted upon shaking him by the hand.

He saw Eloise standing with the champion and Tim Hearn, and for the moment the champion attracted no attention. Roger waved to her, and she made signs that she would see him later.

He did his best to ignore the plaudits of the mob as he had ignored their gibes upon his entrance, and the fact that it nevertheless made a pleasant impression caused him to chide himself. He was not proud of the finish of that fight. Not even the fact that Crowe had not hesitated to floor him when he was off guard because of a woman's cry that he was about to be shot justified his use of hypnotic suggestion.

It was the first unsportsmanlike thing Roger had done in the ring. He was convinced he could have beaten Crowe fairly and squarely, and he had wanted to do it; but the cry of Eloise, the murderous assault on himself, the brutality of Crowe—well, all he wanted was to wind up the fight business as quickly as possible and go after E.H. Mason, who had resumed his attack on him.

The shooting would be explained as the act of a gambler who had bet heavily on Crowe at long odds, and thought he was likely to lose his bets, and Mason undoubtedly figured that it would be so explained. All Mason's thrusts at him were ingeniously conceived, and that they failed of execution was not his fault but his bad luck. That blow of Crowe's, now; had Roger been on his feet the bullet would probably have hit him, so his opponent, quite unwittingly, had saved his life by endeavoring to knock him out. In return—well, after-all, Phil Crowe's intentions toward him had not been benevolent.

It was Eloise who had saved him, Eloise who had watched the slugging match from the chair next to that of the superslugger, Steve Haverty. And it was Haverty's turn now. After what he had said before the fight to thirty thousand people he could not refuse the match.

While he lay with closed eyes upon the massage table under the hands of Whiz, whose status as manager of a coming champion did not prevent him from feeling honored at the privilege of rubbing his winner, Roger thought of that afternoon six months ago when he lay beside the window in his chamber trying to will himself to death, only to have Dr. Marvin intrude and talk him out of his resolution.

Clever, clever physician, Dr. Marvin; he was one who could minister to a mind diseased. What a diseased mind Roger's had been! What an arrogant, supercilious and absurd pedant he had been—so confident that there was no achievement beyond the reach of his genius that he had boasted he could win the love of any woman and knock the champion heavyweight of the world from his throne. He had despised his devoted father, sneered at every decent human motive, considered the world an unfit dwelling place for a superman like himself.

Now? He had plowed his way through the ranks of pugilism and forced the champion to meet him, but could he actually defeat Steve Haverty? He doubted it. Haverty was supposed to be a far better man than Phil Crowe, and he had not been beating Crowe when the battle came to its curious end. Even had he not been knocked down as a result of his inattention during the incident of the gunman, it was very doubtful if he could have won from Crowe. He had overpowered him by mental suggestion. It was like taking an ax into the ring against an unarmed man. He had failed.

And he had boasted he could make Eloise love him. He had received three or four polite notes from her during his training period in return for a dozen long and almost affectionate epistles, and she had not hesitated to disregard his wishes about attending the fight. She had come with Haverty, shown herself in public with him, got her name coupled with his. No doubt some of the papers would declare that she was the fiancée of the champion.

True, she had shrieked a warning when the gangster pointed his weapon at him, but that meant nothing; she would have tried to save a stranger just as quickly.

Thirty thousand people around the ring, and they had allowed the daring gunman to escape. An outstretched foot would have knocked him over in that tightly packed mob, and none had dared to thrust out the foot. Cowardly rabble! He was a coward himself—he did not want to go into a ring with Steve Haverty; he didn't want to fight any more.

His father had been murdered more than three months ago; he knew the murderer, and he had shirked a settlement with him. His vaunted intelligence had not enabled him to get the evidence to send that murderer to the chair. Nor had his supposed sapience permitted him to plumb the depths of the girl he loved. For months he had been associating with Eloise Lane, and for months she had concealed from him that she had some sort of relations with his father.

While the multitude was scattering all over New York singing the praises of the Mental Marvel, that conquering genius lay upon a rubbing table and called himself a coward and a fool.

ELOISE LANE STOOD with Steve Haverty and Tim Hearn near the ring as the fighters and the crowd departed. She was still quivering with the thrill of her first prize fight, the excitement of the moment when the man with the gun pointed it at Roger, the hysteria of the knock-down of her friend, and his amazing recovery and victory.

Eloise was womanly in all her instincts, tender-hearted and humane, and her years in the theater had given her only a surface veneer of sophistication. She had arrived with the champion and his manager a few moments before the beginning of the main bout with only a nebulous notion of what she was going to witness. She saw Roger Thule enter the ring, self-possessed, handsome, clear-eyed and cold, and she had admired him more when he threw off his bathrobe than she ever had before. Roger was tanned and glowing with physical fitness. His broad shoulders, his finely molded arms, his powerful torso with its slender waist and hips, his shapely but powerful legs; these purely physical attributes carried a vigorous sex attraction.

She glanced at Steve Haverty; even more beautiful must the champion be when stripped for action, even bigger and stronger; but that round, flat, stupid face was not to be compared with the face of Roger Thule, nor his bullet head with Roger's splendid head. She looked at Phil Crowe, a blond Viking, low-browed, savage, brutal, lacking in intellect, sinister, dangerous. She was indignant at the mob which rooted so vociferously for the blond beast against the Greek god, and she feared for her friend. Tim and Steve were laughing over the prospect of a speedy finish for the Mental Marvel. In the whole audience perhaps she was the only adherent of Roger Thule. It was unfair—oh, it was unfair! She felt like clawing Tim Hearn and Steve Haverty.

And then the fight began. For five rounds she watched the gladiators, and she saw a dreadful thing—the degeneration of two human beings into snarling beasts. As the men fought, and perspired, and battered each other, their faces underwent a hideous change.

Roger's clean-cut, cultured countenance became strained and ugly. His lips drew back from his white teeth. He seemed to leer. Though no blows disfigured his countenance—Crowe never laid a glove upon his face during the contest—the face was disfigured by strain, fatigue, and gore from the bleeding cheek of Crowe.

She watched him as he lay back in his corner, completely relaxed while rude and sloppy aid was given him by his seconds, and the wickedness of the participation of a man like that in such a struggle grew upon her when he leaped like a wolf at the throat of Phil Crowe in the second round, and then, with gleaming eyes and a snarl on his lips, smashed away with both fists at the tottering blond man. She shuddered to think that she had permitted such a creature to be her friend.

She suffered as the battle continued and the man whose mentality she had unconsciously worshiped wrestled and pounded at the fighting machine opposed to him, and she actually prayed that Crowe would punish him for his self-degradation. She hated Roger Thule. Oh, how she hated him! Her little hands were clenched, her nails, manicured to sharp points, cut into the palms of her hands, and she bit her lower lip until the blood came. The beast, the beast, the *beast!*

And then the man in front drew a gun. He pointed it at Roger. He was going to kill him. The warning shriek tore out of her throat, she reached for the gun arm, but the weapon had been discharged, and the would-be assassin was running, menacing the crowd with his weapon.

Roger heard her voice, he looked toward her, and then the fiend in the ring with him struck him in the head when he wasn't looking, and he fell. He fell.

"Oh, you brute!" shrieked Eloise, standing on her chair. Everybody else was shrieking and bellowing and standing on chairs; she was not conspicuous. Even Steve Haverty was shouting, but he was shouting for Crowe.

And now Roger was getting up. A woman howled. It was Eloise.

"Kill him, Roger! Kill him!" she raved.

The bell had brought the round to an end. Roger was

in his corner. He must not lose now. After that cowardly blow he must go back and beat that brute.

In fiction stories of prize fights the sweetheart's cheers send the fighter out to win, but Roger did not hear Eloise. She was one voice among ten thousand.

And then the last round. The men rushed into a clinch. Eloise was weeping with excitement. She didn't hate Roger. She wanted him to win, to win. And suddenly he had won. Phil Crowe was lying on the canvas. He was counted out.

Roger was leaving the ring from the other side. Thank Heaven, he had not seen her nor heard her! She dropped back in her seat, weak from the reaction.

"SOME COME-BACK," SAID Steve Haverty with an excited laugh as he clapped Tim Hearn on the shoulder. "How did he do that?"

"That's what I'd like to know," said Hearn. "You idiot, who told you to go in there and challenge the winner of this fight?"

"Why, I thought it would be a good idea. I had to say something," stammered the champion.

"Do you think you can lick him?"

"Sure." Steve was always confident.

Tim laughed. "Well, I don't. I'm not sure anyway. Never mind, I'll wriggle out of it."

"I said I'd meet him," replied Steve.

"It was a fluke knock-out. I don't know how he did it. He'll have to take on somebody else."

"Well," grinned Steve. "It's O.K. with me. I can do without him."

A pair of small hands grasped the big arm of the champion. "Steve Haverty," accused Eloise. "You're afraid of Roger Thule."

"Who, me? Aw, go on, Eloise!"

"You are," declared the small blond termagant. "You're terrified of him. You know he'll knock you into a cocked hat."

"Say, listen," said the champion loudly. The trio were now alone at the ringside, save for a few admirers of the champion lurking a score of feet away. "I ain't afraid of nobody, see. This guy might take Phil Crowe that I can lick with one hand tied behind my back but he'll never see the day that he can stand up to me."

"Big words," sneered Eloise. "Let's see you beat him."

"Nix," interposed Tim Hearn. "You mind your own business, Eloise. I think you're stuck on this Thule. Steve could take him, but I'm not risking the championship. He ain't going to fight Thule, see."

"Are you stuck on Thule, Eloise?" demanded Haverty angrily.

"No," denied Eloise. "But I'm not admiring anybody who is afraid to meet him. You told the crowd and Roger that you would meet the winner of this fight, and now you're welching. You profess to be in love with me. But I could never love a welcher."

"I'm no welcher, Eloise," protested the big fellow whose face was crimson. "You don't understand business. The championship is worth millions and I ain't giving it away, see."

"I want Steve to be champion twelve years," explained Tim. "It's business, Eloise."

"Bah," exclaimed Eloise. The girl was beside herself,

trembling like a leaf and obsessed by an idea. Roger had set his heart on meeting Steve Haverty, he had gone through this frightful ordeal for no other reason, and now this pair were prepared to cheat him out of the fruit of his victory. "You're afraid of him."

"You're stuck on him," accused Steve.

"I hate him, I tell you. I want to see him beaten," she protested. "Steve, you want to marry me."

"You bet," declared Steve Haverty.

"Then you've got to beat Roger Thule."

Steve turned upon his manager. "Get him for me, Tim," he commanded.

"But, Steve—"

"You heard what I said," snapped the champion of the world. Eloise began to weep in her excitement.

"Come on, kid. I'll take you home," said the champion.

"Women," observed Tim Hearn bitterly, as had many a boxing manager before him. "Women!"

"You see Whiz Malone," Steve growled, "and tell him I'll be ready in three months. Come on, Eloise."

Tim made a gesture of resignation. "Well, probably you can take him, at that," he said sullenly.

27

A SHOW-DOWN WITH ELOISE

WHEN ROGER THULE called upon Eloise next afternoon, he bore no visible marks of the grueling-contest of the night before. His body and arms were covered with bruises and there was a lump on the side of his head which was concealed by his hat, but he seemed once more a scholarly person and not at all like a pugilist. Eloise had expected him to look rather badly and she had suggested tea at her apartment when he telephoned. She had her reaction and recovered some of her distaste for his personality.

"I hoped you would come around to the dressing room after the contest," he reproached when they were seated at the tea table. "Any number of people in whom I was not interested did."

"I was terribly upset. It was a frightful affair," she said. "I made Steve take me home immediately. Permit me to congratulate you upon your victory."

"Oh—er—thanks," he said with some confusion. "I want to tell you that you probably saved my life when you screamed. How did you happen to know?"

"He was sitting directly in front of me. Don't let's talk of it."

"I certainly am pleased you're back in town. I'm going to

have lots of leisure, Eloise, and you'll be glad to know that my share of the gate last night after splitting with Whiz was over fifty thousand dollars." He said this significantly. "So that money in escrow needn't bother you any more."

"Fifty thousand dollars! Well, your experience last night was terrible. You earned it."

"I suppose I did. Crowe got just as much. I'm glad of that. What do you think of prize-fighting?"

"I was just as disgusted as I possibly could be."

He nodded. "I think that should be the reaction of a decent woman. Let's talk about another matter, Eloise, the attempt on my life last night is the fourth since my father's death. You knew of the first two. Next we caught a man engaged as one of my sparring partners with a chunk of lead concealed in his glove. If he had struck me with that in a vital spot it would have finished me."

"How dreadful!" she exclaimed.

"It's my opinion that these attacks are inspired by a person who fears I shall discover who killed my father and bring him to justice. I have made quite a little progress in that direction but I am handicapped by a certain thing. I wonder—Eloise, did you ever happen to meet my father?"

His keen eye was on her and she flushed. "You—you know I didn't, don't you?"

"I never could understand the presence of that handkerchief with your perfume on it in my father's chair."

"No. It was very strange."

"Just before I went into training and before you left for Chicago I discovered something else. A letter."

"Really?" She tried to sound indifferent.

He thrust his hand into his breast pocket. "This letter," he said.

Eloise took it, inspected it and returned it. "Extraordinary, isn't it," she said in a voice which shook a little.

"Eloise, did you write this letter?" he asked sharply.

"I—I refuse to answer that question," she stammered.

"It is in your handwriting and was scented with your perfume," he said gravely.

"I have nothing to say." Her voice was very low and her eyes were covered by her long lashes.

"Good heavens," he exclaimed. "I can't understand. I am compelled to believe that you knew my father, called on him by appointment upon the night of his murder, and left your handkerchief in his chair. I can't refuse to credit such evidence, Eloise."

"DO YOU THINK I murdered your father?" she asked wildly.

"Of course I don't. I know better. Eloise, I love you, don't you know that by this time?"

"No," she denied. "You say you love me, yet you cross-question me and you believe dreadful things of me." Tears were coming to her aid.

"I believe nothing dreadful of you but I can't understand why you should conceal the fact that you knew my father, or why, since you have certain information about him, you won't confide in me. You must have been there within an hour of his death, Eloise."

"I admit nothing, do you hear?" the girl cried defiantly.

Roger looked very grave. "You don't know how you hurt me by taking this attitude."

"I suppose you are going to call in the police," she retorted, trying to keep up her bravado.

"Eloise!" cried the agonized youth. "If I believed you killed him, I would accuse myself to save you. Now will you tell me the truth?"

"Roger," she exclaimed. "I never thought you liked me like this. I—I didn't think you were capable of any real friendship. You used to boast you were immune to such things."

"Won't you tell me?"

She rose and went to the chair in which he had slumped and laid a white hand on his shoulder.

"I knew your father and I called on him at his request that night," she said. "Our interview was amicable and, when I left at eleven-thirty your father personally let me out of the house. He also admitted me. That's why the servants didn't see me. I don't know any more about his death than you do, my dear."

He grasped her hand. "But why didn't you tell me at the time?"

"I couldn't tell you. I'm only admitting this because you know it. And I can't tell you any more, Roger. I have given my word."

"That's good enough for me," he said, his face lighting up. "Since father let you out, it's obvious that your visit had no connection with the plot against him. Only tell me, does this secret of yours have even the slightest bearing upon his death?"

"I'm sure it doesn't, Roger. If I thought so, I wouldn't have remained silent. I couldn't. It was hard enough to pretend with you and Dr. Marvin."

"Well, I'm glad we've had this out. Now I can go straight

at Mason and get the goods on him. I'll do nothing else for the rest of my life, if it takes that long to run him down."

"But you'll have to train again."

"Oh," he said easily, "I probably won't fight any more."

She looked astonished. "You forget you intend to beat Steve Haverty."

"I made a lot of wild statements when I was young and foolish," he smiled. "Whiz is certain that Tim Hearn won't let Haverty in the ring with me, and I find I don't care."

"You don't care? I thought it was your life's ambition, that and—and—"

"And making you fall in love with me," he finished for her. "I am most humbly paying court to you and hoping that, some day, you will realize I am sincere in wanting to marry you. That's why I am so happy about winning this big purse, but, between ourselves, and not to be repeated, I'm not sure I can beat Haverty. I am not sure I would have beaten Crowe last night. I'm not half so good as I thought I was, Eloise."

THE GIRL DID not smile; she was growing pale.

"You mean you will refuse to fight Steve if you get an offer?"

"I won't get it," he laughed. "Hearn's ambition is to keep Steve champion for twelve years."

"You will get an offer," she said in a low, tense voice. "And what will you do when you get it?"

"Frankly, I don't know."

"I do," cried Eloise shrilly. "I do. You'll accept it, Roger Thule, and you'll go into the ring with him and beat him. You've got to."

"Why? And why the agitation?"

"Oh!" exclaimed Eloise. "Oh, you are the most exasperating, the most infuriating person in the whole world. I'll tell you why. You convinced me that your ambition was to meet Steve. I saw you, last night, go through a horrible ordeal for the privilege, and then I heard Steve and Tim calmly deciding to cheat you out of your reward. I thought your heart was set on it, Roger Thule. I thought you were a person who finished what he started. Instead you are a coward. You are a quitter and I—I made a fool of myself."

Roger grasped both her wrists.

"How did you make a fool of yourself? In what way?"

Eloise hung her head. "I wanted you to have your chance. I—I told Steve he'd have to beat you to marry me."

Roger looked incredulous for a second, then gave a whoop and drew her to his breast. She struggled desperately but ineffectually.

"You darling," he exclaimed. "You precious, marvelous darling. So you held yourself up as bait for a match for me with the champion! Eloise, you have forfeited a hundred thousand dollars. I'll give it to you for a wedding present."

"I think you're crazy," retorted Eloise, who was as red as a peony and who deftly avoided his lips. "Let me go. Let me go, do you hear?"

Roger released her, laughing contentedly. You're not going to deny you're in love with me?"

"I certainly am."

"Why? I'm in love with you."

"I don't think you're capable of it," she retorted. "You are still utterly cold and inhuman. You say you love me, but you wouldn't dare fight Steve Haverty for me."

"It won't be necessary," he said with a warm smile. "Now

that we understand each other, I don't care anything about being champion. I have plenty of money. You will have a dowry of a hundred thousand dollars. All's well that ends well."

Eloise sat down, rested her elbows on her knees and cupped her chin in her hands while her violet eyes gazed searchingly at his face.

"I thought that fight last night was a perfectly horrible spectacle," she said slowly. "I was disgusted at first and I hated you for degrading yourself and then it came to me that it was heroic in a way because you were fighting for what you considered a big purpose. Well, I tried to aid you to gain your purpose. Steve Haverty, in perfectly good faith, agreed to give you a match. He loves me and he is willing to risk his championship for me. I didn't exactly say it in so many words, but he assumes that I will marry him if he beats you. You say you love me. What are you going to do about it?"

Roger Thule got upon his feet, stood over her and smiled down on her. "Suppose I fight him and he beats me. He's bigger, more experienced, stronger and you have given him a marvelous incentive to win."

"He won't beat you," said Eloise. "I learned last night that nothing, nobody can beat you." She said it as simply and sincerely as a child says his creed, and the dark eyes of Roger suddenly suffused.

"God bless you, Eloise," he ejaculated, "I'll be just as medieval as you and Steve Haverty. Beauty, the prize of victory! I'll fight him and beat him."

And then Eloise burst into tears. "I think it's dreadful

that two men I like should have to batter each other. No, you mustn't, Roger. It isn't fair."

"Well, would you like me to kiss you if it were fair?"

She smiled through the tears. "Perhaps."

28

FLIGHT

DESPITE TIM HEARN'S unwillingness to match the champion against Roger Thule, he would have been forced to bow before the storm of popular demand even if Eloise had not delivered her ultimatum. The fight between Roger and Phil Crowe contained such sensational elements that the newspapers screamed about it and the prowess of the Mental Marvel lost nothing in the stories of the sporting writers.

While Roger felt in his heart that Crowe would probably have beaten him on points if the fight had gone the limit, the press completely lost sight of the big lead Phil was piling up because of the terrific finish.

There was the Mental Marvel, fighting furiously against a great battler, when a gunman rose and pointed a weapon at him. A woman's scream warned him, he looked into the crowd and was immediately felled by Phil Crowe with a blow to the head which would have finished an ox. As he fell the bullet winged its way over him. That any ordinary pugilist would have been finished by the double experience, they took care to point out; and even the accident of the long count would not have enabled him to stage a comeback. The Mental Marvel had come back so marvelously during the minute's rest at the end of the round that he was able to knock out Phil Crowe a few seconds after the bell rang for the next round.

"Roger Thule knows everything in the world except when he is beaten," declared one historian of the battle.

The experienced fight-writers had watched closely during the contest for some evidence of scientific trickery, but all agreed that Roger had won because he was the better fighter and all were in accord in demanding that he be given a chance to show himself against the champion.

It was evident to Tim Hearn that the boxing commission would order Steve to defend his title against Roger Thule; Steve was demanding a match along with everybody else; still, he temporized. What decided him was a sudden flop in the stock market in which the whole list sagged from ten to forty points. For that caused the crash of the firm of Evans & Mason.

After several years of bucketing buying orders against a persistent bull market, Mason had suddenly turned bull and plunged desperately to get cash to meet the demands of some of his customers for settlement. He was caught long when the bears assumed control, and at the closing of the market the firm assigned. Mr. E.H. Mason had left for parts unknown.

Upon the books of Evans & Mason there was a credit to Tim Hearn and Steve Haverty of over a million and a quarter dollars, and the receiver reported that the bankrupt house appeared to have no assets whatsoever save its seat on 'Change.

Steve had trusted Tim implicitly and Tim had trusted E.H. Mason. Three-quarters of their accumulated wealth had been swept away, and the blow almost killed the veteran manager. Steve had completely forgotten Eloise's warning that Mason was not to be trusted; he had forgotten to send Tim to see her as she had requested, and he was afraid to tell Tim Hearn now that he was to blame that they had not withdrawn in time from their arrangement with Mason.

"Well," said Tim sorrowfully, "I hate to risk you against as good a man as this Roger Thule, but there is no doubt, Steve, that the match will draw the biggest gate since Dempsey-Tunney. We'll get back the money we lost through my folly, boy, and you can probably beat him at that."

"Beat him? Say, I'll pulverize him, Tim. I got to lick him to marry Eloise."

"And why does she want him beat?" demanded the manager. "What's she got against him? Or does she think he can trim you?"

"I suppose this guy gives her a pain and she wants to see his block knocked off," said the eminent psychologist Steve Haverty. "I studied him during the fight, Tim. He had all he could do to stand off Phil Crowe, and I could drop Phil Crowe in three rounds. He's shifty, quick as a flash, but only a fair hitter; and if he had any funny stuff he certainly didn't pull it on Phil Crowe. Don't be afraid. Sign him up and forget all about this bum Mason. We got some money left and we'll get a barrel out of the next go. Get it quick. The Yankee Stadium about the first of September, and we put this money into savings banks and government bonds."

He threw his big arm around the manager whose false

shrewdness had just lost him most of what he had accumulated during years of fighting.

Tim drew out a handkerchief and wiped his eyes. "Guess there isn't anybody like you in the world, Steve," he declared.

ARTICLES WERE SIGNED two days later. The champion got a guarantee of half a million dollars or forty per cent of the gross. Roger Thule was guaranteed two hundred thousand dollars on a twenty per cent cut and the fight was to go fifteen rounds at the Yankee Stadium on September 10th, just nine weeks distant.

Whiz Malone folded up his contract reverently and privately pinched himself as soon as he got out of the promoter's office. He sought out Roger at his new apartment on East Fifty-eighth Street, only to find it closed, and then he returned to his gymnasium, wondering what had become of his fighter. He had not seen him for two days. There was a letter. Whiz read it.

"Oh, my God," he exclaimed, then buried his face in his hands and rocked back and forth in his chair.

The letter was dated the previous day and its contents were appalling:

> DEAR WHIZ:
>
> When you get this I shall be twenty-four hours on my way to Rio de Janeiro. That's where Mason has gone and I'm after him. He killed my father. I don't know how long it will take me to deal with him and get back, but nothing is as important as this. Two months ago I turned my back on my duty to train for Phil Crowe, and my negligence permitted this murderer to escape justice.

I shall positively be back for the fight with Haverty, but I may not return much before; a round trip to Rio takes about five weeks, and I may not get Mason immediately. I won't return without him. Establish secret training quarters, give out that I am hard at work, and be sure I won't let you down. I didn't tell you I was leaving because you were sure to try to prevent me. This is my job, Whiz. Forgive me, old man, and carry on for me.

ROGER THULE.

Whiz stopped rocking and drew the signed articles from his pocket. Now he knew why Roger had refused to attend the meeting with Tim Hearn and Haverty; why he had signed two days in advance.

"Matched to meet the champion of the world in nine weeks, and goes to South America. No chance to train. Liable to get a bullet in him. Maybe get killed. Secret training quarters. It can't be done. Well, maybe it can be done. I got to do as he says. Oh, doc, this was a tough break for me."

29

THE GLASS BOWL

DURING ROGER'S TRAINING period for the Phil Crowe bout, the detectives engaged by Dr. Marvin had been busy, and had turned up much information about E.H. Mason. Dr. Marvin placed the reports in Roger's hand the day after the big fight, and they had discussed them at length.

"No doubt," said the physician, "that the man is a criminal; no doubt he is responsible for the various attempts on your life; and no doubt he killed your father. But we have no evidence of his connection with the murder. Apparently it was a crime without a clew. The handkerchief with Eloise's perfume was a herring drawn across Mason's trail. It's still a mystery to me where he got hold of that perfume."

It was no longer a mystery to Roger, for he had just come from having tea with Eloise. He was satisfied now that her skirts were clear, and he was ready to go straight at the real criminal.

"I don't need evidence now," he declared. "I have a lot of weapons in my hand, doctor, weapons of a sort that would astonish you. I propose to get at this murderer and make him confess. I have no doubt I can do it."

"But how?"

"I'll explain when I have done it," said Roger. "I've got

some preparations to make, but about the day after to-morrow the show-down will take place. What did you think of the fight?"

"I marveled at your prowess, my boy. It looked to me as though he was going to be too much for you, and when he felled you treacherously and brutally I never thought you could come back."

Roger flushed, hesitated, and determined to make a clean breast of it.

"I didn't, really, doctor," he confessed. "When I went out for the last round my legs were gone, my resistance was very nearly at an end, and I couldn't possibly have lasted three minutes. I didn't know what happened after Eloise screamed her warning until Whiz told me during the intermission that Crowe knocked me down as I turned to see what was happening in the crowd. I staggered out into a clinch, furious at what I considered an unfair blow."

"It wasn't unfair according to ring ethics. Dempsey knocked out Sharkey when he turned his head to speak to the referee."

"I thought at the moment it was unfair. I clinched with Crowe, forced him to look into my eyes, and put into his mind that a man with a gun was pointing it at his back. He took fright for a second, looked over his shoulder, and I threw everything I had into the punch that finished him. I'm not proud of the way I won that fight."

"You have nothing to be ashamed of. It was tit for tat, it seemed to me."

"But I had prided myself upon using nothing in the ring but boxing science, knowledge of anatomy, and superior intelligence. This was hypnotic suggestion."

Marvin laughed easily. "No rule against it, as far as I know. Better try it on Haverty; you'll need to."

"Never again. Not if he beats me to a pulp. Do you know why I am going to get a match with Haverty? His manager had no intention of giving me one, and Eloise promised to marry him if he beat me."

MARVIN LOOKED ASTONISHED. "She is carrying her senseless antagonism to you too far. This is awful. I'll talk to her."

"Don't, doctor," he said contentedly. "Eloise and I understand each other at last. Eloise loves me. She thought I was wild for this match, and she made the deal for my sake. Now she requires me to go through as a test that I love her. You see, she has ample reason to doubt that I am capable of an honest, unselfish affection. Like a fool, I had persuaded her that I wasn't,"

"But you can't beat Haverty. In this day and age, she can't be staking herself on the outcome of a prize fight."

"That is just exactly what she is doing, and I've got to go through. Under ordinary circumstances I don't think I could beat Haverty. The Crowe fight showed me that. These first-class heavyweights are terrific, doctor; they are built of steel and concrete, and it was just part of my old-time arrogance to suppose I could measure myself against them. With what is at stake, I've got to win, and I shall."

"There is a lot of steel and concrete in your own construction, my boy. I am going to lay a bet on you. I ought to get good odds."

"It will be everything or nothing, I'm going to bet my

"You're wanted for murder!"

winnings on the Crowe fight. If I win I get a fortune and Eloise. If I lose, nothing matters."

Roger went to bed early that night, and woke up to read that the firm of Evans & Mason had been forced to assign, as a result of the drop in the market. It was a five or six million dollar failure, according to the newspapers, and E.H. Mason, head of the firm, had absconded.

Roger knew what that meant—the criminal had fled with plenty of funds, and would settle in North Africa or South America to live for the rest of his life comfortably and safe from punishment for his crimes. He, Roger Thule, had set himself the task to get the conviction of his father's murderer, and had allowed the man to slip through his fingers.

More self-abasement, recriminations, useless regrets, and then the need for action. Ransome was still in town, probably not connected in any way with the failure of the firm of Evans & Mason; but Roger was certain that Mason and Ransome had been confederates in the despoiling of Theobald Thule, and Ransome might know where he had gone.

At ten o'clock he phoned Ransome at his office.

"Can you call on me at my new address this afternoon, Mr. Ransome?" he asked suavely. "As you know, there is a matter of a hundred thousand dollars of my funds in escrow. I would like your advice regarding getting this money released."

"Why, certainly. Of course, Mr. Thule," exclaimed the lawyer, who scented a big fee; "I was going to call you, regarding the fight, night before last. I was there, and I want to tell you you were marvelous."

"I won, and that's all there is to that. Suppose we say two o'clock." He supplied his new address.

A FEW MINUTES later Whiz Malone burst in upon him, highly jubilant.

"We've got Steve Haverty," he declared. "The biggest promoter in America wants the fight for the Yankee Stadium; but it has to take place in two months."

"All right," said Roger, distrait.

"Tim Hearn is crafty," explained Whiz, throwing himself into an armchair. "He figures you'll go stale if you have to start training right away. Steve has been resting for months. I would refuse, except that the only way to get the big money is to fight outdoors, and even September 10th will be a little late.

"There's probably three hundred grand in it for us, doc. Hearn thinks we'll get the biggest gate yet for this scrap.

"Of course, Steve will pull out twice what we get, but he's entitled to it because he's the champ."

"All right, Whiz. I'm going to be very busy on private

matters for several days, but I give you full authority to act for me.

"Wait, and I'll scratch you off a power of attorney."

"You'll have to come with me to sign the articles."

"Of course, but if anything should prevent me, this authorizes you to sign for me."

"You're a cool customer," commented Whiz. "Ain't you excited at getting a match with Steve Haverty?"

"Naturally I feel complimented. However, you know I'm going to get licked, don't you?"

He grinned quizzically at his manager.

Whiz cocked an eye at him. "Rub it in," he advised. "I got it comin' to me. I been wrong on every one of your fights. I was sure Crowe would slap you down. Now I don't know nothing. I wouldn't be surprised if you'd K.O. Steve Haverty. You've got somethin', doc, that nobody can figure out. By rights you ought to have been trimmed by everybody you went up against, and you massacred them all.

"So I guess you're going to be the champion."

"You think science has something to say for itself?"

"It ain't science; it's you. Nobody can down you, doc."

This was so much like the assertion of Eloise that Roger was impressed by it; however, he made no reply, and wrote rapidly the authorization for Whiz to represent him.

When he had got rid of his manager he went into the living room of his apartment and made some changes in its arrangement; removed a table and several chairs, and removed the bulb from a reading lamp and substituted one that was much stronger. This done, he went out to lunch.

At two o'clock he was waiting for the arrival of Attorney Ransome, and Ransome did not keep him waiting more than five minutes. Roger's one servant ushered him into the living room, the curtains of which were all drawn and which was illuminated only by the powerful reading lamp.

Philip Ransome bustled in with a glad hand. "My, Mr. Thule," he exclaimed heartily, "you certainly don't look like a man who went through a terrific battle a couple of nights ago."

"Sit right down, Mr. Ransome—right here by the table. That fight you speak of is in the past, and we have other matters to consider."

"Why the artificial light?" asked the attorney, as he took the chair indicated, which brought him into the full illumination of the big bulb in the reading lamp. "It's sort of spooky, isn't it?"

"I prefer artificial light to daylight for study purposes," said Roger smoothly, as he seated himself facing the lawyer, but in the shadow.

"Now, regarding that check in escrow—" began the lawyer.

"Yes. Pardon me if I remove those flowers. The maid insists upon sticking flowers in vases upon my study table." He lifted a bouquet of carnations from a plain glass bowl filled with water, and tossed them into a wastebasket, but did not remove the bowl which sat on the table between them.

"I WANT YOUR attention for a few minutes," Roger said brusquely. "I don't want you to reply to me until I'm through. You were my father's friend. You are naturally interested in the capture and conviction of his murderer, and you would be the first to assist me in recovering that part of his fortune which I am convinced was stolen.

"Don't answer; listen. Now, you told me you never knew of a woman in my father's life, and you were as much astonished as I when a woman's handkerchief was discovered upon his chair by the assistant district attorney, Mr. Quinlan. You went very carefully over my father's papers with Quinlan. You told me you had never met him before, and I am certain that is true."

Roger's voice was curiously and monotonously pitched, and he droned on and on in a stupid and uninteresting fashion. Meanwhile the light from the reading lamp struck the bowl filled with water and was reflected in the face of the attorney, who stirred uneasily at first, but was held by the monologue just as the wedding guest was gripped by the Ancient Mariner.

A trifle suspicious at first, Ransome was lulled by the repetition of dull and familiar facts until, without being aware of it, he was concentrating upon the point of light in the bowl of water.

"Now," exclaimed Roger suddenly, "I want the truth, Ransome. Who killed my father?"

Ransome, whose eyes had closed, stiffened, and the eyes opened.

"I don't know," he said heavily, monotonously.

"But you suspect E.H. Mason."

"Yes; I suspect E.H. Mason."

"Because Mason owed my father eight hundred and fifty thousand dollars which he could not pay."

"Yes, he owed your father eight hundred and fifty thousand, and more."

"How much more?"

"Over two millions, altogether."

"And you and Mason plotted to kill Theobald Thule and destroy the evidence of the debt."

"No; I didn't plot to kill your father, but I felt sure that Mason was planning it."

"Why?"

"Because he emptied the box at the Grandison National Bank the day your father was murdered."

"And you and he destroyed all my father's papers."

"Yes."

"When was this done?"

"The night your father died Mason or his agent destroyed those in his house. I destroyed all in my charge, and when I examined his safe and desk I was supposed to remove anything that had been overlooked, but there was nothing."

"What were you to get out of this?"

"Half your father's original investments with Mason."

"Do you know how my father was killed?"

"No; I refused to have anything to do with it."

"But you knew he was going to be killed."

"I knew that it was inevitable."

"Why?"

"Because he had decided to stop speculating and demanded the securities in Mason's charge."

"Do you think Mason killed him personally?"

"Yes."

"Why?"

"Because he was capable of anything, and he wouldn't trust a confederate."

"And you knew of the attempts on my life."

"Yes."

"Why didn't Mason try to kill me personally?"

"Because he was afraid of you."

"How did he arrange these attempts?"

"Through Antonio Guerro, an Italian bootlegger who is the head of a mob of killers."

"WHERE IS MASON?" Roger demanded.

"On his way to Rio."

"Did you arrange a method of communication before he left?"

"Yes."

"What was it?"

"I am to address him as Philip Brown, care Palace Club, Rio de Janeiro."

"Did he split with you before he fled?"

"He gave me fifty thousand dollars."

"How much money did he take with him?"

"He told me he had only fifty thousand for himself, but I suspect he had more."

"How did he go to Rio?"

"On the Vedado, which sailed yesterday morning."

"Booked as Philip Brown?"

"Yes."

"Sleep," commanded Roger harshly. The lawyer's eyes closed.

Roger moved the glass bowl to the other end of the table, switched off the reading lamp, and lifted one of the window curtains, and then he touched Ransome on the shoulder.

"Wake up," he commanded. The attorney, whose head had fallen on his breast, lifted it and opened his eyes.

"What—where—have I been asleep?" Ransome demanded. "I beg your pardon."

"I must have been very stupid, or you didn't get much sleep last night," smiled Roger.

"That's a fact, I didn't," Ransome said with an embarrassed laugh. "I only dozed, though. I heard most of what you said."

"I asked you how to deal with Dr. Marvin, who refuses to release the check in escrow."

"All you need is the consent of the other party concerned, and then he will be compelled to do so," Ransome said glibly.

His face was red, and he was mortified at his inattention. That he had been the victim of a master hypnotist who had emptied him of his secrets he did not dream, for Ransome, like most men, considered hypnotism a trick known only to showmen, and half fake anyway, and he had the popular notion that only a willing subject could be put under the influence.

He had been up very late the night before, and he attributed his doze to the closeness of the room and the artificial light. While a crystal ball might have awakened his suspicion, the presence of a glass bowl filled with water upon the table in front of him had no significance in his mind. After all, he was a shrewd middle-aged attorney, and Roger was a boy, unusually clever, but still a youth.

"Suppose you put me in touch with the other party in this deal, and I'll arrange everything," he suggested. "And I'll charge a nominal fee—five per cent."

"Well, I'll have another chat with Dr. Marvin, and let you know. I'm very much obliged to you, Mr. Ransome."

Hardly was he out of the house, when Roger had a tourist agent on the phone. The Vedado would touch at

Barbados, he learned. There was no sailing for Rio for a week. Was there any way of reaching the Vedado at Barbados? No. Wait. The agent consulted his sailing lists, and in five minutes had a suggestion, Roger might take train to Miami, airplane to Havana, and catch the Resolution, a touring steamer which sailed from Havana in three days, and which was scheduled to arrive at Barbados upon the same day as the Vedado. It would be close, but he had a good chance to get on board the South American boat in Barbados.

He hung up and considered. What he had got out of Ransome had maddened him so that he was hardly able to keep his hands from the fellow's throat; but Ransome was only an accessory before and after the fact. Roger wanted Mason. There was the fight with Steve Haverty, upon which everything depended, but it was nine weeks distant. He had time to get to Rio, perform his act of justice, and return with two or three weeks to spare. Of course, he would lose his training period, but with Roger training was not a matter of camp routine; he could condition himself anywhere. Whiz would try to restrain him by force, therefore Whiz must not be told of his intention.

Eloise? A line to her, assuring her of his love and his determination to go through with the Haverty contest; asking her to forgive him if he did not see her for several weeks—that was all he dared write to the girl who was so intimate with his coming opponent.

He packed a couple of bags in great haste, put into one of them a revolver and a supply of cartridges, and sent his servant out for accommodations on the Florida express for that evening.

When he had dealt with Mason he would have plenty of time to punish Ransome. In the meantime the lawyer had departed unaware that he had betrayed his fellow conspirator. No danger of a warning being radioed to Mason. And it was up to Whiz to conceal his flight.

When the Florida express departed Roger Thule occupied a drawing room. It was characteristic of the new man he had become that he had not thought to take a book with him to read upon the long, tedious journey.

30

ARRESTED FOR MURDER

AS EVERY NEWSPAPER reader knows, it is customary for pugilists in training for a championship fight to establish themselves in training quarters and prepare for the contest in the full glare of publicity. Steve Haverty moved over into a New Jersey village, set up his usual elaborate establishment, and began work at once.

A corps of newspaper writers followed him, and the papers began to be filled immediately with the doings at the camp of the champion.

Whiz Malone was besieged immediately for news of the plans of the Mental Marvel, and poor Whiz was at his wit's end.

"You mean to say," demanded the *Sun* sporting editor, "that this fellow Thule has gone off somewhere, and doesn't propose to let us know where? He can't do that!"

"Isn't he going to let us see him in training?" demanded the *World* man.

"Listen," said the unhappy manager, "I argued with him, but the doc isn't like any scrapper that ever lived. I do as he says, not him as I say."

"You're going to be with him, of course?" snapped one astute journalist.

"Oh, sure, but not for a week or two. You see, he's just through a hard grind, and he thinks he might go stale, so he won't put in two solid months of training. He thinks five weeks will be about right."

"But where will he train?" barked another.

"I can't tell you that. He hasn't let me know."

"Where is he?"

"He's left town."

"When is he coming back?"

"I don't know, but when I hear from him I'll send out a statement to you boys."

"Well," declared one of the writers, "this bird has to be taught how to treat the papers. If he doesn't know the value of publicity, he's no Mental Marvel. Why didn't he show up to sign the articles?"

"He had a'ready beat it out of town."

"It's my opinion he's afraid of Steve Haverty," said one man angrily.

"You boys ought to know he isn't afraid of anything," replied the unhappy Whiz. "I'm just as much in the dark as you are, but you can be sure he'll be in the ring when the time comes, giving Steve the fight of his life."

With that they had to be content, but they agreed to put watchers on Whiz Malone, who would try to slip out of New York and join his fighter, and who would probably leave a broad trail to the secret training camp. The various wire services notified their correspondents all through the East to keep a sharp lookout for the Mental Marvel and notify headquarters at once.

In the next fortnight a dozen Roger Thules were reported between the Atlantic and the Rockies, and star men went shooting off to remote hamlets, to return angry and baffled. Whiz remained in New York, reported every day at his gymnasium, and worried himself thin, despite his big bank balance and the great prosperity of his athletic institution which had come as the result of his connection with the challenger for the championship.

NO WORD CAME from Roger. Dr. Marvin called up Whiz several times, and declared himself very much hurt that the boy had treated him like the general public; and one day Eloise came to call on Whiz.

Eloise had become a public figure, for she was generally believed to be engaged to the champion. There were plenty of photographs of her in the newspaper offices as a result of her theatrical endeavors, and she found herself exploited almost every day as about to marry Steve Haverty after he had disposed of the Mental Marvel. Steve practically admitted that he expected to marry Miss Lane; and Eloise was getting tired of telling reporters that she had nothing to say.

She bearded Whiz in his den, and several reporters who had followed her hung about outside.

"I want to know where Roger is," she pleaded. "Really, Whiz, it's most important."

"I wish I knew, Miss Lane. Didn't he tell you where he was going?"

"He sent me a letter that didn't say a thing," she said indignantly. "It isn't possible he has run away?"

"Who, doc? You know better than that, Miss Lane."

"But he's not training, is he?"

Whiz shook his head.

"And he wasn't very anxious to meet Steve, was he?"

"Sure he was," said the loyal manager.

"I can't understand it," she complained. "It was tremendously important that he be in the best condition of his life. There is more at stake than you imagine."

"Three hundred grand at stake," Whiz said grimly.

"More than the money. Much more. Oh, Mr. Malone, can't you tell me where I can reach him?"

"Listen, Miss Lane," Whiz said in a low tone, for the reporters were not far from the door of the little office. "I don't know any more than you, honest. The doc knows more than all of us put together and you bet he isn't doing anything that will hurt his chances. He give me his word he would be on hand for the fight and that's all I can tell you."

"He told me that, too, but do you mean to say you don't expect to see him until then?"

"Sure, I do. I'm liable to hear from him any time and I'll call you up just as soon as I do."

"You promise?" she pleaded.

"Bet your life."

When she left the office she had to fight off the reporters who were curious to know why the fiancée of Steve Haverty had called on Whiz Malone, the manager of his opponent.

"You gentlemen may not know that I am a friend of Mr. Thule's also," she said. "I just wondered where he was training."

"Did you find out?"

"No. Mr. Malone wouldn't tell me."

"Will you let us take your picture?"

"You have so many now," she sighed. "Very well."

SHE ACCOMPANIED THE reporters and two cameramen

to the street and patiently posed for the snapshots she knew from experience would turn out terribly. A machine drew up at the curb as the shutters clicked and from it descended two persons whose membership on the police force was as obvious as though they had been in uniform.

"Just in time," observed Inspector Horton.

"You said it," remarked Sergeant Jones. "Are you Miss Eloise Lane?" Eloise inspected them and her eyes narrowed.

"Yes. I am," she admitted.

"We been trailing you for a couple of hours. You're wanted, Miss," said the inspector.

Eloise grew pale and her hands fluttered. "I—I don't understand."

"Look here, Horton," truculently declared one of the reporters. "You watch your step. This young lady is the fiancée of Steve Haverty."

"Tell me something I don't know," snorted the inspector.

Eloise drew herself up and looked very stately for a small young woman.

"And why am I wanted, may I ask?"

"You wouldn't want us to tell this gang, would you?"

"I certainly have no objections to your telling them why I am wanted by the police."

Horton looked at Jones, who nodded. "You asked for it and you can have it," he said politely. "You're wanted for the murder of your stepfather, Theobald Thule."

Eloise tottered, her eyes closed, and a reporter caught her in his arms.

"You'll be broken for this," he warned Horton. "Haverty's got influence."

"Put her in the car," said Horton calmly. "You boys

can follow along. Guess it's a bigger story than you'll get around here."

Eloise recovered in a few minutes to find herself in a closed auto with one policeman sitting by her side and the other on the folding seat in front.

"Might as well make a clean breast of it," said the inspector, who sat facing her. "We know everything, how you were with him in his library and how you shot him when he wouldn't do the right thing by your mother."

"Sure. Tell us all about it, kid," urged the sergeant. "You're young and pretty and your fiancée Steve has a big pull and you certainly had every reason to plug the old man."

Eloise gazed at them with large blue eyes that were almost black from fright.

"How can you say such things," she protested. "I didn't shoot Mr. Thule."

"Of course you did. We know all about it. I don't blame you a bit. He had it coming to him."

The girl closed her eyes again, but her bright little mind was working clearly. She had heard of police third degree methods and these were the methods.

"I have a right to have a lawyer and I am not going to say anything to you two men."

"It'll go hard with you if you take this kind of an attitude," Inspector Horton assured her.

"Where are you taking me?" she demanded with spirit.

"District attorney's office first, then to the Tombs."

Eloise sank back against the cushions and during the remainder of the ride she preserved silence.

AT THE COURT house she alighted, refusing their aid, and walked firmly into the office of the district attorney. Mr.

Quinlan met her, nodded to the officers and led her into his office. A moment later five reporters stormed the outer office. Quinlan was closeted with Eloise for less than ten minutes and found her as uncommunicative as had the policemen.

"I want Dr. Thomas Marvin sent for," she said. "He will get me an attorney and I positively won't say one word until my lawyer advises me to."

"You are making yourself appear guilty," the district attorney warned her.

"I am not guilty and I demand the right of an innocent person to be protected." Eloise was herself again.

"Take her to the jail," said Mr. Quinlan. "I'll have this Dr. Marvin notified at once."

When the girl had been led away, he admitted the reporters.

"What a bone you fellows have pulled," exclaimed the *Journal* man. "That's Steve Haverty's girl and anybody can see by looking at her that she never killed anybody."

"Make yourselves comfortable, boys," said Quinlan. "I've got a strong case against her. I'm going to give you the facts in our possession, to show you that the authorities of this town are always on the job."

"Hear! Hear!" said one of the newsgatherers satirically. The district attorney went on:

"On March 6, Theobald Thule was murdered. Shot through the heart just before midnight while sitting in his library. The only clew was a handkerchief with a peculiar perfume. We took it to the perfumers, who assured us that it was a private perfume, a composite of some kind and unknown to them. That meant a lot, you understand.

Now it happens that I have—ahem—a friend who was playing at the Fairmont Theater. A couple of weeks after the crime I happened to be dining with her and I showed her the handkerchief. She recognized the perfume."

"Aw, say, no perfume would last as long as that," protested a cynical reporter.

"This perfume seems to be everlasting. My friend said it was the same as a perfume used by Miss Lane who was in the show, but that Miss Lane had stopped using it. We knew that the girl was acquainted with the son of the murdered man, Roger Thule."

"The Mental Marvel?"

"The same. That meant that she might have been the old man's visitor the night he was killed. Well, we proceeded very carefully and investigated her past life. She was the daughter of Mrs. Hester Thomas, formerly an actress named Hester Price, and we found that Mrs. Thomas had been living in a small apartment on Riverside Drive. We searched Miss Lane's quarters and found nothing, but in Mrs. Thomas's apartment we found letters from her former husband, Theodore Thomas, letters four or five years old, in the handwriting of Theobald Thule."

He paused and smiled to see that the journalists were skeptical no longer.

"Now it was this woman's daughter whose handkerchief was found on the chair in which the dead man was found sitting. It took time, but with luck we located the taxi driver who took her from the theater to Thule's house and the taxi driver who carried her from the house to her apartment on March 6 around midnight."

"Still circumstantial," observed the *Times* man. "What was the motive?" Thule had deceived her mother.

The girl was trying to force him to do the right thing. He refused and she lost her head and put a bullet in him.

"We have other evidence, but what I have told you justifies holding Eloise Lane, don't you think?"

"What does the mother say?" asked one reporter.

"She left town a couple of weeks ago and we haven't located her, but when she finds out that the girl is in jail she'll come forward."

DR. MARVIN READIED Eloise in her cell in the Tombs half an hour later, opened his arms and the girl slipped into them, laid her head on his shoulder and sobbed for five minutes.

"It's all some terrible mistake," he soothed. "I've got Amos Craft to look after your interests, the best criminal lawyer in town. I'll pay him out of the hundred thousand dollars. Roger would insist on that."

"Do you think they can con—convict me?" she wailed.

"Of course not. Why, you never saw Theobald Thule in your life."

"I've known him for years," she said. "He was my step-father."

"I don't understand!" gasped the physician. "It's not possible you saw him that night."

"Yes, I saw him. It was my handkerchief. I felt dreadful at having to lie about that to you and Roger, but Roger knows that now."

"He knows that you are his stepsister?"

"I'll tell you, doctor. We're not related at all, Roger and I."

Dr. Marvin took her hand in his and made her sit with

him on the cot. He observed a policeman lurking in the corridor close to the grilled door.

"Just a minute. Is there anything incriminating in this?"

"Of course not," she replied wide-eyed.

"Well, fire ahead."

"About eight years ago my mother and I were living in Elmira when she became acquainted with a man named Theodore Thomas. Mother was very pretty and only thirty-three years old. He was middle-aged but very kind. Well, he married my mother. He was a traveling man and he made a good income and he gave her a nice home and he was very good to me, but he wasn't home much. After two or three years mother discovered something about him which shocked her frightfully, but she would never tell me what it was and she forbade me ever to mention his name. She left our home with all our things in it, just locked the front door and left the key with the agent addressed to Thomas. We had a hard time for several years and then I went on the stage as a dancer and began to make money. Eloise Lane is a stage name, of course.

"One night, it was the fourth or fifth of March, a man knocked at my dressing room door and it was my stepfather, who had bribed the stage-door man to let him come back. He had dropped in to see the play and recognized me, though it was four or five years since he had seen me. He wanted to know where mother was and how he could reach her. I refused to tell him. Then he told me the whole story. He was Roger's father. He had always posed to Roger as so faithful to his dead wife's memory that he would not dream of marrying again. And he was so afraid of his son, who was only about thirteen or fourteen years old, that, when he did fall in love with mother, he married her under an assumed name.

"It was very pathetic, doctor. I wept about it, and knowing the way Roger was a few months ago I could understand that he dominated his father.

"Mother discovered his real identity through some letters he had left in an old coat and she supposed he had never really married her. That's why she was so shocked and why she left our home and concealed her tracks. Mr. Thule assured me that they had been legally married and he loved her and wanted her back. He pleaded with me to give him her address. I told him that he would have to tell Roger he was married and bring his wife to live with them.

"Doctor, he was afraid. I said some scornful things, and then I told him I knew his son. He implored me not to tell Roger and I said that was his business. I finally gave him my solemn word not to betray him. I had to. He was so pathetic.

"Next day he wrote me imploring me to come to his house. He had another plan he wanted to discuss with me.

"I wrote him that I would come, but nothing he could say would change my attitude in the matter. I called on him after the theater and talked with him for fifteen or twenty minutes and I think persuaded him to tell Roger and acknowledge mother as Mrs. Theobald Thule.

"Mr. Thule let me out of the house himself, and that's all I know. Of course, after my promise, I couldn't tell Roger, could I?"

"IT'S A WONDER they didn't find your letter," said the doctor thoughtfully.

"Roger found it and concealed it. I had to refuse to give

him an explanation. Now, I suppose everything will come out."

"It's a strange story. Where is your mother now?"

"She came to New York a few months ago and took a little apartment on Riverside Drive to be near me. She is away now, visiting some friends. Of course she doesn't know that Theobald Thule who was murdered was her husband."

Dr. Marvin looked very grave. "Your visit so close to the time of the murder, and the fact that he had done your mother a grave injustice, makes a fair case for the police," he said. "However, Craft will know what to do."

"Where is Roger, doctor?" she asked pitifully.

"I don't know, but I suspect he is in pursuit of Mason. I was hurt that he didn't let me know his plans."

"Can you get me out of this frightful place?"

"There is no bail for a murder charge, my dear, but we can make you much more comfortable."

"Do you think—suppose they make it look as though I did it."

"Eloise, there are things about Roger that may repel you, but in this situation, no other man in the world is so dependable. He believes Mason killed his father. Mason has fled and Roger is on his trail. He'll know how to find Mason and how to make him confess. Roger is rather terrible, but he's your champion in this and he'll save you. Remember that, no matter how black things look."

Eloise smiled bravely. "Nothing can stop Roger. I'm not afraid now."

"Do you love him, dear?"

She nodded.

"Then why did you promise to marry Steve?"

The girl smiled again. "I only promised in case he beat Roger, and he can't do that. Nobody can beat Roger. I saw him fight that terrible Phil Crowe and I know."

"You've set a terrific task for one young man—to clear you of a murder charge and beat the champion of the world."

"Do you think Roger loves me?"

"I know it. He has told me so."

Eloise laughed her silvery little laugh. "This old jail isn't so dreadful," she declared.

31

THE LAST CARTRIDGE

ON A BRANCH of the Iguaro River in the province of Santa Caterina, which is down near where Brazil meets Uruguay, two white men, sheltered each by a wide-spreading banyan tree, were shooting at each other. The hunter had trailed his quarry for weeks, by steamship, by train, by automobile, by mules and, on the last lap, through the jungle on foot.

Now they were within a few rods of each other, the wolf at bay, haggard, bleeding, unshaven and unshorn, clothing hanging in shreds, the eyes bleared, the hands trembling, but the revolver spitting fire and lead. In equally sorry case was the hunter, but his black eyes blazed with indomitable fires. They had been sniping at each other for an hour and Roger Thule had only one cartridge left.

Thule had missed the Vedado at Barbados by two hours, but he had caught a coaster two days later for Pernambuco and there he had the luck to make connections with a fast Royal Mail boat from Plymouth for Rio, which landed him in the Brazilian capital three days behind the New York liner.

E.H. Mason, a fish out of the water, speaking no Spanish or Portuguese, having no friends in Rio de Janeiro, stood on the quay watching the steamer land her passengers and he saw Roger Thule stride down the gangplank. He left by rail for Sao Paolo within an hour and the next day Roger, whose perfect Portuguese stood him in good stead, followed.

Mason was already going south by automobile and Nemesis was only a few hours behind him. Roger heard of him at Parangua, actually caught sight of him at Itajahy, but Mason had secured a mule and escaped into the back country, while the avenger was held for several hours in a vain effort to secure a guide and horses or mules.

The hard-boiled, cold-blooded absconder by this time had lost all stomach for battle with his pursuer. He was weakened by drink and malaria and fled insanely into the pathless jungle. In New York he had feared young Thule so much that he had put himself into the power of gangsters to compass the man's murder; now he faced danger from natives, wild beasts, poisonous insects and reptiles in preference to a meeting. His guide deserted him, his mule died, and he pushed on afoot, continued for days with the endurance of insanity.

He was lying exhausted in a small clearing fringed with great banyan trees when the enemy appeared. Cornered at last, he took cover and drove the pursuer back with bullets.

At the end of an hour Roger Thule had one cartridge; Mason appeared to be well supplied still with ammunition.

The murderer fired steadily, but so far Thule was unwounded. Now he slipped back into the thick forest and began to circle the clearing. Two-thirds of the way around his departure appeared undiscovered, for Mason still fired at the tree behind which he had been hidden. Roger could see him fairly well, but, with only one bullet in his revolver, he dared not risk a shot.

The banyan is one of the strangest of all trees, for it shoots out horizontal branches from which drop limbs which sink into the ground, take root, and become trees themselves. There are banyan trees which grow to forty or fifty feet in diameter through this curious system, and their limbs spread sometimes to a hundred feet.

In time the hunter reached the farthest offshoot of the great tree which was Mason's refuge, and lifted himself up into its branches. Cautiously he worked his way toward his enemy, and was within a few yards of him when a branch gave way beneath his weight and betrayed him. Immediately Mason sprang back and emptied his gun wildly where shaking limbs and falling leaves located the hunter; and then Roger Thule dropped upon the ground, rose, still holding his weapon, and sent the last bullet into the breast of E.H. Mason.

"Got you," he cried hoarsely.

MASON LAY UPON the moss, blood gushing from his bare chest.

"Help me," he pleaded. "It's in the right side. I've got a chance."

"You killed my father, and you tried four times to kill me. Why should I try to save you?" Roger asked.

"For God's sake," moaned Mason, "don't let me die like this."

Roger knelt beside him and examined the wound.

"It passed beneath your right lung," he stated. "You might recover under proper conditions. Are you ready to admit your crimes?"

"I admit nothing, see? You've got to save me. Humanity demands it," panted the wounded man.

Roger got upon his feet. "I am certain you either killed my father or had him killed, but I have no proof of it. A life for a life, Mason. I can leave you here. I consider I have done an act of justice. You will bleed to death or wild beasts will devour you. I assure you my conscience won't trouble me."

"You ain't human," whined the absconder and murderer, who began to sob like a child.

"I am a physician, as you may not know. I can stanch the bleeding, transport you to the village, eight miles back, and then bring about your recovery; but I have to have a full confession. Will you make it?"

"Might as well die here as go to the electric chair," retorted Mason, who was very white and growing weak, but was still defiant.

"I am satisfied either way," said Roger coldly. "Good-by."

A sound between a howl and a whine came from the creature on the ground. "I'll do anything. I'll make a full statement. For the love of Heaven, don't leave me here. It will be dark in a couple of hours. There are jaguars in these woods."

Roger tore off the remnants of his own shirt, got down on his knees, and with skillful hands and sure knowledge stanched the flow of blood from the hole in the man's chest. When this was done he lifted him tenderly in his arms and slowly but steadily moved with him into the forest. Mason weighed a hundred and fifty pounds, and it was eight miles to the village.

32

THE FIGHT

EIGHT DAYS BEFORE the battle in the Yankee Stadium the well-nigh insane Whiz Malone received a cablegram from Roger Thule. It was dated Santos, the day before.

> Successful. Returning by airplane. Carry on.

There was no signature.

Whiz for weeks had fought the good fight, stood off hordes of curious, steadfastly maintained that Roger was in secret training and would appear at the proper time; but his assurance was oozing steadily out of him. Something had happened to Roger. Mason might have got him. He would be too late for the match with the champion at any rate.

The mail boat from Rio de Janeiro, which came in ten days before the battle, had been his last hope. No other steamer was due until after the fight, and Roger was not on board, nor was there any message from him.

The promoter had been pounding Whiz steadily for information. He, too, was alarmed, for the sale of tickets was enormous, and his loss would be correspondingly great if the Mental Marvel failed to appear.

"Listen," Whiz told him defiantly. "If Roger Thule was

a regular scrapper, you wouldn't have a house at all. He's queer; he never does what anybody expects, but he's getting ready for this fight, and he'll be there. No, he isn't scared. All he has to do is to walk into the ring and play dead and get three hundred grand. He knows that. Now, Tupper, don't you worry."

"Well, even Tim Hearn and Steve are getting worried. And this business of Eloise Lane has played heck with Steve's morale."

"That makes it easier for Roger to take him," said Whiz.

"Another thing," whispered the promoter. "I have it on good authority that the police are looking for him. He and Eloise Lane were intimate friends as well as stepbrother and sister, and the district attorney's office think Thule knows something about this murder. They think he may have disappeared because of that.

"I got a whale of a pull in this town, and I have it fixed for the police to keep their hands off him until after the fight. Pass the word along to him, Whiz. That may bring him back to town."

"You can bet your life Roger isn't hiding from the cops. And everybody knows that Miss Lane is as innocent as you are. If you and Steve have such a big pull, why didn't you get her out on bail?"

"Can't be done on a murder charge. We've tried."

Whiz took his cablegram to Dr. Marvin, and they studied it together. "If he went south after this Mason because he thought it was him killed his father," said Whiz, "this 'successful' means he's got him; and that lets Miss Lane out, don't it?"

"I don't know, Whiz," the doctor replied slowly. "You see,

Roger isn't an ordinary sort of individual, and man-made laws don't bother him much. He had no proof that Mason killed Mr. Thule. This may mean he found a way to get a confession from Mason, or it may mean he has fought and killed him. We'll soon know."

"Yeah, but lookit here, doctor. This coming from Brazil to New York by airplane is dangerous. A lot of fellows have fallen into the sea. Roger may never get here. Ain't that right?"

The physician closed his left hand and slapped it nervously with the palm of his right hand.

"There is a heavy percentage against him," he admitted.

"Oh, Lord," groaned the manager, "And if he gets here, what condition will he be in? The boy probably hasn't had the gloves on since he fought Phil Crowe. Maybe he's sick, or suppose he fought this Mason and got wounded?"

"In that case, I don't think he would have cabled. He evidently intends to go through with the fight."

"How long does it take to come by plane from Brazil?"

"If he starts from Santos, it may take four or five days. He will probably have to land several times to refill his gas tanks. Doubtless he has a competent aviator with him."

"Doctor, can you do anything for me?" asked the harrowed man. "I'm sick. I don't think I'm going to live till the fight, honest, I don't."

"You're not sleeping, are you?"

"Ain't had a good night's sleep for six weeks."

"I'll give you a prescription. In return, give me this telegram. It's going to do wonders for Eloise."

FIVE DAYS. A week. John Tupper, the fight promoter,

haggard, the muscles of his lips twitching, his eyes wild, appeared suddenly at the elbow of Whiz Malone.

"Where is he? Where is he? You can't keep this up any longer. I'll call the fight off."

"If you do, you must pay us our guarantee," replied the stalwart. "According to the articles, Roger don't have to show up till eight o'clock on the night of the fight. Weighing in waived at request of Steve Haverty."

"But the mob will tear me to pieces if he doesn't come."

"He's coming. He's on his way."

"How? When?"

Whiz waved a piece of yellow paper at him. "By airplane, John. Got this message an hour ago. I was as scared as you."

He handed the promoter a cablegram which was dated Port au Prince, on the island of Haiti.

Forced down. Lost two days, repairs. Take off immediately.

"Where in heck is Haiti? What's he doing in a plane? Suppose he gets killed! I'll murder you if he does!"

"Don't blame you," agreed Whiz. "But you ain't suffered like I have. This Haiti is in the Caribbean Sea, and he ought to get here in thirty-six hours anyway. I looked it up."

"He's got to cross the ocean. The crazy scoundrel! Every nickel I have in the world is at stake. How did he get away down there?"

The agony of the promoter was balm to the agonized Whiz, who was now able to smile.

"Eight days ago he started in a plane from a joint called Santos, away down at the end of Brazil. He's come

three-quarters of the way, and I guess he'll make it. I'm
always pulling for Roger to win."

Tupper wiped his forehead vigorously. "That's where he's
been? What for?"

"Chasing the man that killed his father. He got him, too.
Don't worry any more, John. That boy always does what
he sets out to do."

"Thirty-six hours. That will bring him in day after
to-morrow in the morning. For what he made me suffer I
hope Steve Haverty murders him."

But upon the morning of September 10 there was no
Roger Thule. Nine, ten, eleven—no word. Nothing. The
stadium was sold out. The papers had accepted Tupper's
statement that he was in touch with Thule, and the Mental
Marvel was certain to appear. The newspaper attitude was
very unfriendly, but unsuspicious. There was speculation
as to the effect upon Steve Haverty of his worry about his
fiancée, who was in jail charged with murder. The stepsister
of one fighter, the fiancée of the other—a strange meeting
for the champion and the Mental Marvel.

Whiz had been without sleep for two days. Dr. Marvin
was spending most of his time with Eloise, who was frantic
with fear lest Roger had fallen into the sea.

At four o'clock came a telegram dated Baltimore. Whiz's
hands shook so he could hardly tear it open.

> Forced landing in field near here. Coming by special train.
> Due Pennsylvania Station at eight ten.
>
> ROGER.

Tupper fainted when the good news was telephoned.

Whiz, Tupper and Dr. Marvin were in the station half an hour before the train was due, and at that time a hundred thousand people were trying to get into the stadium forty minutes uptown.

No newspapers had been notified, and Roger had engaged the train under an assumed name, so word of his coming had not been wired from Baltimore. When he came up the stairs into the waiting room he was fallen upon and embraced by Whiz, who was weeping salt tears. **THE PROMOTER GAZED** at him and shook with alarm. Roger was thin, pale and drawn. There were dark circles under his eyes and his skin was sallow. This was the man who was to face the champion of the world in an hour and a half!

Dr. Marvin grasped Roger's hand.

"Where's Mason?" he demanded.

Roger smiled grimly. "Dead."

It was the doctor's turn to lose his color. "How did he die?"

"I shot him. He died of his wound."

"Dead. Do you know that Eloise is in jail for the murder of your father? Mason was our only hope, Roger."

Roger looked petrified.

"Eloise? Eloise charged with my father's death? Then they found out that she had been at the house!"

"They found out everything. I have the best lawyer in New York for her, but the State has a very strong case, Roger."

"We'll have her out in fifteen minutes," he said with a strained laugh. "Mason died, doctor, but before he died I carried him eight miles through a jungle and got a sworn confession from him before witnesses."

"Glory be!" shouted Whiz.

"Come on. Let's go to the jail," commanded Roger.

"Wait a minute," roared Tupper. "You come with me. The crowd is already in the stadium. You've hardly time to get there. Let Dr. Marvin take your affidavit. For Heaven's sake, Thule, don't make me suffer anymore!"

"Sure. The doctor can do it, and he'll have Eloise at the ringside in an hour," pleaded Whiz. "You *got* to come with us, Roger."

Roger drew a long envelope from his pocket and gave it to Dr. Marvin.

"Please explain to Eloise," he asked. "I owe it to Mr. Tupper and Whiz to go right to the stadium."

On the way uptown in the taxicab Whiz looked disconsolately at his fighter.

"You can't put up an argument," he sighed. "Say, I don't believe you can pass the physical examination. You been sick, Roger."

"Had a touch of malaria, but I'm all right. Of course I'm tired. I haven't slept much for a week."

"You won't last a round," groaned Whiz.

Roger set his jaw. "I'm going to win this fight. I've got to."

"He'll pass the physical examination," declared Tupper. "You leave it to me. Do you think I'll have this fight called off now?"

THE BATTLE BETWEEN the champion, Steve Haverty, and Roger Thule is ring history now. Ninety thousand people saw it and talked about it for weeks. Roger was rushed through the physical examination. Whatever the physician thought, he dared not prevent a bout with a shrieking multitude ready to destroy the stadium if they were balked.

Steve Haverty entered the ring at nine fifty-one, and received the greatest ovation of his career. Experts thought he looked a little drawn, but he was smiling contentedly and seemed debonair. Five minutes before going on he had been informed that Eloise had been set free and would be at the ringside.

Roger entered the ring two minutes later, and he also was given a wonderful reception by the crowd, which was mindful of his battle with Phil Crowe.

Steve Haverty crossed to his corner immediately, threw an arm over his shoulder, and said in a low tone:

"I got to lick you, kid, but I'll never forget what you done for Eloise."

"Thanks," Roger said curtly. "You do your best, and so shall I."

Roger looked fairly well when he threw off his bathrobe. His splendid physique was unimpaired, but he was fully conscious that he was minus half his strength, his nervous condition was frightful, and he was dying for sleep. At the bell, however, he rushed to meet the champion, and there was fast work in the center of the ring.

Steve was six or eight pounds heavier and an inch and a half taller, and he looked in the pink of condition as he was. He boxed cautiously for a minute, parried easily a series of jabs from Roger's left, and then was stung by a right hook to the ribs. Immediately he lowered his head, snorted with rage, scowled savagely and forgot that he was full of good will toward his opponent.

Whang, slam, bang! His mighty arms worked like hammers, smashed against Roger's guard, broke it down and sent the challenger to the mat with a right to the stomach. Roger took the count and got up. He went down again immediately. He leaped to his feet without waiting for the count and drove a right against Steve's chin which jarred him a little, and a second later planted a solid right to the ribs. Steve laughed. He wasn't hurt.

The second round went to Steve by a slight margin, and the third was his by a mile. He sent Roger down twice for the count, while the blows of the Marvel seemed to have no effect upon him.

Whiz saw that his man's legs were buckling, that his punches lacked steam, and that the blows of the champion were hurting him badly.

"You can't keep it up, doc," he pleaded. "I'm going to throw in the towel if this keeps up."

"I'm going to win," Roger muttered. "I've got to win."

The crowd sat silent during the next two rounds, for the punishment which the Marvel was gamely taking was so terrific that even the most brutal did not have the heart to cheer. Again and again Roger went to the canvas, and always he was up and in for more. The innate decency of Haverty caused him to let up after a while, whereupon the Marvel was upon him like a tiger, and to save himself Steve had to take the offensive again.

By the fifth round people were shouting, "Stop it!"

In a clinch Haverty whispered, "Quit, kid. You can't lick me. Take a dive."

Roger's reply was an uppercut which stung the champion, who responded with another wicked body blow. Only the bell saved Roger that time.

IN THE MIDDLE of the sixth round the referee interfered and started to point to Haverty, but Roger pushed him violently out of the way and tore in so ferociously that the champion had to give ground for the moment.

Both eyes blacked, his forehead bleeding profusely, his lip split, and his body crimson with blows and gore, the Mental Marvel was a fighting demon attacking a bronze statue. Steve had marks on his face and body, but as yet he wasn't even in distress. He kept pleading with Roger to quit. Between the rounds Whiz, the tears rolling down his cheeks, was imploring him to end it, and Roger Thule only-scowled and set his jaw.

Dr. Marvin had arrived with Eloise at the end of the fifth round, but Tupper, who knew the situation by this time, refused to permit them to go down to their seats.

"It's a slaughter, I tell you. I won't let Miss Lane in," he declared; and when the girl insisted he called an officer to keep her out of the arena.

In the seventh round the men were clinched, and Haverty was holding Roger on his feet.

"Please, kid, stop it," he pleaded. "I'd let you win, but I can't give up the championship."

"Damn you," snarled Roger. "Do you think I'll give you Eloise?"

Comprehension dawned upon the battered face of the champion. "You fool, she gave me the gate a week ago," he whispered.

Roger's grip on his arm loosened, his jaw dropped. Haverty pulled himself free and brought up his right glove against the chin of the Mental Marvel, who slid to the canvas, mercifully and completely out.

The referee lifted the glove of the greatest living fighter, and the storm of cheering split the sky. And then Steve Haverty stooped and picked up in his great arms the unconscious foeman. He stood holding him until the uproar stilled, and then he stepped to the ropes.

"Now, folks," he shouted, "I want you to give three cheers for the gamest man that ever set foot in a ring, the Mental Marvel."

And the cheers that followed were even greater than those which had greeted his victory.

Roger Thule came back to life in his dressing room. Dr. Marvin was bending over him, and Whiz was bathing his head.

"Knocked out," he said with a hideous smile, for his upper lips was as big as a sausage.

Whiz wiped away the tears with the back of his hand.

"Seven rounds you stood up to the best man in the world, and you sick and dying on your feet," he sobbed. "Doc, I've seen them all. If you had been right you would ha' licked him."

"Eloise?" demanded Roger.

"She's outside," replied Dr. Marvin. "As soon as we get you fixed up I'll bring her in."

"Better not. If she sees me like this—"

"That kid's a thoroughbred," declared Whiz. "She saw us bringing you in, and we had to pull her away from you. Say, doc, what happened to your mental an—an—anaesthetic stuff?"

He grinned. "My nerves were all shot. I had no control.

I'm only a shell, anyway, Whiz. I started from Santos full of malaria."

"Some shell! Seven rounds against Steve Haverty. You shook him up some in the early rounds. I guess you didn't have anything in the ring with you but your nerve."

They had patched up the wounded warrior, painted his eyes, dressed and gauzed his cuts, massaged him, and got him into his street clothes.

He was able to sit up on the side of his cot.

"THERE'S A MOB outside," Whiz reported. "Reporters, women, and the district attorney. They want to get the story of how you caught Mason."

"Get rid of them," commanded the Mental Marvel.

"And Jake Fulbert wants to sign you for a return match with Phil Crowe."

"That's out," he cried. "I am through with this. Send in Eloise, and keep everybody else out."

Whiz and the doctor shook hands and departed, and a second later Eloise slipped in. Her pretty little face was wrinkled with woe at the sight of him.

"You poor, bruised, battered darling," she moaned. "Oh, Roger, they wouldn't let me down to the seats. A policeman kept me in the club office. I almost died."

"I'm a pretty terrible looking object," he muttered. "I took a frightful licking, Eloise."

"What do I care?" she cried passionately. "If there was any decency or any law in the land they would not have permitted you to fight after what you had been through."

"I'm glad they did. I made three hundred thousand dollars. We'll be able to use it when we're married. Won't we?"

She came to him and put her arms around his neck and softly touched the poor bruised face with her lips. "I saw Steve when he came out," she said, "and he told me everything. He told me how you fought when you were hopelessly beaten, and how you wouldn't quit when he pleaded with you, and all the time you thought you had to win on account of me. I never intended to marry Steve, Roger; and I told him a week ago, when he came to see me in the jail, that I couldn't possibly."

"It hurts me to think that they had you locked in a jail, darling," he said. "How could they have been such fools as to think that you killed my father?"

"My lawyer said they had a very strong case of manslaughter."

"But what motive? I don't understand."

Sitting beside him, she told him what she had told Dr. Marvin. Roger bowed his head when she had finished. "What a terrible person I am!" he sighed. "My poor father! Imagine his being afraid to admit to me that he was married. Of course I wouldn't have objected. I want to meet my stepmother. If she is like you, I shall love her."

ELOISE RAN HER fingers through his thick hair, "You were rather terrible when I first met you. I hated you. But you have changed so, Roger. You're adorable now. Tell me: Dr. Marvin said you fought with Mason in the jungle and wounded him and then carried him eight miles."

"That was when I picked up malaria."

"You would have beaten Steve if it wasn't for that. I'm glad, though, that the poor boy kept his championship."

"Eloise, I couldn't have beaten him if I had been in perfect condition. My poor tricks wouldn't have sufficed.

Since I've got you, I don't care anything about the championship, and I would have retired immediately."

"How was your father killed? They didn't show me the affidavit."

"Mason and a bookkeeper called on father about twenty minutes of twelve, having made an appointment on the telephone after you left. The book-keeper was a tool of his and had to do what he was told.

"Mason pretended he wanted to go over father's accounts before the market opened next day, as he expected everything to slump and wanted to sell out immediately.

"Father got out all his own books and records, and while he was busy with the bookkeeper Mason shot him.

There was a silencer on his revolver, which explained why the report of the gun was not heard.

"They immediately collected all father's papers, looted his safe, which was open, went through his desk, and then walked out of the house. That's the story. Mason shipped the bookkeeper out of the country the next day."

"If you hadn't carried him eight miles in your arms, I would still be in jail," she exclaimed.

"It's very extraordinary that I persisted," he said. "I had no suspicion you were in danger. I supposed the police had dropped the case long ago, but I was determined to make Mason confess and then drag him back to stand trial. I fought hard to save him, but the conditions down there were against recovery. He died the following day."

"And your fortune is lost," she sighed.

"We won't do so badly. We'll turn that hundred thousand over to your mother as father's widow, and we ought to get along on my wages for serving as a chopping block to Steve Haverty."

"Are you sure you are not hurt internally?" she asked anxiously.

Roger laughed. "Steve would have needed a battle ax to injure me like that. I'm all right, sweetheart. In a couple of weeks these marks will disappear, and then—"

"And then," she finished, "we'll be so dreadfully happy!"

www.ingramcontent.com/pod-product-compliance
Lightning Source LLC
Chambersburg PA
CBHW051142030726
47504CB00004B/993